T0208458

"Let me in, Miss McKendrick."

The moment Augusta heard the deep male voice, she hugged her arms around her waist. He couldn't come in here. He mustn't.

But how was she going to keep him out? If there was anything she was beginning to learn about the Major, it was that he had a will of granite. Her lips pursed. But then, she had a stubborn will of her own.

"Surely you don't mean to deny me the privacy of my own room," she challenged.

"Yes. I do. I've been given the task of guarding you, and I intend to do so."

She scrambled to find some tangible reason for him to stay away. "It wouldn't be proper for you to come in here at night, Major."

"No. It probably wouldn't be, Miss McKendrick."

The relief his statement brought was banished when she heard an awful crash. The wood splintered near the lock, the knob bouncing to the floor. Within seconds, the door was open and she was face to face with Major Jackson St. Charles. . . .

Critics Cheer for Lisa Bingham!

SWEET DEFIANCE

"Enjoyable! Pleasurable reading. . . . Ms. Bingham writes a good yarn . . . [and] weaves an exciting story in history."

—Gloria Miller, *The Literary Times*

"The provocative plot and lavish detail provide a colorful backdrop which further envelops the reader."

—Melissa Bradley, *Rendezvous*

SWEET DALLIANCE

"A fast-paced, action-packed western romance that will leave readers breathless from its gait. Lisa Bingham is to be commended for also providing her audience with two enchanting lead characters. Readers will surely look forward to the next in what looks to be an exciting trilogy."

—Harriet Klausner, *The Paperback Forum*

"A light, humorous tale in which Ms. Bingham illustrates the power of love to treat wounded souls and mend broken hearts. Lizzie's brothers are a delight, stealing the show with their winsome antics."

—Lizabelle Cox, *Romantic Times*

SILKEN PROMISES

"Ms. Bingham weaves an exciting tale. . . . This novel will grip you as few thrillers can, pushing the reader to look for the unexpected. The action is exciting, the characters believable and compelling. You will not put this one down."

—*Rendezvous*

"*Silken Promises* is Lisa Bingham at her talented best— a wonderful example of Americana. Filled with excitement, danger, and passion, it captures perfectly the spirit of late-nineteenth-century America, a land on the verge of being tamed by those who believe in honor and love."

—Harriet Klausner, *Affaire de Coeur*

"Exciting, humorous, and utterly delightful. . . . This marvelously fast-paced, often funny, and yet tender romance is an ideal read for a cozy afternoon when you need to fill your heart with love and laughter."

—*Romantic Times*

TEMPTATION'S KISS

"Vibrant, sensitive, brimming over with delightful characters and sweet love. . . . There won't be a dry eye in the house when readers come to the end."

—*Romantic Times*

"Don't miss this one—it's a definite 'must-read.'"

—*Rendezvous*

Books by Lisa Bingham

Silken Dreams
Eden Creek
Distant Thunder
The Bengal Rubies
Temptation's Kiss
Silken Promises
Sweet Dalliance
Sweet Defiance
Sweet Decadence

Published by POCKET BOOKS

LISA BINGHAM

SWEET DECADENCE

POCKET BOOKS
New York   London   Toronto   Sydney   Tokyo   Singapore

This book is a work of fiction. Names, characters, places and incidents are either products of the author's imagination or are used fictitiously. Any resemblance to actual events or locales or persons, living or dead, is entirely coincidental.

An *Original* Publication of POCKET BOOKS

POCKET BOOKS, a division of Simon & Schuster Inc.
1230 Avenue of the Americas, New York, NY 10020

ISBN: 978-1-4767-1587-2

First Pocket Books printing April 1996

10 9 8 7 6 5 4 3 2 1

POCKET and colophon are registered trademarks of Simon & Schuster Inc.

Cover art by Bill Dodge

Printed in the U.S.A.

To Isolde,
thanks for the "T"
and sympathy

Prologue

Wellsville, Kentucky
1865

The two women stood motionless in front of the cracked mirror, gazing at their own reflections. It was a position they'd taken innumerable times—one which, in the past, had helped them to draw strength from what they saw there. A living confirmation that although fate might have decreed them sisters, a bond much stronger than blood had made them friends.

"Gus? Gus, I don't think I can bear it much longer."

The voice was more plea than whisper, barely heard over the sigh of the wind and the scuttling of dry leaves being blown down the drive.

A draft seeped through the windows and the curtains quivered. The lamplight trembled and spat, causing the features reflected in the cracked glass to ripple and dim, then bloom into focus again more sharply than before.

Augusta touched her younger sister's cheek, filled with wonder when she found the skin warm to the touch. After all Effie had been through this evening,

Augusta had expected to find her sibling chilled. Augusta herself felt cold to the bone. But not Effie. Her shoulders were drawn back to a proud angle, her chin tilted ever so slightly—even though she must have seen the truth in the mirror.

The way they both looked so pale.

Surreal.

Ghostlike.

"What are we going to do, Gus?" Effie cried, her facade of strength melting away, her body beginning to tremble. She sank onto the chair in front of her dressing table, clutching her hands together.

How alike they were. Of about the same build, nearly the same coloring. But there the similarities ended. Where one was strong, stubborn and willful, the other was fragile, genteel. Almost childlike.

"Nothing," Augusta McKendrick stated firmly. "We're going to go on as we always have. No one needs to know that Armiture wrote to us or that he insisted on meeting with us personally."

"But . . ."

"It never happened. We never saw Senator Armiture. If anyone asks what transpired tonight . . . the occupants of Billingsly were all in the salon sewing together."

"But, surely—"

"Please, Effie. Just this once. Do as I say."

Augusta saw the way Effie's eyes flared. Then, as quickly as the rebellion had appeared, the fire was gone and she became submissive.

"Very well." Effie glanced down at the vanity table draped in a lacy shawl. Nervously fingering the bottles and pots and china containers, she finally grasped the handle of a sterling silver brush. When she lifted it to her hair, her hand shook so violently she cried out, "I can't stand this! I want it to go away!"

Effie's eyes grew wide and haunted and Augusta feared she might swoon. Effie's heart wasn't as strong as it should be, and strain of any kind often heralded some sort of illness—a reaction Augusta must guard against at all costs. After a bout with scarlet fever when she was fourteen, Effie's health had not been the same.

"Hush, Effie." She bent to hug her sister close in order to calm her, to no avail. "Don't carry on this way. It isn't good for you. Not when you've been feeling so poorly the last few weeks."

Sensing that Effie had barely heard her, Augusta held her until the wild trembling of her body subsided. All the while, she studied their reflections as if they were strangers in a play.

Augusta wished it were a play. Then she would have some sort of script, some idea of what to expect in the days to come.

But life rarely evolved so tidily. It scared Augusta how unpredictable fate could be and how much a turn of bad luck affected her sister. Effie felt things much too deeply. She carried her emotions in her hands, never having learned as Augusta had that sometimes it was easier not to feel. Better not to dream. The future, after all, wasn't always a nicer place to be. She'd learned such a fact some time ago when her own hopes for the future had been sacrificed to the necessity of making a living for herself.

It took a considerable amount of time and coaxing, but when Effie grew calm, Augusta pried the brush from her fingers. "Hush, now. Nothing will come of this. You'll see that I'm right. No one will dare to blame anyone at this school of wrongdoing, let alone make an accusation."

"But the authorities will try to find Senator Armiture! They'll come here to search!"

"If they do, there'll be nothing to find but a half-empty finishing school tottering on the brink of ruin."

Slowly, methodically, Augusta began to run the brush through her sister's hair. The tresses was soft and pretty, like butternut-colored embroidery silk. Augusta had always wanted hair like that, but hers was too curly, too thick. Simply one more reason why Effie McKendrick had been considered the pretty one—gathering beaux like a blossom gathered bees—while Augusta had been forced to content herself with the leavings.

She hadn't minded really. Even then, all those years ago—when such things as balls and clothes and gentlemen callers had mattered—Augusta had never been able to deny Effie the best of whatever the world had to offer. Not when Effie struggled each day with her weak lungs and fragile heart. If their situation was different, Augusta would have moved them to a warmer climate where it wouldn't be such a struggle for Effie to maintain her health.

"Do you remember that apple tree behind our house, Effie? Do you remember how I caught you once, sitting in the crook of that withered branch, holding court to nearly a dozen boys? A dozen!"

"Yes," Effie answered hesitantly. "Yes, I remember."

"Unfortunately, Mama saw you too. That's when she sent word to Papa that we would have to board at Billingsly until we learned to behave properly. How we fought her! We even talked Clarence into helping us run away. You couldn't have been more than fourteen at the time."

"Thirteen. It was before the fever."

"Yes, that's it."

Bit by bit, as Augusta deliberately forced Effie to recall their childhood, her sister began to relax, the rhythmic brush strokes lulling her to a near trancelike state.

"Better?" Augusta asked.

Effie nodded.

"Then climb into bed," she ordered as if Effie were a child. "Dawn and its duties will be here soon enough."

When Effie tried to protest, Augusta placed a finger on her mouth to stop her.

"Don't. Don't argue. You need the sleep—more desperately now than ever before. I'll take care of everything. Leave it to me."

Effie hesitated, obviously torn between what she thought was right and her own exhaustion.

"Please," Augusta urged. "Do it for me, if not for yourself. You know we've an embroidery class scheduled for tomorrow. You're the only one who can teach it. I'm hopeless with a needle."

Her sister's lips twitched, ever so slightly. It was a flimsy excuse and both of them knew it. But it was what Effie needed to save her pride.

Slipping the wrapper from her shoulders, Effie stood, allowing the garment to drip over the chair like a layer of silk icing. It was then that Augusta was reminded of the bruises which were darkening Effie's skin. Violent marks that curved around her neck and arms.

Effie padded barefoot to her bed, using the cherry wood stepping block to climb onto the puffy feather mattress. Augusta pulled the blankets over her sister's shoulders and tucked a strand of hair behind Effie's ear—as she had done when they'd first been sent to Billingsly and Effie had suffered from bouts of homesickness.

"Sleep," Augusta whispered.

When she tried to leave, Effie grasped her wrist. "You're sure we're doing the right thing?"

Augusta nodded, forcing her lips into a smile. "Yes. I'm sure." She blew out the lamp and went to the door, waiting there for several minutes. Long enough to hear Effie sigh and settle deeper into her pillow. Then Augusta tiptoed from the room and down the stairs.

Hesitantly, she approached the study, her stomach knotting in anticipation, her hands growing clammy. As silently as she could, she slid the pocket doors wide. Padding forward, she peered around the brocade settee.

Armiture was there, lying in the darkness, a pool of blood seeping from the gunshot wound to his head.

"Is he dead? Is he really dead?"

She should have expected the voice. Although she'd ordered the students to leave the room and return to their own quarters, she shouldn't have assumed that they would. Not when they'd proven to be stubborn on countless occasions.

She saw them huddled near the sideboard and knew immediately that the whisper had come from Revel-Ann Tate. If possible, her dark eyes had grown even blacker, sparkling with a mixture of horror, determination, and intrigue.

6

Thank heaven most of the girls hadn't been in the room when the shooting had occurred. Otherwise, Augusta knew the students would be far more difficult to handle than they already were.

"Well? Is he?"

Before Augusta could respond, the oldest girl, Buttercup Browning, shot Revel-Ann a withering glance. "Of course he's dead, you dolt. Most of his brain matter has been splattered all over the—"

"Enough!" Augusta scolded, but it was too late. Thelma Richter was wilting to the floor. Thankfully—due to the experience they'd gained after many similar swoonings—Aster and Pansy Browning grasped her arms, holding her in a limp, upright position.

Positioning herself between her students and the body on the floor, Augusta drew herself to full height, donning the intimidating mask she'd worn often enough in her role as their teacher and guardian. Since the owner of the school, Mrs. Marble, had suffered a stroke and moved to town, Augusta was the only adult influence in their lives other than Effie—and Effie was far too indulgent with them to count for much in the way of moral guidance.

"Go to bed. All of you."

"But—"

She wasn't sure who uttered the automatic protest. Augusta simply interrupted it with, "Go . . . to . . . *bed.*" Her glance became steely. "Nothing has happened here. Nothing at all—do you understand?"

The thick pall that settled over the room was the only answer she needed. These girls knew what she meant. If anyone were to come and ask about Senator Armiture, none of them had seen him, none of them

7

had even heard of him. Her students had experienced enough of the war's repercussions to sense the inherent danger they faced as soon as this man's disappearance came to light. The war might have ended between the Union and Confederate armies, but it was far from over for them. It would take years to put their lives back together and build some sort of future.

"Good night, Miss Augusta." Buttercup was the first to speak, her glacial blue eyes skipping from girl to girl in such a way that Augusta knew they would soon follow her out the door.

"Yes, ma'am. Good night."

"Good night."

One by one, they went into the hall, the trio formed by Pansy, Aster, and the reviving Thelma the last to go.

Augusta waited, listening to their footsteps on the staircase, the creaking of the floorboards, and the slam of their bedroom doors. Then finally . . . quiet. Blessed quiet.

Again, she regarded the man on the floor, the man who had put them in so much trouble, who had made them so frightened. She knew she should be sorry he was dead, but somehow, she couldn't summon the emotions. Not after all he'd done. All he'd tried to do.

"Miz 'Kendrick?"

The whisper caused Augusta to jump. Whirling, she faced the tall black man who stepped out of the shadows pooling under the threshold.

"I brought de buggy back here like you asked. I left it out front."

"Thank you, Elijah." Her throat grew tight, but she swallowed, forcing back the fear, the worry, the nausea, and the weak display of tears.

"You'll be wantin' me to take him away?"

Elijah had always been so kind. Unlike the rest of the slaves and servants who'd helped with the work at Billingsly, he hadn't fled the moment he'd heard about Lincoln's Emancipation Proclamation. He'd been given such a chance long ago when Mrs. Marble, the owner of the Billingsly School for Young Ladies, had given him his papers. He'd stayed because he was needed here. He'd stayed because this was his home.

"Dump him in the pond, Elijah."

"Dey'll find him dere, Miz 'Kendrick," Elijah warned. He then added, "Let me take care of him. Dat way, if anybody asks, you don' know where de body is."

He crossed the room in lithe, noiseless strides. Tall to a fault and built with shoulders which could have rivaled Atlas's, he was a picture of strength. Rolling the dead man in the rug where he lay sprawled, facedown, Elijah hefted the body over his shoulder. At the door, he paused, turning to regard Augusta quite seriously.

"He won't be botherin' you or Miz Effie anymore, Miz 'Gusta."

Augusta nodded, her gaze drawn to the tiny droplets of blood which created a trail from the place the man had fallen to where Elijah held him now.

"No. He won't."

"An' Miz Effie . . ." The question he wanted to ask hung in the air, too horrible to be spoken aloud. "Was he . . . dat is . . . did we stop him in time?"

Augusta nodded, the tears crowding so close they burned the back of her throat. "She has a few bruises and scrapes but . . . he didn't hurt her any more than that, Elijah."

His relief was obvious. "Den de Lawd is good, Miz 'Kendrick. De Lawd is good."

"Yes, Elijah," she echoed as he backed from the room. Moments later she heard the click of the front door closing behind him. "But if the Lord is so good," she whispered to no one but herself, "then why didn't He stop this before it started?"

Why hadn't He struck Senator Tobias Armiture down with a bolt of lightning instead of arranging for the man's life to be ended with a bullet to the brain?

The tears came, first one, then another. Wrapping her arms around her waist, Augusta sank to the floor, sobbing, trying to reassure herself that everything she'd told Effie was true. No one would discover what had happened. No one would trace Armiture here.

So why didn't she believe it?

Why was her heart so filled with dread?

1

Augusta! Soldiers are coming down the front drive!"

After the first few words, Augusta barely heard the rest of Pansy Browning's warning.

Eight months. It had been eight months since the war had ended, but the cry of alarm from the young girl had the power to jar Augusta to the core of her soul. Especially now.

The precious bag of clothespins she held fell from her too-cold fingers to scatter onto the frozen ground. They were a luxury in times like these and she couldn't afford to lose a single one. But even as she lamented their loss, the sound of approaching horses crescendoed in her ears.

"No, no!" she whispered under her breath. This couldn't be happening. Not after two weeks of blissful peace. She'd been so sure that they were safe, she'd unconsciously allowed her guard to drop.

Augusta felt the panicky glances from the two students who had come to help her with the task.

11

Buttercup glowered in a way that was much too severe for a girl of nineteen while Aster blinked with something akin to shock.

"Miss Augusta! What shall we do?" Pansy ran to lean over the back verandah, her face white with terror.

Augusta felt an answering horror bubbling inside her. The urge to shepherd the inhabitants of the Billingsly School for Young Ladies inside and lock the doors swept over her, immediately, overpoweringly.

As soon as it came, Augusta thrust the instinctive reaction away, reminding herself that there was no reason to respond too hastily. The Union soldiers weren't necessarily here for anything of a serious nature. The area was filled with the troops who aided the provisional government. These men could be harmless—merely passing through on their way back to town.

Unfortunately, her heart didn't have the same confidence as her brain. She found herself dropping to her knees and searching blindly for the clothespins. It was the first thing that came to mind, the first task she felt would appear honest and aboveboard. Innocent.

The moment she was committed to the exercise, she realized her error. Even Buttercup and Aster gazed at her in astonishment. Over an inch of snow had fallen the night before and the chill weather had not allowed it to melt. Since Augusta had run outside to remove the laundry from the line without donning her mittens, she was forced to sink her fingers into the white powder, causing her hands to grow even more numb. Too late, she realized she should have remained standing. To be found kneeling this way, for whatever reason, put her at an immediate disadvantage.

The clop of hooves grew louder, their gait quick and urgent. Gasping, she saw a trio of horses rounding the corner of the house and galloping in her direction.

"Buttercup, Aster, get into the house!"

Augusta struggled to stand, but the tangle of her skirts and the weakness invading her limbs held her down as the three Union soldiers brought their mounts to a skidding halt mere inches away. The girls, too terrified to move, stood where they were.

No. No! Augusta thought frantically when she saw the hard set of the soldiers' features, the determined glint of their eyes. She offered a quick, silent prayer. Please, let them be here for water, or a quick warming by the fire. Please, please, don't let them be here on some government errand.

But most of all . . . *don't let them be here for any of us.*

"You, there!"

She couldn't move. The last breath she'd taken was wedged in her throat. The man in charge hadn't spoken to the young women. His call had been directed at her.

"Are you Augusta McKendrick?"

She looked up into an implacable face and a ferocious scowl barely concealed by a weather-stained hat.

Dear Lord above, she thought as she met the man's gaze. *He was going to shoot her. Here and now. Before she even had a chance to defend herself.*

"You are Augusta McKendrick, are you not?" the man asked again, his tone as crisp and sharp as flint to stone. His gaze was direct and penetrating, as if he meant to peer into her very soul.

"Yes. Yes, of course." The reply was barely a whisper, but somehow she knew he'd heard it.

"Get up. The rest of you stand back out of the way."

The clipped commands he issued were barely civil in tone.

Buttercup and Aster cautiously stepped toward the house, then turned and ran the rest of the way.

Breathing more easily now that the girls were gone, Augusta rose as gracefully as she could from her position.

The leader of the group turned his head briefly, issuing some sort of muffled order. Immediately, his men dismounted, their boots crunching in the snow.

Augusta hoped that since the soldiers were on the ground, she would feel less intimidated. But she was wrong. There was no comfort to be found in the way they watched her, their hands slipping into their jackets and resting on the butts of their revolvers as if they were prepared to shoot her at the slightest provocation.

"What's this about?" she asked, her voice stronger, but still not emerging as unaffected as she would have wished.

The soldier in charge—a major, judging by the decorations on his coat—didn't even glance her way. Instead, his eyes restlessly roamed the yard as he ordered softly, "Search the area."

The strength rushed from her body. "I *beg* your pardon!"

The man didn't pause in his instructions to his men. "According to the records, there are two teach-

14

ers in residence. There's also a Negro handyman, and five young girls ages thirteen to nineteen. If you find anyone who doesn't fit those descriptions, apprehend them immediately for questioning. We'll deal with those who do belong here later, after we've made our search."

The two men split up, one in the direction of the outbuildings, the other making his way toward the three-story dwelling that served as both school and dormitory.

"Now wait a minute!" Lifting her skirts, she took a few quick steps to intercept the two soldiers, but such actions were futile, so she whirled to face their leader. "What is the meaning of this? I demand to know why you feel you have the right to barge into our affairs and send your men poking through our buildings!"

But she knew. The pounding of her heart told her plainly enough.

The major withdrew a stiff envelope from his coat pocket. Bending from his vantage point on his horse, he held it in her direction. "I have written permission from a Mrs. Willard Marble—Agnes Marble—the owner of this establishment. Such permission is hardly necessary, however, since a warrant is being signed even as we speak."

Augusta took the note, immediately recognizing the spidery script. After her stroke, Mrs. Marble had gone to live with her daughter, leaving the Billingsly School for Young Ladies in the hands of her staff. A staff which had dwindled to Augusta and Effie, both of whom had originally been hired to teach little more than literature, art, and women's handicrafts.

"Why is it necessary to search the property at all?" she asked coolly, handing the letter back to him.

15

He took it with a hand sheathed in worn, stained leather. Augusta shivered at the sight. After she'd spent so many years of war and fighting to survive the conflict, those gloves told her a lot about him. More than he would have realized had he cared about such things. She knew in an instant that—to this soldier— appearances meant nothing compared to comfort and practicality. That he worked hard. And that he'd killed. The darker splotches near the wrist could only be blood.

"A month ago, Senator Tobias Armiture and two of his aides began a fact-finding tour in order to determine what relief funds would need to be sent to the area."

"I don't see what that has to do with this school." But she did.

It had been about a month ago that she'd received the first missive informing her that Senator Armiture planned to make a personal visit to the school. She'd immediately known he intended to question her about her brother, Clarence, and his activities during the war. Armiture had sent a half-dozen letters inquiring when she had seen Clarence last and how long he'd stayed to visit. He hadn't believed her when she'd responded and told him she hadn't seen Clarence in years. He kept insisting that she must have some of Clarence's personal papers and correspondences. He wouldn't believe that she'd never seen them while Clarence was alive, and he was even more adamant that they must have been forwarded to her once Clarence had been listed among the Confederate casualties.

Augusta had immediately burned Armiture's letter

in the fireplace in case Effie should find it and worry about the impending visit. Watching it being consumed had momentarily eased Augusta's frustration at the time, but she could do little to prevent the man from coming to Billingsly as he'd planned.

The major watched her so carefully she wondered if he had somehow read the guilty thoughts which shot through her brain.

"Although this school was not involved in the hospitals and refugee camps he was sent to investigate, the senator did make it clear that he wished to visit Billingsly for personal reasons."

"We never saw him."

"We've been retracing his appointment schedule as he outlined them to one of his aides. This is the last stop he intended to make on the day he disappeared."

Damn. Trust Armiture to have left a record of where he was going for all the world to find.

Augusta's hands were growing clammy and it took every ounce of will not to wipe them down her skirt.

Offering the man a quick smile, Augusta shrugged with more nonchalance than she felt. "I'm afraid we haven't seen the man, Major. I had no idea that our school was to receive so influential a visitor. Had I known . . ."

He interrupted her before she could finish. "You'll pardon me, ma'am, if I don't believe you."

Her mouth parted in a reflexive action. Never had a gentleman said anything so completely and utterly rude to her. Even if he doubted her sincerity, the major shouldn't have voiced such objections aloud. It simply wasn't done.

The man abruptly touched a finger to the brim of

his hat. "Good day, Miss McKendrick," he said, dismissing her without bothering to explain. "And please . . . allow me to complete my search in my own way"—he added pointedly—"without your interference." Then he urged his horse away from her.

Augusta stood stunned, the cold seeping through her shoes as the major led his mount slowly around the perimeter of the property, then began to retrace his own path as if examining the area for clues.

"What's he doing, Gus?"

Augusta hadn't heard Effie approach. She'd been too busy watching the major navigate the front drive.

"He's come for us, hasn't he?"

"Shh, Effie." Augusta cast her gaze in the direction of the other two soldiers to ensure her sister hadn't been overheard. "Keep calm. We must appear as if we haven't a clue as to why the soldiers have come."

"Just why *are* they here?" Effie whispered fearfully. "Did they tell you what they want?"

Only then did Augusta allow herself to meet Effie's gaze, knowing that to hide the truth would only make things worse. "They're searching for some sort of evidence to prove that Senator Armiture came to Billingsly two weeks ago."

Augusta saw the way Effie blanched. Pressing a hand to her chest, she fought to breathe.

Watching her sister, reminded again of Effie's frailty, Augusta wished she could wrap her arm around her sister's waist and offer her a tiny bit of strength. But she couldn't do that. Not here. Not so near to the men who were scouring the area.

"Go inside where it's warm, Effie."

"But—"

"It's almost time for the poetry class. Gather the girls together in the salon and keep them away from the windows. I don't want these men questioning them."

Effie nodded, clutching the collar of her bodice to shield herself from as much of the winter chill as possible. Augusta couldn't allow herself to watch her progress, but she heard each squeaky footstep in the snow, the thump of Effie's shoes against the verandah, her murmurs as she led the students inside.

Then the yard was quiet. Even the clop of hooves, the creak of leather, was absorbed by the cold. If she closed her eyes, she might be able to fool herself into believing that he'd never come here, never jerked the foundations from her tenuous belief that the worst was over.

Augusta delayed her own return to the house as long as possible. She worked quite slowly at peeling the laundry from the line and folding the stiff, frozen articles of clothing into the basket at her feet. She even took a few extra minutes to search again for her clothespins, kicking the snow aside with the toe of her boot until they'd been found. Then, realizing she couldn't stay in the yard any longer without appearing much more apprehensive than she would like, she made her way to the front door.

Since the major had stopped his horse a few yards away, she hoped her proximity would force the man to speak. But he didn't approach her, didn't motion for her to approach *him*. Instead, he watched each step she took with those dark, hooded eyes. By the time she reached the portico, the hairs at her nape stood on end. She had to resist the urge to shiver at the way he made her feel—as if he were examining her like a bug on a pin. As if he knew she was afraid of him and what he represented.

Turning her back to him, she slipped into the house, shaking her head at such nonsense. The man didn't know anything about her. He didn't know anything at all.

Jackson St. Charles watched her go, absorbing the brittle quality of Augusta McKendrick's shoulders and the steely length of her spine.

As soon as the door closed behind her, the gruff and grumbly facade he employed as an interrogator dropped and he found himself looking at her much differently. More thoughtfully.

She was nothing like what he had expected from the file he'd gathered about her. He'd thought she would be much older, for one thing, and more hardened by the war. He'd imagined a sour-faced spinster toting a rifle in one hand and a book of prayers in the other.

He should have learned long ago not to make snap assumptions based on paperwork alone.

Shifting, he eased the stabbing pain in his thigh and rubbed at the tension gathering between his brows.

Actually, Jackson wasn't the officer who was supposed to investigate this situation. Another man had been assigned to search for Senator Armiture, but as soon as Jackson heard about the man's disappearance, he'd arranged for a change of orders. Then, he'd traveled the thirty miles to Wellsville to take care of the matter himself. As soon as he'd seen the file on Augusta McKendrick and the way she'd been accused once before of hiding her brother, Jackson had known his instincts had been right to bring him here.

The instant Jackson had looked into Augusta McKendrick's eyes and sensed her uneasiness, he'd known she was somehow involved with this whole affair. Despite what she'd said to the contrary, Jackson knew she'd seen Armiture and knew exactly what had happened to him.

What no one else was aware of, was that Jackson had his own reasons for tracing Senator Armiture's path to this school. But at the moment, he had more than a missing government official on his mind. He intended to find Clarence T. McKendrick, convicted Confederate spy and assassin, come hell or high water.

"Sir?"

Jackson shook himself from his musings to find one of his men riding toward him.

"What is it, Boyd?"

The soldier dropped a button made of heavy brass, very masculine in appearance, into Jackson's palm.

"What do you think, sir?"

Jackson nudged the button with his thumb, noting the black threads still attached to the shank. A voice in his head nagged that it could only have belonged to Armiture. The button was in far too good condition to have been on the ground for long and its workmanship was elegant and expensive, fairly screaming of a wealthy owner.

"I think I'll have a word with Armiture's valet," Jackson said. "Finish up here, then guard the property from the outer gates until I get the warrants we need from French."

Boyd nodded. "Yes, sir."

As the man rode away, Jackson stared in the direction of the school. He was sure Augusta McKendrick was watching him from behind one of those curtained windows, her hair drawn back in a loose knot, her brows creased, the cool gray eyes giving nothing away.

It was a pity, really. If he didn't know so much about her past, about the trouble she'd been in with the army once before, he might have allowed himself to . . .

To what?

Straightening, he growled in disgust at his own thoughts. He didn't have the time for a woman—especially one like Augusta McKendrick.

No, there was much more happening here than appeared on the surface.

"Damnit, man! What in hell do you think you're doing?"

Jackson barely glanced up from the files spread on the desk in front of him when General French stormed into his temporary office at Army Headquarters. As usual, the man brought with him the scent of cigar smoke and whiskey, as well as a nature that was habitually foul.

"Well?"

Sighing, Jackson stood, using his hands to take most of the weight from his bad leg as he limped past the general to the door, shutting it.

"Why don't you have a seat, sir?"

"A seat? I'll have your head on a platter if you don't tell me what in the Sam Hill you think you're doing, boy. You're supposed to be in Jonesboro."

Nevertheless, the general settled his stocky frame into the chair Jackson had vacated and opened the bottom drawer. Without asking, he withdrew the bottle of liquor that Jackson had put there to dull the pain of his leg. How he knew it would be there was anyone's guess, but the general seemed to have a homing instinct for good whiskey. Before Jackson could say a word, he'd removed the cork and taken a healthy swallow—not that Jackson *would* have said anything. The general did not tolerate any comments on his drinking. As far as he was concerned, if Ulysses Grant imbibed now and then, why couldn't he?

The older man swiped a hand over his lips and glared at his protégé.

"I thought I sent a wire to you in Jonesboro telling you to stay away from that Armiture mess," the general grumbled.

Jackson sank into the opposite chair. "You did."

"Then why do I hear that you dismissed Elliot from the investigation and went out there yourself?"

"I thought such an important matter deserved my personal attention."

"Personal attention, my aunt Fannie. Hell, boy. You'll be discharged in three weeks."

"That's plenty of time."

The general paused in his blustering tirade. "For what?"

"For a confession."

French's fingers tapped the bottle. "A confession of what?"

Jackson considered his words before saying, "Murder."

The general's brows rose. "You think it's come to that, do you?"

"Yes, sir."

"Why?"

"Armiture has been gone for two weeks. For a man

accustomed to being the center of attention, that's an awfully long time to be missing."

"What makes you think it was murder?"

"Gut instinct."

The now-empty bottle was abandoned as French's pudgy fingers reached into his blouse pocket, snagging a cigar. Using the silver smoking set attached to his watch chain, he snipped the end of the rolled tobacco and withdrew a match, striking it on the edge of the desk.

"Much as I've come to trust your twinges of indigestion, son," he said between puffs, "what evidence do you have to support your suppositions?"

"Nothing concrete."

"Then what sort of flimflam, stack-'em-up rumors have you collected?"

Jackson pointed to the papers on his desk. "What you have there, copies of Armiture's schedules—times, dates, locations. His last known destination was at the Billingsly School for Young Ladies. The reason: personal."

"So?"

"So who should be one of the teachers at that school, but a Miss Augusta McKendrick."

French scowled at the tip of his cigar. "I don't get your meaning."

"According to our records, Augusta McKendrick is the older sister of Clarence T. McKendrick."

"The Confederate spy?" French was giving Jackson his full attention now.

"Yes, sir. As you well know, Clarence McKendrick spent most of the war stealing munitions, supplies, and medicine, as well as gathering information for the South. He developed a web of operatives that some people suspect extended nearly to the White House staff itself."

"I thought they caught the bastard midway through the war."

"Yes, sir. They did. But he escaped three days before his execution. It is believed that McKendrick went to his sister for help. She was questioned, but denied that she'd seen her brother at all."

"You doubt her testimony?"

"Yes, sir. Especially in light of the fact that once Clarence continued his espionage from a safer distance, her school directly benefited from his activities. We have documented reports that he regularly supplied her with food and medicine until his reported death in May of 'sixty-four."

"So what does that have to do with Armiture?"

Jackson sifted through the papers on his desk, unearthing a telegram he'd read so many times he had it memorized. "This is only one of a dozen such reports I've received over the last six months."

French clamped his cigar between his teeth, held the paper at arm's length. Jackson knew when he'd finished reading by the way the cigar dipped. "Clarence McKendrick is alive?"

"So it would seem."

The general squinted at him through the smoke. "You're sure about this?"

"As sure as I can be without seeing him myself."

"I'll be damned."

"It is my belief that Armiture has friends who are still well-placed in the military. I think one of them received similar information and passed it on to Armiture. I think he went to that school in the hopes of interrogating the McKendrick women on the whereabouts of their brother. During the time Clarence was incarcerated, Armiture was a colonel in the army. It was his unit that was put in charge of guarding McKendrick and organizing the firing squad. It has always been a sore spot to him that Clarence escaped during his watch. The press made quite an issue of the fact during his election."

"But if Armiture were able to find the man and bring him to justice . . ." French said, thinking aloud.

"He would be hailed as a conquering hero."

French's eyes were narrowed now, hiding his thoughts, passing no judgment. "What else have you added to your theory?"

"Armiture had a reputation for having a temper, for being violent when provoked. There were even rumors that he and his men beat Clarence while he was awaiting trial." He tossed another paper in French's direction. "I interviewed Matthew Scott, Armiture's personal aide. He distinctly remembers mailing a letter to the McKendrick sisters weeks before the senator's scheduled visit. Suppose, sir, that he told them he planned to meet with them. Maybe he spooked her, causing Augusta McKendrick to send word to her brother. If he was hiding nearby, he would have seen to it that she was protected."

The chair creaked as the general leaned forward. "Good hell, Almighty," he breathed. "Clarence McKendrick hated Armiture. The man wouldn't have a chance. Clarence would have been there waiting for him."

French pondered that fact for a moment, then waved his cigar dismissingly. "But even if Clarence McKendrick was bent on retribution, he would be long gone by now. He's not stupid enough to stick around, you know. It would be nearly impossible to prove that he was responsible for Armiture's disappearance, even if we found a body and could prove foul play."

"That's true. Unless we use what we know to set a trap for him, sir."

The cigar paused halfway to French's lips. "A trap?"

"Yes, sir. If what I believe is true, one of the McKendrick women at that school must have notified Clarence of Armiture's arrival. That means they know where to find him."

"And if you can get that information . . ." French began, his expression brightening.

"We'll be able to apprehend a traitor."

The general made a hissing sound as he inhaled. "You know your rationale is weak as marsh water, don't you, boy?"

"Yes, sir."

"You must know that we have nothing to back up your ideas but hearsay and idle gossip?"

"Yes, sir."

"Senator Armiture may come blustering back into town bold as brass and the both of us will have egg on our face and a good deal of explaining to do to the McKendrick women."

"I know that." Jackson leaned forward. "But I don't think that's going to happen. Do you?"

The general took a deep drag of his cigar, exhaled, and squinted against the smoke. "Probably not." He took another puff. "But give me one good reason why I should send *you* to trap the man. Damnit, boy, after everything you've been through, you should spend the last few weeks of your army career here, out of danger.

If Clarence does come back, he'll be mean and ornery, and ready to shoot anything in blue."

Jackson felt a small glow of victory. He would return to Billingsly by sunup.

"That might be true, sir. But you know as well as I do that I'm the only man you can afford to send." This time, it was Jackson who leaned forward to make his point. "I'll get the confession you need to prove a member of the McKendrick family killed Senator Armiture. Whether it be from Clarence himself . . . or one of his sisters."

French regarded him for some time before nodding. "Very well. I'll let you take your own lead on this, boy. As long as you remember who you're dealing with, son. Don't trust 'em. Not any of 'em. No matter how pretty or how desperate they appear to you at the time."

After giving Jackson one last frown of warning, he stood, striding from the room with the same efficiency he'd once used on the battlefield.

It wasn't until he'd gone that Jackson realized he'd been holding his breath. He'd known that French could be irritated with the way Jackson had assumed control of this investigation. It wouldn't have been unusual for French to fly into a rage for having his original orders altered.

But Jackson had been willing to take the risk.

Just as he'd already taken so many risks.

He sighed, raking his fingers through his hair, wondering how much longer he would have to live under an assumed name and identity. Years ago, he'd dropped the "St." from his name to avoid suspicion and began tracking down the bastard who had stolen boxcars of munitions and sent faulty equipment to

Union troops in their place. Once he'd obtained proof that Clarence T. McKendrick had been responsible and that the man was alive and hiding somewhere behind Southern borders, Jackson had known it would only be a matter of time before he tracked the man down.

He could thank Armiture for giving him the proof Jackson needed that McKendrick was in touch with his sisters.

Jackson rubbed at the ache in his thigh. It was only a matter of time now. Soon, Jackson would be meeting the man face-to-face; he knew he would. At that moment, he would demand an explanation as to why Clarence had infiltrated Jackson's platoon as a bewildered soldier in search of his battalion. Then, after pumping Jackson's men for what information he could obtain, after living and sweating with them for weeks, he had turned on them and returned to the South, only to reappear weeks later to steal their munitions.

Yes, once he saw him again, Jackson would demand an accounting of the trust he'd betrayed—as well as for the deaths of Jackson's platoon and his own shattered leg.

2

As soon as the Union soldiers galloped away, Augusta wilted in relief—even though she instinctively knew they would be back. It was only a matter of time.

Her fears proved correct. The following morning as Augusta locked the garden shed behind her and made her way to the main building carrying a basket of dusty potatoes, the three men appeared on the main drive. The same man was at the head of the group. The *major*, as she'd begun to call him in her mind.

"Miss McKendrick!"

As the horses cantered up the drive, Augusta steeled herself to keep from bolting. She schooled her features into a semblance of calm. She mustn't give anything away. Not by so much as the twitch of a muscle could she reveal that these men frightened her to the bone.

"Morning, ma'am," the major murmured as he brought his horse to a stop mere yards in front of her.

But the commonplace greeting was in no way reassuring.

The man had come for her.

Her.

She knew it as surely as she knew her own name.

"Major. What brings you back to Billingsly so soon?"

"I'm afraid we have more business to conduct, ma'am." The comment was idle, his posture relaxed, but she sensed the steel behind the tone.

"Oh?" She was proud of the way her voice didn't shake even though she feared her knees would not be able to hold her. "Another search?"

Crooking one finger, he gave a tacit command to his men, one which caused them to circle her on either side, and then dismount. It was a clear sign that this time they would not be leaving so quickly.

"No, ma'am. We won't be conducting another search. At least not for an hour or two."

The major took his time swinging to the ground, his movements slow and deliberate. Augusta thought she saw a slight flinch tighten his features, a twinge of some inestimable pain, then he planted his boots solidly in the snow.

"I think we found what we needed yesterday to proceed with a more thorough investigation."

"What exactly did you find, Major?"

He slid a hand into the pocket of his coat, removing a tiny round object. The moment she saw it, Augusta's blood turned to ice. It was a button. A shiny, brass button. One she recognized from the frock coat Senator Armiture had been wearing when he'd come into the school. The night he'd tried to rape Effie.

"I don't understand." They were the only words she could force from bloodless lips.

"It's a button. One that an aide identified as

matching those on Senator Armiture's coat the day he left for his appointment with you."

She forced a wry smile. "Come now, Major. A button such as that could have come from any one of a hundred sources other than the senator's coat."

"Perhaps."

The major adjusted his stance so that most of his weight shifted to his right leg. Inexplicably, she found her gaze sliding to that point, where the dark blue wool of his uniform clung to strong legs, muscular thighs.

He flung one arm casually across the pommel of his saddle, his fingers rubbing against the stock of a rifle in a way she knew was completely planned. Despite any attempts to the contrary, there was nothing casual about his stance. He could have been carved from a solid block of granite for what softness he displayed.

"But we both know differently, Miss McKendrick. You know what happened to the senator. Just as you know precisely why *you* are the first person in the area to be suspected of any wrongdoing." He paused purposefully before adding, "You've been in trouble with the army before, haven't you?"

Augusta took an instinctive step back, one which caused the soldiers to grow even more tense and ready. In a flash, the unpleasantness she'd experienced two years ago at the hand of the Union army raced through her head. The accusations that she had consorted with her brother, a Confederate spy, that she had accepted gifts of food and medicine from him.

She studied her accusers. A tall, deathly thin sergeant and a short, bandy corporal. And the major.

The man who drew her attention time and again and held it fast.

At that precise moment, the two of them locked gazes. The major's stare was so piercing that she was sure he'd fathomed at least a portion of her thoughts, her fears. She grew even more disturbed when it became apparent that he was not completely adverse to the idea of scaring her.

"Allow me to introduce myself," he finally said.

"Since you didn't bother to do so before," she added caustically, feeling the need to point out his breach of manners.

His lips twitched, then resumed their firm line. "Yes, ma'am." He propped one hand on his hip, pushing the placket of his greatcoat aside enough to reveal the holster strapped to his hips. "I'm Major Jackson Charles, ma'am."

"Am I supposed to know you?"

"No, ma'am." But the reply was slow. "I don't suppose you would. I'm an aide to General French."

"I don't understand."

"It's simple, ma'am." Major Charles straightened, reaching over the saddle to pull the rifle from its scabbard. Although he didn't point it at her, it was clear that he wouldn't object to doing so if need be.

"Major—" she began, but he interrupted her before she had the opportunity to protest.

"Miss McKendrick, I've been instructed to put you under house arrest."

The words echoed in the frozen silence like a gunshot.

House arrest.

Too late, Augusta noted the young girls who'd

gathered in a huddled group on the verandah. Could they hear what was being said? Did the crystal silence of the late winter afternoon carry this man's voice that far?

She licked her lips, but her mouth had grown dry.

"Major Charles, I wonder if you would be willing to step inside." She nodded in the general direction of her students. "As you can probably see, we've drawn an audience and I don't wish to needlessly worry my charges."

Judging by the flicker of annoyance on his face, she guessed that he probably didn't give a damn about what her students did or did not hear. But Augusta refused to give him the opportunity to buck her own meager authority in this matter. Holding her head high, she made her way to the side of the house.

"Girls! I believe that you were assigned tasks in the kitchen, isn't that so?"

"Yes, ma'am."

"Go find Effie then, and get to work."

The young women meekly subsided, disappearing into the school.

"I'd like to speak with your sister too, Miss McKendrick."

"Later," she stated firmly, not about to let him bother Effie.

"This way, Major," she murmured, the words nearly sticking in her throat. She didn't want him in the school or in her office. But there was no way around it. Not if she wished to avoid a scene.

Ushering the man inside, she closed the heavy wooden door behind him, then gestured for him to precede her down the hall toward the front of the building.

"No, no. After *you,* Miss McKendrick."

The words were mocking, clipped, as if he'd seen through her pitiful display of control.

Augusta led the man into her private office. Once he'd followed her inside, she shoved the basket of potatoes onto a small bookcase and gripped the doorknob with more force than was necessary. Keeping her back to the man, she eased the portal shut and waited for the latch to click.

For several long, agonizing seconds, she didn't move. She couldn't. It took all the will she could muster to remain stiff and proud when every nerve in her body begged her to give in, surrender, and sink to the floor in defeat.

But she would not do that.

She *could* not.

"Now, Major," she said, taking a quick, fortifying breath and turning to face the man who had rattled her so completely. "Since we're finally away from the prying eyes and ears of my students, perhaps you would care to explain yourself. I'm *sure* you've made some horrible mistake." Somehow, she found the audacity to offer a gay laugh. One of those coquettish whispery peals of merriment that women of means were taught to use with men from the moment they graduated to long skirts.

If her feminine machinations had any effect on *this* man, she saw no evidence. Indeed, he appeared removed from the situation, looking far more intrigued by the decor of the room than any womanly wiles she'd displayed.

"This school has fared very well, despite the war."

His meaning was clear—that when most of the country wallowed in need, Billingsly looked quite comfortable. But he had no idea. She and Effie—the only employees remaining other than the proprietor, Mrs. Marble—had taken great care in cleaning and decorating the office and front parlor so that no evidence of hardship could be found. These were the rooms which would be seen by parents and prospective students. They must gleam with pride and apparent opulence. If this man were to investigate further, in the students' rooms, the kitchen, the larder, he would find the rest of the furnishings to be quite spartan—if not missing altogether.

When she didn't immediately reply, Major Charles gestured to the blaze roaring in the fireplace. "Do you mind?"

She wasn't entirely sure what he was asking. Did she mind if he moved closer to the fire? Sat in a nearby chair? Arrested her? Tore her life asunder with a few quick words?

But good manners prevailed. "No. Please."

He stepped closer to the flames, parting his greatcoat to the warmth, but not removing it. Nor did he sit, despite the prominent limp he displayed as he walked. Funny how she hadn't noticed that weakness until now, hadn't even heard the irregular *clomp* his boots must have made on the verandah and down the hall.

But this wasn't the time to think of such things.

Folding her hands in front of her, squeezing them tightly to keep them from shaking, she offered him her most dazzling smile. "So, Major Charles, what is this nonsense about arresting me?"

As if it were an afterthought, the major swept the hat from his head, revealing dark chocolate brown hair that was too long and wavy for any kind of a fashionable statement. Tossing the hat onto a nearby chair, he propped his elbow on the mantel.

"It isn't nonsense, Miss McKendrick. You are under arrest, by orders of General French."

Again, she offered a coy laugh.

Again, it had no effect.

"What is my supposed crime?" But she knew. She knew what he would say. Just as she knew he must be able to hear the thunderous beating of her heart.

"*Crimes* would be a better description, Miss McKendrick."

"Crimes?" she echoed weakly, feeling a trembling invade her lower limbs. "I can't imagine—"

"Perjury being right at the top of the list," Charles continued without pause. "Added to that is a host of accessory charges: espionage, aiding the enemy, and murder. The cold-blooded murder of Senator Tobias Armiture."

A cold fear rushed through her body.

"Does any of this sound familiar, Miss McKendrick?"

"Oh, dear." Augusta sank onto a worn velveteen chair, her display of weakness only partially an act. Slipping a handkerchief from her sleeve, she waved it in front of her face as if she were faint. She had to buy some time to think. Why hadn't she even taken into account that the events leading up to the senator's death would unearth the old accusations as well?

Closing her lashes, she took quick shallow breaths, dabbing the handkerchief across her brow and upper lip. "Oh, my, oh, my, oh, my," she gasped while her brain whirled. Think. *Think!*

An irritated sigh split the silence of the room. "An excellent show of dramatics, Miss McKendrick, but highly unnecessary."

Opening her lashes a bare slit, she found that Major Charles's expression hadn't altered. It remained hard, cold. Unaffected. But Augusta didn't immediately give up in her attempt.

"I assure you, sir. I feel . . . faint."

"I doubt it."

This time her eyes opened completely and she glared at him. Not even a cad of the highest caliber would dare to refute a woman in the midst of the vapors.

"I've been warned, Miss McKendrick." He didn't bother to move from his position by the fireplace, but somehow, his gaze became even more intent and even more powerful. As if he were stripping away the layers of clothing she wore, the wool and flannel and cotton, to inspect the quivering woman beneath. His tone dropped, ever so slightly, becoming husky, willful.

Dangerous.

"You are very beautiful. And extremely clever."

She froze, the handkerchief growing damp in her clenched fist.

"Where are you from, Miss McKendrick?"

The sudden change in topic caused her to frown. "From?"

"I detect a slight . . . drawl. A distinctly *Southern* drawl, if I'm not mistaken—no matter how hard you've tried to disguise it with that almost British intonation—but I doubt it originated here in Kentucky. No, it's not quite the same as the local folk. Your vowels are much softer, much more genteel."

She didn't reply, choosing to take the offensive.

"And you, sir. Virginia, I believe? The western portion of the state? Your own lazy tones reveal the truth."

She was surprised by the way he became still, almost wary. It gave her the courage she needed to goad him.

"A Southern state as well, by all intents and purposes," she asserted. "I believe General Lee hailed from there, as well as General Pickett."

"Which has nothing to do with my original question. Where are you from, Miss McKendrick?"

He knew the truth. She was sure he did.

The silence grew brittle and snapped with sparks of tension before she offered, "South Carolina."

"Ah," he drawled. "The first state to secede, the first state to declare war."

"Facts which can hardly be attributed to *me!*"

His lips twitched ever so slightly, but it was not a pleasant smile. More of a bitter twist. "How extremely Southern your pronunciation becomes when you're angry, Miss McKendrick. It fairly reeks of magnolias and Spanish moss."

She snapped her teeth shut, struggling for control.

"Perhaps I lack the 'cleverness' you accuse me of, Major Charles," she said after taking a calming breath. "After all, it is difficult for anyone to wipe away the speech patterns of their youth, no matter how much one might have been taught to do so. Nevertheless, I fail to see how such a topic of conversation has any bearing on the issue at hand. Just as I don't understand how you, or General French, or the army, can accuse me of anything untoward—let alone the crimes you've listed. My father fought on behalf of the—"

"On behalf of the North. I know. But your father is dead and can not help you now."

She gasped at the stark effrontery of his remark.

"This has to do with *you*, Miss McKendrick." His eyes, dark brown with flecks of blue, glittered as harshly as the frozen pond beyond the carriage house.

"Me? Why would you or the Union army have any interest in me?"

"We are acting on behalf of the provisional government in the area."

"And what have I done to merit such treatment?"

He made a *tsk*ing sound that she found incredibly irritating.

"I see that I shall have to remind you of the facts as they were related to me. In 1861, you made a trip across enemy lines—"

"In an effort to contact my father."

"In the summer of 1862, you made two more trips."

"For medical supplies."

"Medical supplies obtained from the 'enemy,' so to speak."

"My father lived and worked in Washington. He was the only person I could go to for help. My sister, Effie, has a heart condition which sometimes requires doses of laudanum."

"So when your father died of cholera, you accepted help from another source. That of your brother, Clarence."

"No."

"We have the necessary proof, Miss McKendrick."

"Those charges were dropped long ago."

"But they may be reopened." He took a step toward her. "For over a year, your brother ravaged the

Northern supply lines and carried information to his Confederate commanders. Then he was captured."

"As well as beaten," she inserted hotly.

"When he escaped, mere days before his execution, he came to you."

She studied him then. Fully. "It isn't true."

"Isn't it?"

As if sensing he had her complete attention, Major Charles finally moved away from the fire. But Augusta found the change in position less than reassuring when he began to prowl toward her with that uneven gait of his.

"After your brother escaped, you were accused of aiding the enemy. During the hearing, you testified that you hadn't seen him, but no one really believed you, Miss McKendrick. Instead, the army was quite sure that he *did* come here, that you *did* offer him medical aid, helped him flee to safety, then lied in a court of law when you were asked if you'd seen your brother."

"I *didn't* see him."

"He was your brother."

"He *didn't* come here."

"We have evidence to the contrary."

She sniffed in disdain. "From whom?"

"From one of your students at the time. A Miss Cordelia Bryer."

Augusta's stomach roiled with a sudden bout of nausea. She remembered that girl. Remembered her well. Remembered her churlishness, her selfishness, her tantrums when the last of the household servants had disappeared and those students living at the school had been forced to divide the chores among themselves.

"My brother was never here," Augusta stated again. "We were separated years before the war began when my sister and I came to Billingsly as students. I didn't even know he'd joined the Southern cavalry until I received notification that he died near Atlanta nearly a year before the war ended."

The major inched closer, crowding her.

"But he isn't dead, Miss McKendrick."

One of Major Charles's dark brows cocked in supreme enjoyment.

"Your brother is very much alive. He masterminded his own 'death,' then fled." His tone dropped. "I believe he came here, Miss McKendrick. I think he's hiding somewhere nearby."

3

The girls ironing in the kitchen area first heard the shouts of disbelief, then the cries of rage.

"What do you suppose he's doing to her?" Pansy whispered.

Buttercup shot her friends a quelling glance, gesturing with a slight tip of her head at the way Effie had moved from her station at the table and crept to the door.

They waited, paying only half a mind to their laundering duties, until Effie walked into the hall and closed the door behind her. As soon as the creaking of the floorboards informed them that she was safely out of earshot, they ran to the back staircase, made their way through the dormitory wing to the "spy glass."

Nearly three decades before, several additions had been made to Billingsly—one of which being the rooms for the younger girls boarded at the school. Because a staircase and doorway had once been situated at the spot which was now the main wall of an open foyer, Mrs. Marble had ordered the steps removed and a window installed in the yawning aperture. For years, it had become the place where the younger students gathered to watch the older girls in the vestibule below with their gentlemen callers and ballroom chaperones. The lookout afforded a good view of the foyer, the doors to the parlor, and Miss Augusta's office, but the lace panels covering the glass allowed little more than shadowy shapes of the students to be detected from the opposite direction.

"Can you see them?" Revel-Ann gasped, trying to wriggle nearer.

The young women pressed close—all but Thelma, who hung a little way back. "We shouldn't be looking," she whispered.

"Why not?" Revel-Ann demanded, her eyes sparkling. "He's probably torturing her—or better yet, he's drawn her into a passionate embrace that will make her his slave."

Buttercup frowned. "You've been getting into Mrs. Marble's trunk of dime novels again, haven't you?"

"So what if I have?" Revel-Ann retorted. "A girl's got to know what to expect from a man, doesn't she?"

"That isn't real life," Aster added primly.

"How do *you* know? The closest you've ever been to spending time with a boy is by mooning over those art books you're always reading—the ones with those Greek statues and naked Romans. It's a wonder you haven't tried to kiss the page."

"Enough!" Buttercup snapped. "We're supposed to be looking after Miss Augusta, not bickering among ourselves."

"That's right, Revel-Ann," Aster concurred.

Revel-Ann stuck out her tongue.

"Can you see anything?" Pansy interrupted, vainly trying to peer through the sliver of window she'd been given access to.

"No. The door is closed," Aster stated, returning to the matter at hand.

"What do you suppose is happening?" Pansy murmured.

Buttercup huffed indignantly. "He's interrogating her, that's what he's doing."

"I told—"

"He's not torturing her, Revel-Ann," Buttercup interrupted her quickly. "And he's certainly not kissing her."

Revel-Ann sniffed dismissingly. "I'm sure he's trying to force her to bow to his wishes, at any rate."

Pansy stood bolt upright, her hands plunking onto her hips. "But he can't *do* that!"

Buttercup offered another *harrumph*. "He can do whatever he wants. He's an officer of the Union army. They're law unto themselves 'round here. Why, he could take her outside and shoot her, if he wanted."

Thelma moaned, bracing herself against the faded silk wall coverings. "No, please. Don't say things like that!"

"Don't be such a goose, Thelma," Revel-Ann chided.

But Thelma had spent the better part of her early years being raised by a maiden aunt and she was invariably squeamish about anything unpleasant. She was also prone to lacing her corset too tightly. The combination was enough for her to keep a supply of smelling salts handy.

"Can you see Effie?" Aster whispered, standing on tiptoe.

Revel-Ann peeked through the lace. "I can't see *her,* but I think . . . I can see the tip of her shadow."

"Wait! The door is opening."

"Miss Augusta is coming out—she's . . . oh, my, she's *angry!"* Aster whispered as they heard the head-mistress storm up the stairs.

"Now that . . . that *man* is coming out," Pansy supplied.

"The major," Buttercup clarified with extreme disdain.

"He hasn't hurt her, has he?" Thelma gasped from her spot farther away.

Buttercup shook her head. "I doubt it. She acted mad enough to spit nails, but I didn't see any marks."

Pansy gasped. "He wouldn't strike her!"

Buttercup's lips thinned. "Why not? Those Union soldiers have done worse before."

"So what are we going to do?" Aster inquired.

Buttercup folded her arms under her breasts, assuming a militant pose. "We're going to help her, that's what we're going to do. After all she and Effie have done for us, it's the least we can do." She speared each girl with a pointed look. One which caused even Thelma to put some starch to her pose. "Tonight, after Effie and Augusta are asleep, we'll meet in my room and make plans. Understood?"

It was Thelma who whispered what they were thinking.

"What sort of plans, Buttercup?"

"We're going to drive them away, Thelma."

"Who?" she hissed, even though she knew.

"Those men, that's who."

* * *

"I don't care who you are, Major Charles. I don't have to listen to any more of your lies!"

The slam of Augusta McKendrick's bedroom door could be heard quite clearly through the entire house, but was especially loud to Major Jackson Charles. He'd followed her as far as the foyer, then watched her run the rest of the way up the curved staircase to the second floor.

Jackson allowed the slightest lightening of his expression. In fact, he was surprised by the satisfaction he felt at having unsettled the woman. Until the moment he'd informed her that her brother was alive, she'd been so calm, so unaffected.

Unreachable.

But deep down, he knew her surprise was false. She'd known her brother was alive. She'd known because she'd contacted him when Senator Armiture had notified her of his visit.

"Major?" The low call was uttered by Frank Conley, one of the soldiers assigned to Jackson's command. He was a tall, gangly man with cadaverous features who invariably spoke with the reverent tones of a minister. In fact, before the war, he'd been a mortician's assistant. A job which Jackson thought befitted him.

"Sir, what's our plan from here?"

Jackson abandoned his thoughts about the woman who'd barricaded herself in her room. There was plenty of time to confront her again.

Motioning for Frank to follow him, Jackson stepped outside, whistling for Boyd. As soon as he had joined them, Jackson stated, "I'm sure that the local folk in the area will pick up on what's happened here—and if Clarence is the man I think he is, I'm sure he has his local contacts informing him about the well-being of his kin. He'll try to come here. There's no doubt of it. Once he hears his sisters are in trouble, he'll have to make some sort of effort to help them. According to our records, they're the only family he's got. Until such time as he makes his appearance, it is our job to keep Miss McKendrick under house arrest and make sure the students remain within the confines of the property. Meanwhile, the three of us are to blend into the scenery as if we've always been here."

"How are we supposed to do that, huh?" Boyd quipped. "This is a girls' school, for cripes' sake."

Boyd Peterman was the antithesis of his deliberate companion. Quick and sharp and bursting with energy, he had trouble keeping still. He darted from place to place, idea to idea, like a moth dancing against a glass chimney. Jackson was not looking forward to having the young man closed up in a girls' school for the next few weeks. In his opinion, that was like putting a bear cub near a hive of honey.

"Change your clothes, both of you," he ordered sternly. "I don't want you wearing anything that can be interpreted as military issue. Then find a way to keep yourself busy with some sort of chore—chopping wood, fixing fences—whatever it takes. Boyd, I want you to cover the perimeter of the schoolyard as much as possible. Concentrate on the carriage house especially. With the weather the way it is, it's a logical place for McKendrick to hide until he can approach his sister. Frank, you'll spell Boyd every three hours so he can come inside and get warm. In the interim, I want you to search the house, inside and out, for any evidence of Senator Armiture's having been here. If we can implicate the woman, we can begin prosecution—which would be an even better incentive for Clarence McKendrick to make an appearance."

"Yes, sir."

"But won't we look suspicious, Major?" Boyd asked. "The last thing a girls' school needs is a couple of men wandering around outside looking busy."

Jackson's smile was slow. "That's the point. We want Clarence to think his sisters are in danger."

"What about you, Major?" Boyd asked with a grin. "What task will you be given to complete?"

The question was rhetorical, since they knew what Jackson had been assigned to do. It was his job to interrogate the reluctant Miss McKendrick. After spending a scant quarter hour with her in the office, he was feeling energized. Why, he wasn't sure. He'd done his best to appear as threatening as possible, to scare her into submission. But as the minutes had passed, she'd grown less and less docile. Her eyes had snapped, color had dotted her cheeks, and her hands had balled into fists that he knew she'd wanted to aim in his direction.

His smile widened. She was like a wildcat guarding her kittens. So completely adorable.

Jackson's thoughts screeched to a halt. Adorable? Augusta McKendrick? Out of the question. What had come over him?

Bit by bit, Jackson became aware of the fact that the silence had continued far too long and his men were eyeing him strangely.

"Get going," he said, with a jerk of his head. "I want the horses bedded down in the carriage house before anyone else can see them—and for hell's sake, keep an eye on the rest of the inhabitants of Billingsly. We can't have anyone trotting off to warn Clarence McKendrick, can we?"

After exchanging curious glances, the two men set off for the carriage house, leaving Jackson alone to contemplate the frozen grounds in front of him.

No, not alone. Not quite.

He turned in time to see a woman peering at him from one of the parlor windows. She was a beautiful thing, slim, slight, fragile. A more ethereal copy of Augusta McKendrick.

So this was the other sister, Effie, Jackson thought, going back into the house. Moving as quickly as the pain in his leg would allow, he blocked the entry to the parlor, just as Effie McKendrick attempted to leave.

"Good morning, Miss McKendrick."

She grew so pale that he wondered about the state of her health. According to Agnes Marble, she'd been hired to teach needlepoint and elocution—hardly the most rigorous tasks.

Effie's hand fluttered against her chest like a captured butterfly, and he heard a faint wheezing as she took a breath, but she held her ground. Indeed, her own eyes flashed with a defiance he wouldn't have thought possible of so fragile a woman. "I don't believe we've been formally introduced."

Jackson bowed shallowly from the waist. "Major Jackson Charles, ma'am."

"Are you really keeping my sister under house arrest?"

Jackson surmised that the word had been passed to her by one of the students.

"Yes. I'm afraid so."

"Why? She hasn't done anything." There was a thread of iron to her tone despite the way she fought to keep her labored breathing under control.

"General French believes that your sister lied on the witness stand during the hearing. He feels he has enough evidence to prove she directly benefited from his acts of espionage."

Effie shook her head, her hand sweeping in front of her in a disgusted motion. "It isn't true," she whispered. "Augusta would never do such a thing."

"But she's your sister. Don't you think you might be prejudiced in your opinions, Miss Effie?"

"No." Her voice was stronger now, her chin jutting out. "No, I don't think I am. And I think you're horrid to accuse her. Absolutely horrid!"

With that she sniffed, angled her nose into the air, and brushed past him as if he were of no more importance than a fly, her skirts swishing as she disappeared down the hall.

And for the first time in years, Jackson felt the tiniest twinge of discomfiture.

The floorboards squeaked beneath Augusta's feet as she paced the length of her bedroom, turned, then marched to the opposite end.

Damn.

Damn, damn, damn.

What a muddle! What a complete and utter muddle!

Stifling a sob of frustration, she strode to the window, staring out at the frosty yard. What was she going to do? She'd been more than ready to field any questions or accusations which might come her way concerning Senator Armiture. She'd thought of every possible repercussion, rehearsed every answer she might be required to give.

But never in her wildest imaginings had she thought that the army would resurrect the old charges. Charges which they had dropped over a year ago.

How could this have happened? And how could her brother be dragged into it as well? The Union officials were supposed to believe he was truly dead. She'd seen the list proclaiming his demise, she'd even been sent his personal effects should anyone care to check the records. So what proof did Major Charles have that Clarence was alive?

She'd told the truth on the stand. She hadn't harbored Clarence after his escape. Not because he hadn't asked, but because she'd known he wouldn't be safe here. It would be the first place they would have looked for him.

Augusta sighed. Poor Clarence. Poor misguided Clarence. When they'd been younger, he hadn't understood why their parents quarreled so bitterly over everything. He'd felt it was somehow *his* fault that their father had packed his bags and gone to Washington to live apart from his family. As a boy, he'd ached for some sort of masculine approval, and when it had never come, he'd grown angry and bitter, vowing to hate everything their father loved.

But even when Clarence had railed against the injustice of having a Union officer as a father, Augusta hadn't dreamed that Clarence would become a spy for the Confederacy, raiding their supply lines and gathering information for his superiors. If she'd had any idea . . .

What? What would she have done? As much as

she'd disapproved of Clarence's attitude, she couldn't have stopped it. Not with their mother egging him on. While Effie and Augusta had been at Billingsly, Clarence had been exposed to the way their mother railed against the North and glorified the South. Augusta later realized that her mother had used Clarence as a pawn against their father. Too late, Augusta had seen Clarence become brooding and hard, but even then, even when he grew into a stranger, she couldn't discount the fact that he was her brother. Her blood.

Alive. Drat it all, how had the army discovered the truth behind the ruse?

Her thoughts scattered through her head like buckshot and she pressed her hot forehead against the cool glass. The rush of dread she felt was tempered with a rush of determination. Clenching her jaw, Augusta rose to full height.

As a child, Augusta had always been the peacemaker, the comforter. That job had not changed over the passage of years. Effie needed her strength. And Clarence . . .

She would find a way to protect Clarence from these newer threats. She must. No matter the cost to her own standing.

It was her duty.

When she emerged from her room, Augusta had determined that, for the rest of the evening, she would behave as if nothing had occurred. After all, nothing *had* happened. Yet. If she could convince the major that he'd made an error in coming here, in assuming that Clarence was alive, she could keep the army away from him.

The door creaked slightly as she slipped into the hall. But she needn't have bothered with such stealth. The minute she appeared, a shadow loomed over her shoulder and stretched onto the floor in front of her.

The major. He'd followed her upstairs.

She studied him, taking in the lean strength of his body and the quiet seriousness of his expression. There was no anger in the depths of his gaze, no sense of intimidation. He merely studied her as if she were a stranger and he wished to sum up her character.

It was disturbing, that casual scrutiny. She'd felt so sure that whenever they were near each other, battle lines would be drawn. She would remain firmly on one side, he on the other. But the way he watched her now was almost . . . familiar. Intriguing.

Knowing she couldn't allow her thoughts to take such a path, she turned, and without comment, made her way down the hall.

"Miss McKendrick," he called from behind.

She didn't bother to look his way. "Yes, Major Charles?"

"Is there something I can help you with?"

She didn't alter her pace. "It is nearly five. I've duties in the kitchen."

"I would prefer that you stay in your—"

She held up a hand, the same gesture she had used countless times to force recalcitrant students into silence. "As I recall, you mentioned 'house' arrest." Only then did she bother to shoot him a quick glance. "I am assuming that I will be allowed to continue with my duties here."

"Why aren't there any more teachers?"

"Our enrollment this fall was extremely small—

barely a dozen girls—which meant that two instructors were sufficient. After her stroke, Mrs. Marble moved to town. The noise the young ladies make tends to bother her."

"You said there were twelve students. We've only rounded up five. Where are the rest?"

"Most of the young ladies returned home for the winter recess. Those who have stayed here are—in essence—orphans. They have no homes or families to return to. They may not be able to pay anymore, but I will not turn them away."

The information was starkly uttered, as she'd meant it to be. Before the man could ask her anything more, she continued, "Now, if you'll excuse me, I have work to do."

Her heels clicked in military fashion on the bare wooden floor—a floor which had once been covered with a braided woolen runner and crowded with furniture. But the runner had been dismantled, the strips washed and mended to be used as bandages. The tables and chairs had been stolen last winter by a band of ne'er-do-wells who'd broken into the school searching for firewood and valuables. Augusta had thanked heaven above that she and the girls had been in town at church services, otherwise the men might have stolen more than mere material possessions.

Pulling her mind back to the matter at hand, to a new group of soldiers with a fresh batch of trouble, she nearly sighed aloud when the major's shadow dogged her to the lower level, and back to the rear of the house where the kitchen and larder were located.

When they entered, the gaggle of girls whispering over the scuffed table grew silent.

"They cook?"

The major's question rang with too much surprise for Augusta's comfort.

"Yes, Major. They cook. They sew, they clean, they run, they jump, they skip."

He shot her a pithy glance. "I merely meant that this is supposed to be a finishing school."

"Yes," she said, whirling to face him and speaking so low that only he could hear her. "And in my opinion, the most important phase of 'finishing' a young lady's character in this day and age is teaching her how to survive should calamity strike—as it has already."

After pinning him with one of her finest I'm-in-charge-here stares, she faced the girls.

"Ladies, I think it would be best if I introduced our . . . guest." The last word lodged in her throat. "This is Major Jackson Charles. He will be staying here"—she shot him another pointed glance—"for a very *short* time while some clerical errors are being ironed out. Major Charles, these are my resident students."

She gestured to a gangly girl of about thirteen with wide eyes made even more pronounced by a pair of thick spectacles. "This is Pansy Browning, of Vicksburg, Mississippi."

The girl offered a shy curtsy.

"Her eldest sister, Buttercup."

A tall, willowy blond eighteen-year-old glared his way.

"And the middle Browning, Aster." A short, bird-like creature, with a puff of dark ringlets, bobbed in a curtsy.

"Thelma Richter, from New Orleans."

56

The eldest student by a year sank into a chair, her eyes as wide as quarters.

"And this is Revel-Ann."

Revel-Ann plunked her hands on her hips in open challenge and Augusta feared she was up to some mischief. Revel-Ann was *always* embroiled in mischief.

"Where is Revel-Ann from?"

Augusta opened her mouth, then hesitated. Before she could offer a response, Revel-Ann intoned, "I am from the earth and the sky. Nature has suckled me at her bosom and I glorify her name."

The silence of the room was deafening. Then Buttercup snorted in disapproval, Aster turned away, and Pansy giggled.

When Major Charles looked to Augusta for some sort of explanation, she was forced to murmur, "Revel-Ann's parents were part of the recent transcendental movement."

"Ahh."

"Those men with you," Revel-Ann said suddenly. "Are they—"

"Major Charles and his men are of no concern to us, Revel-Ann," Augusta quickly interrupted. "We've supper to prepare."

Buttercup scowled. "They won't be joining us, will they?"

"No."

"Yes," a deep voice corrected.

Augusta glared at the major.

His features lightened for a second and he looked almost pleasant. Handsome.

"If you'll make a list, Miss McKendrick, I'd be

happy to supply any stores you might need for the length of our stay. My men would be willing to chop wood and haul water—as well as do a few odd repair jobs—in exchange for your trouble."

Augusta was so very tempted to take him up on the offer. There was so much at Billingsly that had to be done if they were ever going to attract a paying student body. Not to mention that their food supplies were growing dangerously low and it was only the beginning of winter weather.

"Very well." She marched to the small accounting desk in the corner of the kitchen. At one time, when the school had been bustling with students, it had been used by a housekeeper who oversaw the servants, planned menus, and kept accounts. Now, Augusta did those jobs as well.

Taking pen and ink, she chose the back of an old envelope for her list—about the only blank scrap of paper left in the school.

"We will need flour," she said as she wrote.

"Fine."

"Sugar, yeast, baking powder, salt."

"Whatever you need."

"Good! Then be so kind as to add cornmeal, salt pork, dried beef, beans, oatmeal—"

"Now see here—"

"Raisins, dried apples, apricots, and cherries. At least two live chickens—"

"Chickens!" he barked.

"For a supply of eggs," she replied smoothly. "Your men do eat eggs, don't they? As well as the breads and such which will be made from them?"

"I don't believe—"

"Of course if there's any way you could supply a goat or a cow as well, that would really be a help."

"Damnit, when I offered supplies—"

"Please, Major Charles." She waggled a finger in the general direction of the girls. "Not in the presence of such impressionable young ladies."

He scowled at her, the expression so fierce, so . . . threatening, that Augusta feared she'd gone too far. The affable mood he'd displayed was gone in an instant and the interrogator was back.

Jackson bent close, rasping against her ear, "Fine, Miss McKendrick. I'll get you whatever you damn well want—even if I have to buy it myself. But plan on offering me a bit more than meals in exchange."

His voice was so silky and rich and smooth that a rash of gooseflesh raced up her spine. The double entendre was not lost on her—and to her horror, she was not as affronted as she should have been.

With that, he stormed from the room.

But even as he sent a tall, cadaverous soldier to guard her, Augusta knew the major would be back to confront her. Soon. Much too soon. Perhaps even to claim she owed him something for the supplies.

Her lashes squeezed closed in silent prayer. *Leave it alone, Major. Just leave it alone.*

The school had grown eerily quiet.

Jackson shifted in the wing-back chair he'd pulled close to the fire in Augusta McKendrick's office. His leg was giving him fits tonight, protesting too many hours in the saddle and as many on his feet. It was time he went upstairs to needle Augusta—the best way to get her angry enough to spill her secrets, he was

59

sure. But as the minutes ticked by, he found that he couldn't move. Not yet. It had been too long since he'd been warm. Comfortable.

Sighing, he stared at the flickering flames, wondering why his mind had decided to pester his conscience and remind him what he'd done to reach this point. This place.

This woman.

In the past, he'd savagely kept his thoughts in the present. That day. That hour. Only the present. He hadn't allowed himself to think of his home or the people he'd left behind. Since he'd been sure that the army would have been suspicious of assigning him to an intelligence division if they'd known he had a personal vendetta against Clarence McKendrick, Jackson had changed his identification to read Jackson Charles, not *St.* Charles. He'd kept his service record buried in order to facilitate his own search for Clarence McKendrick. He'd arranged a transfer to French's division since he had been in charge of tracking McKendrick. Then, he'd promised himself that he wouldn't return to his home in Virginia until he'd avenged his comrades' deaths.

If French had been aware of his hidden motives, Jackson was sure the man would accuse him of indulging in "vigilante justice." But Jackson didn't care. He was sworn to obtain retribution for his slain comrades. Even if that vow was getting harder and harder to keep.

Funny, but all those years ago, lying on a hospital cot, fighting for the will to live, he'd thought it would be an easy matter to track down the man responsible for stealing his platoon's munitions and replacing it with faulty cannon. He hadn't realized it would take years to flush his quarry out of hiding.

He was so damned close to finding Clarence McKendrick. His instincts were roused to a fever pitch. The man was close. He could feel it. It shouldn't take long to flush him out of hiding. In the meantime, he had to discover what happened to Senator Armiture, then determine how involved Augusta and Effie had become in their brother's concerns.

Augusta.

Why did her name cause him to hold his breath each time he heard it? She was nothing at all like he'd imagined her. When he'd first encountered her name in connection with her brother's trial, he'd pictured an older woman with graying hair. Not with tresses the color of vinegar taffy and eyes a rich, elegant bluish gray. But now that he'd seen her, he couldn't picture her any other way. She fit her name completely. Cool, elegant, composed.

Feisty.

Damn. She complicated things. Why, he wasn't sure yet.

He only knew he couldn't seem to get her out of his mind.

4

I'll get you whatever you damn well want—even if I
have to buy it myself. But plan on offering me a bit
more than meals in exchange."

The words returned to haunt Augusta as soon as
she'd retired to her bedroom.

What did Major Charles want in exchange for his
largesse? Would he demand something as simple as
extra bedding for his men or a few rooms for their
use? Or would he wish to be paid in other ways? Far
more personal, intimate ways?

The jiggle of her lock put Augusta's nerves on edge.
She whirled, staring at the broad door, picturing the
man who must be on the other side.

"Yes?" she called softly, in case it were Effie or one
of the girls who had come to check on her.

"Let me in, Miss McKendrick."

The instant she heard the deep male voice, she
hugged her arms around her waist. He couldn't come
in here. He mustn't.

But how was she going to keep him out? If there was

anything she'd learned about the man, it was that he had a will of granite. Her lips pursed. But then, she had a stubborn will of her own.

"Surely you don't mean to deny me the privacy of my own room, Major," she challenged.

"Yes. I do. I've been given the task of guarding you, and I intend to do so."

She scrambled to find some tangible reason for him to stay away. "It wouldn't be proper for you to come in here at night, Major."

"No. It probably wouldn't be, Miss McKendrick."

The relief his statement brought was banished when she heard an awful crash. The wood splintered near the lock, the knob bouncing to the floor. Within seconds, the door was open and she was face-to-face with Major Charles. He held his rifle in one hand, obviously having just used it to break the lock.

"You bastard," she whispered.

He merely shrugged, his lips lifting in a wry grin. "I warned you."

"I didn't know you'd break the door down!"

"You should have guessed." He limped forward, closing the shattered wood as far as it would allow.

"Augusta!"

The call came from down the hall and Augusta glared at the man. "I'm fine, Effie. Major Charles merely stumbled and broke some things. Stay where you are."

The answering silence fairly trembled with uncertainty, but Effie finally called, "All right. Good night."

Augusta waited until she'd heard Effie close herself in her room then hissed, "Just what do you think you're doing? I won't have you alarming her."

"You're very protective of her."

"My sister is a gentle creature, Major. Her health is not what it should be. She needn't be caught up in this . . . fuss."

One of his brows lifted. "But this . . . *fuss* may ultimately involve her."

"Nonsense. My sister hasn't done anything."

"That's what she said about you."

Augusta sucked in her breath. "You were questioning her?"

"It's my job."

"Leave her alone, Major."

"Only if you cooperate with me, Miss McKendrick."

Augusta had been backed into a verbal corner and she knew it.

"Has Effie seen the senator?"

Augusta stumbled over a reply and chose to remain silent.

The major limped toward her. "You've been very careful to keep me separated from her, Miss McKendrick. Other than a few seconds with her in the parlor this afternoon, she is constantly accompanied by one of your students or by yourself."

"That's absurd."

"Is it?"

He grew near, too near, crowding her to the point where she couldn't breathe without smelling him— leather and woodsmoke and man.

"I would never harm your sister."

She studied him closely, somehow sensing that what he said was true. She might not like the man, but there was a decency about him, a personal sense of honor, that she couldn't deny.

"You might not strike her, but there are other ways

of hurting her, Major. She's . . . sensitive to a fault. Too giving of her emotions."

"And you think this is a bad thing?"

Augusta stiffened. In that query lurked a challenge that her own emotions were far too cool. "What do you want, Major?"

"I told you. I've been asked to guard you. Around the clock."

"Then you've failed in your task. I've been denied your company several times today."

"Not without one of my men assuming the responsibility in my absence."

"If you feel so strongly about guarding me, you can do so from the hall."

He shook his head. "I don't think so."

Her lips pressed tightly together. "I will not have my reputation ruined by—"

A smile teased the corners of his lips. "Your reputation was ruined long ago, wouldn't you say?"

She gasped. "How dare you say such a thing!"

He eased closer and she found it difficult to breathe.

"It's true, though. Charges were brought against you. You spent several days in jail. A woman's character suffers from far less scandal than that. You've also lived alone in the house with a man all these months without the benefit of a chaperone."

"A man?"

"Elijah Ward."

She waved the thought away with her hand. "Elijah is an employee here at Billingsly. No one would ever believe anything untoward has happened between us."

"Perhaps." The intensity was back. She was being probed for information again. "Where is he, Miss

McKendrick? Where is Elijah Ward? Everyone else has been accounted for."

Augusta didn't answer. She couldn't. She wouldn't have this man chasing after Elijah, asking him questions, insinuating that he had behaved in any way which would damage Augusta's honor. Elijah would be crushed if he thought such gossip was spreading through town.

"Elijah is no concern of yours, Major. He has not been here at Billingsly for some time."

"Where can I find him?"

"I wouldn't know." She did know, but she wouldn't tell this man. As it was, she was going to have to find some way of meeting with Elijah herself.

Major Charles grasped her arm.

"Where *is* he, Miss McKendrick?"

She yanked free. "Elijah is a free man—was a free man before the war. It isn't my place or my business to demand explanations about his personal affairs."

Sweeping her skirts aside so that they wouldn't brush so much as the toes of his boots, she pushed past him. "Now, if you'll excuse me, I'm going to do some accounts. If you will not leave me alone in my bedchamber, then I will have to find a more practical means to fill my time, because I will not—*will not*—allow you to spend the night, in here, with me."

When she would have marched away, he drew her close, murmuring near her ear, "You can run as far as you want, but the facts won't change, Miss McKendrick. I'll be there, a half step behind you. Watching, waiting."

The words were meant to daunt her, she was sure. So why did they bring a strange tingling to her skin and an odd exhilaration to her pulse?

"What do you want, Major?" she challenged. "A confession?"

"Things would go much better for all of you if you would work with me instead of against me."

She faced him then, her hands itching to slap him for his arrogance. "In what way will things 'go much better,' Major Charles?" she retorted mockingly. "Will you see to it that my girls are protected from a world they no longer understand? Will my sister and I be given back the family which was taken from us? I don't see how any sort of soul-baring can alter what has occurred."

There was no softening to his features.

"Maybe it won't, but it could change the way things proceed from here. I could make things easier for you should you cooperate."

She stiffened by degrees. "I wonder, Major Charles, how you intend for me to interpret that remark."

"Any way which might help me to solve this murder."

"Solve this murder," she repeated slowly and carefully. "As far as I'm concerned, you haven't given me sufficient proof that there even *was* a murder."

He pulled her closer, so much so that his breath whispered against her hair.

"Oh, there was a murder, all right. And it occurred right here at your school."

"You've found no proof of that." She could only pray that the body had been hidden well enough that he never would.

"Not yet. But I will."

"How can you be so sure?"

"Because I *feel* it." His voice dropped, becoming husky and low. "It's one of those gut instincts I've

67

learned to trust over the years." Again, he drew her close and she was made aware of the heat of his body, the whipcord strength of his form. "I'll uncover the truth. It's my job. One that I've grown very good at."

She remained quite still, knowing that what he said was true. This man could pull secrets from a block of wood. He need only pierce it with those blazing eyes. But *she* would not give in. She mustn't.

"Go to hell, Major."

"Such talk from a lady."

"You have a talent for provoking me."

He smiled as if pleased. "It doesn't have to be this way, you know. I may not be able to change what has taken place, but if you help me—if you tell me what I need to know now—I could soften the repercussions. I could plead your case."

"There is no case," she insisted again, but he continued as if she hadn't spoken.

"What happened, Augusta?"

It was the first time she could remember his using her name and it startled her. The practice was too familiar. Too intimate.

"Nothing happened," she murmured succinctly. "I haven't seen the man."

"But you're lying. Do you know how I can tell?"

She didn't dignify his question with a response.

He continued nevertheless.

"Your cheeks grow slightly pink, and you begin to breathe erratically, causing the fabric of your gown to shudder. Here." He touched her with the back of his finger just above the edge of her corset.

She tried to yank free, but he slid his free arm around her waist and held her securely, causing her hips to grind against his legs. Those hard muscular legs she'd examined when he'd swung from his saddle.

"It's a circumstance that intrigues a man. All that tight lacing a woman wears. The layers and cinching and ruffles and furbelows—they only make a woman's emotions more patently clear."

"I'm glad you think so, Major," she said lowly, barely able to contain her irritation. "Then there will be no confusion as to my feelings toward *you.*"

He merely grinned.

"No, Augusta. I don't think those feelings *are* clear. Exactly how *do* you feel?"

"I think you're a slimy, no-good, evil, rat-faced—"

His arms snapped around her waist, driving the insults from her lungs.

"You're very vehement."

"I think I have reason to be."

He shook his head in wry amusement. "It never ceases to amaze me how those who have sinned consider themselves so wronged once they're caught."

"I haven't done anything," she ground out through clenched teeth, trying not to think about the way she was pressed so closely to his thighs, his hips, his chest.

"That's what I'm here to find out. You see, the army considers me an expert, to some degree."

"An expert in what?" But she knew. She knew deep in her soul where a tiny part of her grew quiet.

"I've developed a talent for extracting information from those unwilling to give it."

She would have trembled at the tone he used, but she didn't dare. She couldn't afford the display of vulnerability.

Abruptly, he turned her loose.

"Go to bed," he ordered curtly. "I'll allow you fifteen minutes—alone—to change. Then, if you've followed my instructions, I'll guard you from the hall, door open." His eyes flashed in the lamplight as he added, "But only as long as you prove to me that I can trust you that far. If you try to buck me—or my authority—I assure you, there will be no more reprieves."

He spent the allotted quarter hour in the study. Not so much because it was quiet, but because it was located directly beneath Augusta McKendrick's room. Despite what he'd said, he wasn't about to trust her any more than he had to, and by waiting below, listening to the creaking of the floorboards, he had some idea what she was doing—the way she'd waited as if doubting he was really gone. Then the pacing. Then finally, the hurried steps, the bang of wardrobe doors, and the squeak of drawers.

Sinking onto a settee, Jackson lit a cigar, imagining each move she made. It wasn't difficult to do. The way she must be pulling the pins from her hair, unbuttoning her blouse, peeling the petticoats free, was incredibly clear. He was even able to ignore the unusual chill to the room, as if the area had been shut away for days without a fire in the grate.

Taking a drag of the cigar, he allowed the muscles he'd held in check to relax. But the sounds above him kept drawing his thoughts back to Augusta.

Damn. Why couldn't he get her out of his head? Fifteen minutes. That's all he required. Fifteen minutes of peace. Then he'd be ready to resume his duties, to poke and prod and pester her into admitting the truth.

But try as he might, his thoughts returned to their wayward track.

She was a beautiful woman. Strong. Resilient. Not a bit ethereal and elegant as Effie, to be sure, but he'd never really been drawn to that sort of female. No, Augusta was spunky and stubborn and willful and proud. She wouldn't be easily subdued.

What a pity she wasn't more biddable. The strength she displayed could only get her into more trouble.

Jackson returned to Augusta's doorway at the precise instant he said he would. Setting a ladder-back chair in the corridor, he took two steps into her room.

The lamp at her bedside had been blown out, leaving little more than a faint wash of light seeping in from the lantern in the hall. There was enough of a glow to see that she was lying in her narrow bed, the covers drawn up to her ears.

Jackson knew that the pose was meant to discourage him from lascivious thinking, as was her freshly scrubbed face, the tawny hair drawn into a tight braid, and the sheets and quilts tucked beneath her nose.

But something about the whole tableau was far from off-putting. Indeed, standing there, with the barest glow of lamplight illuminating her figure, he couldn't help but wonder what she'd chosen to wear to bed. Was she completely dressed? Or had she changed into some sort of night shift? Something in flannel. A sheer worn cotton. Silk?

He shook his head at such a fanciful notion. Why in the world would this woman wear silk when she knew she was about to be guarded for the evening by a near-stranger?

Turning, he strode back into the hall, wincing when the actions were performed with more vigor than necessary. Sinking into the uncomfortable chair, he tipped it back against the wall and folded his arms over his chest. Closing his eyes, he tried to get some rest. Just enough to take the edge off his temper.

Even so, time and time again, his lashes opened and he found himself watching Augusta.

He was sure she slept no better than he did.

"Well, girls, what's our plan?"

The students gathered around Buttercup's bed, some sitting, some standing, Thelma gripping the posts as if they were her only means of emotional strength.

"The two soldiers are taking turns at the front door," Pansy volunteered. "The tall one is guarding right now. The other one is bedded down in the rear bedroom the cook used to use."

"Good." Buttercup took a stub of a pencil and made a note on the scrap of wallpaper torn from one of the upper rooms—the only paper she'd been able to find to use for notes at such short notice.

"They've put their clothes and equipment and things in the same back bedroom," Revel-Ann added.

Buttercup scribbled down the information.

"Do you think you can get ahold of some things—bullets, pieces of their uniforms and such?"

Revel-Ann tossed her fiery-red hair over her shoulder. "Yes, ma'am, I do. I could be like the wind, ethereal, unseen, omni—"

"Fine," Buttercup interrupted. "You be the wind—or whatever else you need to be—but get everything I ask for, understand?"

Revel-Ann threw her a cocky salute.

Buttercup then turned to Aster. "What have you been able to find out?"

"The major spent a good fifteen minutes in the study."

They exchanged worried glances.

"Do you think he found anything?"

Aster shook her head. "There's nothing to find, I'm sure. You saw how Miss Augusta scrubbed the place. But come morning, I'll prop one of the windows open a crack so that the room will stay chilly. That should discourage him from lingering inside."

"Excellent." Again, she scrawled a note.

Thelma was the first to disturb her concentration. "What are we going to do, Buttercup? You said you had a plan."

"I do. But for now, we'll bide our time. At least until the 'wind' can get us a gun and some ammunition."

Revel-Ann smirked.

"In the meantime, there's no sense in antagonizing the soldiers if Miss Augusta can get them to go away. But I want you all to spy on those men every minute of the day. Keep them busy, distract them as much as possible."

"How?" Pansy demanded.

Buttercup straightened, throwing her shoulders back and jutting out her chest in a way she'd seen Miss Augusta do when she felt she was bearding a lion's den. "We're women, aren't we? We'll do what comes naturally. We'll trap them in our feminine lairs."

"Oh," Pansy replied weakly.

Revel-Ann grinned.

"But, Buttercup," Astor inserted gently, "Pansy and Revel-Ann are much too young to be consorting with anyone but boys of their own age."

"That's why it will be up to the three of us to tempt them."

Aster stared at her sister in disbelief. "You mean you want us to . . . seduce them?"

"If that's what it takes."

Aster sank onto the bed in disbelief. "Oh, my."

Thelma made a mewling sound and collapsed to the floor in a dead faint.

Poking at her with her toe, Buttercup rolled her eyes in disgust. "Pansy, see what you can do about reviving her—then loosen her corset strings and tie some smelling salts around her neck, for heaven's sake. We can't have her succumbing to the vapors in the midst of our campaign, can we?"

Pansy was on the floor, lightly slapping her friend's cheeks.

Having taken charge, Buttercup pointed at Revel-Ann. "Go get those dime novels you're always mooning over. Before we go into battle, I think we'd best scout out how best to defeat the enemy."

As Revel-Ann ran from the room, Buttercup strode to the bureau and tipped her head, eyeing her own reflection in the mirror. "We can bring these men to heel. I'm sure of it. Wait and see."

Thelma, who had been rousing, took one look at Buttercup as she fussed with her hair and tugged at her bodice. Then her eyes rolled back in her head and she fainted for the second time in as many minutes.

5

At the first pink crack of dawn, Augusta wriggled out of bed—no easy task since she was trying to keep the blankets wrapped around her as much as possible. She didn't want Major Charles to know she hadn't changed into a night rail as he'd probably assumed, but into a simple skirt and shirtwaist. Just in case that man should get it in his head to drag her out of bed.

As she inched toward the door, she could see that he'd tipped his chair back against the wall. His eyes were closed, his face relaxed. Asleep. Good.

Pressing her lips together in supreme enjoyment, she slammed the door closed with all her might.

Bam!

A quick smile of satisfaction creased her lips, but it faded when she remembered the smashed lock. To her ultimate horror, the door quivered against the jamb, bounced, then swung backward.

"Good morning to you too."

The major's eyes were open a mere slit, causing her

to wonder if he'd really been asleep at all, or if he'd been waiting for a show of defiance.

Slowly, ever so slowly, he allowed his chair to settle to the floor with a muffled *thump,* then he stood—effortlessly, despite the uncomfortable evening he must have had.

Bit by bit, he closed the distance between them, and with each step he took, Augusta knew she'd made a mistake. A horrible, horrible mistake.

She shouldn't have defied him so openly. After all, he was pitted against her, determined to find some evidence of her guilt. And she'd just slammed the door in his face.

The major scowled and took her chin, his grip firm, the pressure enough to make her wince, but not sufficient to bruise.

"Never do that again," he said slowly, deliberately.

"Or what?" She knew she shouldn't goad him on, but she couldn't help herself.

Instead of answering her directly, the major said, "You're treading on thin ice, Miss McKendrick." He inched closer, his thighs pressing into the blankets, her skirts. "Somehow, the seriousness of your predicament hasn't sunk into your pretty head."

"Pretty, Major? I wouldn't have expected you to compliment someone you suspect of being a criminal."

"I'm not blind, Augusta."

Just as he had the night before, he'd used her name. It was no less startling, no less overpowering in its effect.

"Moreover, I would be less than honest if I didn't tell you exactly what I think. You're pretty, yes. You're also intelligent, no doubt witty, and full of fire. But those can be dangerous qualities in a woman who's in trouble." His hand shifted, cupping her cheek, making her stare deep into those burning eyes. "Do you know what they expect of you?"

"Who?"

"The authorities who will prosecute you."

"You don't have any proof that there *will* be any prosecution. I haven't done anything that warrants a trial."

He made a *tsk*ing noise with his tongue. "We've been over that. You're guilty of quite a few crimes, and I will prove that fact. It's only a matter of time. When I do, you'll be taken to prison, Augusta. They won't treat you kindly there. Your guards won't appreciate your spirit. They'll break you and purposely mistreat you. All in the name of justice. Then . . . the authorities will probably hang you."

She shivered at the image his words created, but she refused to act cowed.

"Get out of my room," she hissed.

"Why? You're completely clothed. An ivory linen shirtwaist and a rust-colored skirt, if I'm not mistaken. You've even got your shoes on."

She felt a sting of heat touch her cheeks. She'd kept herself completely covered through their exchange, yet he knew what she was wearing. That meant he'd studied her form some time during the night. She hadn't slept very heavily, but now and then, she'd jerked awake, discovering that she'd dozed. At some time during the evening had he gazed at her from a vantage point other than the hall? Had he pulled the sheets and blankets away? If so, what had he been looking for?

The heat in her cheeks began to radiate through her

entire body, making her feel as if a slow fire were being stoked low in her stomach, but she pushed the sensation away. She could not allow him to affect her in any way but anger. Not now. Not ever.

"Get out of my room, Major."

To her surprise, he appeared ready to comply, releasing her and taking two steps back. But the mocking grin he wore robbed her of the triumph she should have felt.

"Very well, Miss McKendrick. We'll shelve this discussion for a later date. You have fifteen minutes with the door closed. Then, if you aren't ready, I'll be checking on you."

The major followed her about the school all day like a silent shadow, dogging each move she made.

By the time evening fell, she was at her wit's end. Too little sleep and too many encounters with the major had contributed to a pounding headache and the uncontrollable urge to wrap her fingers around his neck. Then there was the matter of her three oldest students. They had taken to batting their eyelashes at the Union soldiers, pursing their lips, and giggling. Buttercup and Aster had managed to capture Boyd's attention, but Thelma had succumbed to a blinding headache which had sent her to her room by midday.

Augusta wasn't quite sure what mischief they were brewing. Nor did she understand why Revel-Ann had taken to skulking through the hallways like a thief, but she didn't chide them. Not when they'd managed to create a diversion of sorts with Major Charles's men. Now, if they could only find a way to bring the major himself to heel.

Slamming the last of the dishes into the cupboard,

she ignored Effie's wince at the treatment of their precious crockery. Planting her hands on her hips, she decided that the time had come to take the offensive.

"Well, Major. Was the meal to your satisfaction?"

He didn't even blink at her scathing tone.

"It was fine."

"It would have been much better if you'd given us those foodstuffs you promised to supply."

"Your list is being processed. Due to its length, it took longer than expected."

She snorted in disbelief.

"The order should arrive first thing tomorrow or the next day."

Not sure how to respond to that remark, she pursed her lips together and offered a grudging, "Very well. As long as you remember that I'm not running a hotel here. I don't intend to wait on you."

If she'd hoped to deflate a bit of his air of authority, she was sadly disappointed.

"That's the last thought in any of our minds, Miss McKendrick," he mocked. Then he rose from where he'd been lounging in a chair at the head of the table. "I wonder if you would be so kind as to come with me."

She opened her mouth to refuse, but something in his eyes warned her that it would not be the wisest course of action. Shrugging, as if it were of no concern to her what they did, she followed him into the hall.

"Where are we going?"

"To the study."

Her blood turned to ice and she stumbled slightly against a loose board in the hall. The study? Had he found something? Had she missed some tiny detail in her cleanup? Since it had been years since the floor had been properly finished and waxed, the parquet had absorbed a good deal of blood, but she'd bleached enough of the stains away so that the patches could be passed off as spilled punch from some distant party.

Major Charles slid the door open for her and she passed through. Distantly, she noted that a fire had been lit in the grate and two old leather chairs had been drawn close to the blaze, a small table set between them.

"Have a seat."

She hesitated, wondering if this were to be some sort of inquisition.

"Where?" she asked, trying to avoid the inevitable.

"It doesn't matter."

The pop of a log in the grate caused her to start, and wanting to disguise the telltale movement, she took the chair on the left. The major, his leg stiff, sank into the one opposite.

Augusta's fingers clamped around the arms of the chair and she sat ready for flight, afraid of what he would ask her and how he could discern if she told the truth.

But the major merely bent, scooping a pair of flat objects from the floor. One was a folded checkerboard. The other, a shallow box of playing pieces.

"Black or red."

She blinked, unable to comprehend what he was asking.

"I beg your pardon?"

He jiggled the box to draw her attention down to the wooden discs. "Which color would you prefer? Black or red?"

Augusta could only stare at him, wondering what sort of trick he was playing on her. "Red?"

"Fine."

He dumped the red pieces in front of her in a pile, then began to set the black ones on the appropriate squares. He'd finished arranging his pieces by the time it occurred to her that he meant for her to set up her own side.

"You do know how to play, don't you?" he asked when she hesitated again.

"Yes."

He sat in his chair, resting his elbows on the arms. "Good. I was beginning to wonder if there was some sort of rule against ladies playing checkers."

She finally relaxed, just a bit, and began to slide the red discs into place. "I don't know if there's a rule, per se, but as long as no money is involved, I suppose it couldn't hurt."

"Why the stipulation against money?"

"Gambling for money isn't considered ladylike."

"Hmm." Resting his elbows on his chair, he steepled his fingers together, laying the tips against his lips. "What about a good-natured competition? Is that acceptable?"

"Yes, of course."

"What if a friendly challenge accompanied it? Perhaps even a prize for the winner?"

"That would also be acceptable."

"And what if some wager were involved, but of a nonmonetary variety?"

Augusta trod carefully in her answer. She didn't know why, but she sensed a trap lying in wait for the first wrong word.

"I don't see the harm, as long as any rewards which might be gained are not of a . . . tarnishing nature to a woman's virtue."

"Ahh."

The room crouched in silence as he studied her. It was a lazy inspection, one that was far too personal and curious to be comfortable. It was as if he'd forgotten for a moment that she was his quarry.

"I believe I will allow you the first move, Miss McKendrick."

Allow.

She knew he'd chosen the word with great care, that he'd meant to underscore the precariousness of her position. But she refused to appear unsettled. Not when she was rattled at being forced to spend time in this room. The place where Senator Armiture took his last breath. She felt cold here. As if his ghost lingered in the air.

It took all her willpower to keep her hand from shaking as she reached for one of the checkers and pushed it forward.

The major immediately made his own move.

Again, she paused, then slid a piece forward.

Once more, his move was made with rattlesnake precision and speed.

"Is there a point to the game, Major?" she asked, completing her turn more quickly.

"I believe the object of checkers is for one person to defeat the other by taking all of his opponent's pieces."

"You know that isn't what I meant."

She leaned back, refusing to play anymore. "Suppose you tell me exactly why you think it's so important to sequester me in this room and involve me in this particular activity."

He cocked one brow. Her brother, Clarence, had always been able to do that. It had infuriated her when she was younger because she'd never been able to master the gesture. Both of her brows invariably rose together.

"You sound so suspicious, Miss McKendrick." His voice was low and indulgent, causing her stomach to flip-flop with something other than nerves.

"I think I have a right to be."

"Perhaps. Or perhaps guilt is nudging at your conscience, making more of a simple invitation than was intended."

She sighed in impatience. "Tell me, Major, are you always this infuriating?"

Her accusation didn't appear to unsettle him in the least. In fact, he smiled at her, his eyes growing warm. "So I've been told."

"Is that how you became such an expert at forcing confessions?"

He chuckled, making her even more angry. He found this whole situation amusing, damn his hide. He was the cat to her mouse, pushing her, toying with her, goading her on, and he found it highly entertaining.

"There are many methods of interrogation, Miss McKendrick, but this . . . is merely a game of checkers."

She was breathing hard, her hands clenching the arms of the chair until her knuckles gleamed white.

"Why?"

"Why what?"

She could have slapped him. He was being purposely dense.

"If this isn't some twisted means of interrogation, then why are we doing it?"

He sighed. "I've been ordered to guard you, follow

your every move. But I'm tired, Miss McKendrick. You led me on quite a chase today—from the garden shed, to cellar, to attic, to larder. I have a feeling that your days are not usually so busy. Be that as it may, I'm finished with being run around like a dog on a leash. Tonight, we'll be doing what I say. Sitting. By a fire. Playing checkers."

Her eyes narrowed and she tried to determine if he'd told her the whole truth, but his face was an inscrutable mask. She could only trust her instincts, those which told her that most of what the major had said was true.

Most of it.

"Very well." She leaned forward to push one of her pieces ahead. "But I don't see that it will be a very entertaining evening for either of us."

"We could make it so." He slid a checker forward with swift precision.

"How?"

His eyes glittered in the firelight. Not angrily, but with a certain roguish charm. "A question—honestly answered—for each piece taken from the board."

"What kind of questions?"

"You decide."

The whole situation was dangerous—extremely dangerous. But she couldn't deny that she was curious about why this man had come here, now, when most soldiers had long since returned home. Moreover, she wanted—no, *needed*—to know why his interest in her case appeared more than professional.

She finally nodded, a bit of her competitive nature returning. "Very well," she said slowly, agreeing to the idea, but not without protecting herself first. "I'm assuming that you wish to ask questions of a personal nature?"

"I think that a discussion of politics would be a bad idea, don't you?"

She nodded. "Yes. I do. But I must insist that if your questions are going to be of a personal nature, they must concern my childhood or the school. I won't answer any questions involving the war or the last few months."

"Fine."

His easy capitulation to such a request made her immediately suspicious.

"What of you, Major Charles? Do you have any special requests?"

He shook his head. "You may ask whatever you like, Miss McKendrick."

From that point on, Augusta began playing in earnest, determined that if any of the pieces were to be taken and a confidence forfeited, it would be on the major's part.

As she'd planned, the first piece to go was black. Augusta laughed in delight, swiping the wooden disc from the board. Leaning back in her chair, she measured her opponent, feeling a strange rush of power. For the first time, it seemed, she had him at a disadvantage.

"Well?" he prompted when she didn't immediately speak.

She pondered carefully, wanting to ask something that would strike a crushing blow, but she soon realized that she didn't know enough about the man for that sort of effect, so she had to settle for garnering more information instead.

"Tell me about your family."

"That's a statement, not a question." He grinned. "You forfeit your turn."

When he would have moved a checker, Augusta flung out a hand to prevent it. But the action was a mistake. She knew that as soon as she came into contact with his skin. He was warm, vibrant, the backs of his fingers dusted ever so lightly with dark hair. They were beautiful hands, long and well-formed. The hands of a musician or a doctor. Not a soldier.

"There were no stipulations as to the way information was to be gathered," she insisted. But her voice was weak. Much weaker than she would have liked. Perhaps because she had initiated the contact, she was faced with the fact that Major Charles was a man first and a soldier second. If not for the war, he might have been a scholar or a laborer.

"Your past, Major. How were you raised?"

He stood, crossing to a sideboard. For the first time, she noted that a bottle of liquor had been placed there as well as two shot glasses. She recognized the glasses, but not the bottle.

Major Charles poured a healthy measure of some amber-colored liquor into each of the glasses and returned, setting one of them on the table in front of Augusta before resuming his seat.

"What is it?"

"Whiskey."

Augusta opened her mouth to refuse it, but she sensed he knew that and this was some sort of a test, so she wrapped her fingers around the glass.

"Your family," she prompted when he didn't speak.

"Maybe I shouldn't go into that."

She made a scoffing noise. "Surely it isn't a matter of Union security."

"No. But my family is incredibly normal and mundane—certainly not worthy of a precious question."

"How are they 'normal and mundane'?"

He shook his head. "That would require taking another of my pieces, don't you think?"

Intrigued by his reticence, Augusta returned her attention to the board. Within another three moves she'd taken two pieces in a combined jump. Grinning, she took a gulp of her whiskey, knowing that Major Charles was watching her for the slightest flinch in her expression as the potent liquor burned its way down her throat.

"You're a practiced drinker, Miss McKendrick? How surprising."

"There are many things about me you don't know, Major."

"For now."

It was a promise, reminding her that she was at this man's mercy and he intended to unburden her soul. But before she returned to the subject of his family, there was something else she had to know.

"What made you choose this line of work, Major?"

"Checkers?" he teased.

"Interrogation."

"Is that one of your two questions?"

"Yes."

He took another sip of whiskey, allowing it to linger on his tongue before swallowing. "I've always been naturally curious."

"That isn't an answer."

"It's the one I intend to give."

His gaze was dark and piercing in the firelight. Reflections of shadow and flame licked over his profile and accentuated the rough planes of his face.

"I doubt that 'curiosity' was your only reason, Major. Especially when able-bodied men were in such desperate need in the field. What made you shun battle for a job in an office somewhere?"

"Is this your second question?"

"Yes."

"I was a battery officer. Once."

There was such a haunting sadness to his tone that she was momentarily taken aback.

"Then why . . ."

He didn't allow her to finish the question. "It's your move."

Again, she plotted carefully, this time taking three of his men.

"Continue your story, Major."

"That isn't a question."

She sighed. "What happened next?"

He countered her query with one of his own. "Do you know what it's like to be in pain, Augusta? Really in pain? Have you ever awakened to a grinding ache in your body and known in an instant that you were teetering right on the edge of some black abyss and nothing could ever be the same?"

She shook her head.

"It was early summer in 'sixty-three when I awakened in a field hospital, my leg on fire. I'd broken bones before. I'd been shot, I'd been knifed. But this was different, so different. The pain was incredible, like nothing I'd ever experienced. I remember thrashing against the ropes used to tie me down, and a face, a drunken horrible face wielding a saw covered in rust and blood and grime."

She shuddered, seeing everything he said so clearly.

"I started screaming, knowing he meant to use that saw on me—where, I wasn't sure. The pain was so intense, he would have needed to amputate me at the neck to make it stop."

He rose and limped to the table again, pouring the whiskey quickly and taking a large gulp.

Augusta didn't blame him. The images gathering in her head were enough to make her want to take her own bracing sip. But she didn't. She couldn't. She mustn't do anything that might stop his monologue. She wanted to know what had happened to this man. What made him who he was tonight.

"It was like waking to a living hell, Augusta. Especially when I remembered what had happened, how it had occurred—not by the enemy's hands, but by negligence and flawed munitions."

She didn't really understand the curt explanation, but she didn't interrupt him. Not yet. Not when he'd grown so fierce.

Augusta. Not Miss McKendrick.

"But your leg is intact," she whispered.

"As much as it can ever be." He lifted his glass in a silent toast. "To my good fortune, the surgeon passed out. By the time he'd been revived, he was more sober and decided I might heal after all."

"With such injuries, you should have gone home."

"You are out of questions, Augusta. Indeed, I think you owe me."

Returning her attention to the game, she managed to jump three men the next time.

"Why didn't you go home?" she demanded before he had the opportunity to even prompt her to claim her prize.

He shook his head. "It was never an option. I was groomed to be a career soldier. My family came from Virginia and my father was a died-in-the-wool Unionist. We came from old money, and as such, there were certain traditions to uphold."

"What sorts of traditions?"

"My eldest brother, Micah, was expected to take over the handling of Solitude."

"A plantation?" Her brows rose in surprise.

"We raised breeding stock and racehorses."

"Oh." She couldn't help the disappointment that echoed in her tone.

"The second eldest brother, Bram, was expected to go into business."

"Did he?"

"The war broke out before he could."

"And you?"

"I was to be the soldier. Had there been a fourth son, I fear he would have been doomed for the clergy even though my father was not a religious man."

"What about your mother?"

"She died some time ago."

Augusta offered a weak, "I'm sorry." She too had experienced the death of family members firsthand. First her father, then her mother—she'd even believed Clarence had been killed until he'd managed to send her word to the contrary. Through it all, she'd learned that such platitudes were far from comforting.

"When the war broke out, my course was clear. I

90

had been destined to enter West Point, but the conflict merely hastened my enlistment into the army. By that time, my father had also passed away, but I felt honor bound to obey his wishes. It would have been a disgrace to abandon my country's needs when I could use this." He tapped his forehead with his finger. "So I asked for a transfer to an interrogation corps."

"So all this"—she waved an arm to encompass the room, herself, and her situation—"is merely a way to satisfy some responsibility you feel you owe to your father? You must enjoy the career well. You must delight in making my life—and those of the others you interrogate—miserable."

"No, Augusta." He braced his hands on the table, leaning toward her. "I despise being a soldier; I loathe the interviews I conduct. I hate the necessary brutality it sometimes takes to force a confession, the waste, and the cruelty." He drew nearer and nearer, cutting off her supply of air, filling her with a raging tension that she didn't fully understand. "In three weeks I'll be released from it all. I'll finally have the peace I need to pick up whatever threads of my life I can salvage. I can go home and see what has become of my brothers, my home."

"Then why do it? Why come here to me? Why not spend your three weeks in some office in town?"

"Because this entire affair has become strangely personal."

"Personal?" she echoed the word in an incredulous whisper. "How? Why?"

He abruptly stood. "You're out of questions and I think it's time you retired."

"But—"

91

He strode to the door, opening it for her. It wasn't until then that she realized how quiet the school had grown around them.

"Good night, Miss McKendrick."

She stood, draining the rest of her whiskey in one gulp. She had sipped liquor before—usually after Clarence had dared her to do so. Even so, she wasn't prepared for the way it slipped down her throat like liquid fire. Nevertheless, it emboldened her, gave her the courage she needed to say, "No. I will not leave this room until you explain. Why would you feel some vendetta toward me? Are you somehow related to this . . . this senator you think came here?"

He moved toward her then, more quickly than she would have thought possible with his injury. Before she knew what was happening, he'd grasped her by the wrist and yanked her against him.

"No. It's personal because of you, Augusta."

Her brow furrowed in confusion. "But we've never met!"

Broad arms wrapped around her waist and she was pressed so tightly against him that the buttons of his vest ground into her sternum.

"No, ma'am. We haven't."

Gooseflesh peppered her arms.

Major Charles's head bent, his breath brushing her cheeks, creating in her a storm of confusion. It wasn't supposed to be like this. He wasn't supposed to hold her so intimately. Just as she wasn't supposed to feel . . .

What?

Fear? There was a sliver of that, yes, but what she was experiencing was far more complicated, far more dangerous.

Her fingers curled into the fabric at his shoulders in an attempt to push him away. She didn't want this—the confusion, the anticipation, the exhilaration. This man was her enemy.

But he was immovable. Strong. A force to be reckoned with. The arms around her waist grew tighter, pulling her so close against him she could barely breathe. His buttons were biting into her skin, through the layers of clothing she wore, underpinnings and all. It wasn't difficult to imagine what it might be like if he held her this way without the garments that separated them.

No!

She grew light-headed as the thought raced through her brain. She mustn't think like that. It was wrong. Completely and utterly wrong.

But similar ideas must have crowded into the major's head, because he was bending toward her, closing the last bit of distance that remained.

Augusta knew she should retreat, turn her head to the side, something—anything! But she couldn't move. She was mesmerized by his approach, caught in a web of sensation that she could not escape. When their lips touched, she could only sigh. Her arms wrapped around his neck and she was returning the caress full measure, without thought to proper behavior or future consequences. She wanted this. Dear heaven above, how she wanted this.

His lips were warm and sure, his kiss passionate. The warmth the whiskey had brought to her veins exploded into a raging inferno. Standing on tiptoe, Augusta strained against him until he took most of her weight, pressing her so firmly to his hips that she could feel the ridge of his arousal through the layers of her skirts. Rather than frightening her, it excited her even more. That she could bring such a man to this state of desire.

Her fingers plunged into his hair, satisfying her curiosity about its weight and texture. Soft, so soft. And when he drew away to run his lips over her chin and down her neck, she gasped at the pure pleasure of it. She'd never known, never dreamed, that intimacy could be like this. Not sweet and innocent. But bold. Daring. Suffocating.

Her fingers dug into his scalp, forcing him to rise, to take her lips again, to mold her to him, hip to hip. Her heart was pounding so wildly, she knew he must feel it, and the thought excited her even more.

But then he was pushing her free, leaving her to feel even more isolated. Alone.

Their gazes locked, and she saw in his eyes that he'd never meant for such a thing to happen. But it had. And he was no less affected by it than she.

"Go to bed, Augusta," he ordered firmly.

But she could hear the lingering traces of desire coating each word.

She knew what he wanted.

For her to leave him.

Alone.

Now.

Without another word, she brushed past him, abandoning him in the flickering firelight. Not so much because he had ordered her to do so and she felt compelled to obey, but because, deep in her heart, she knew that to stay would spell both their dooms.

As the sound of her footsteps disappeared down the hall, Jackson leaned against the mantel, staring into the fire. With each tick of the clock, he willed the raging passion in his blood to still and his body to cease tormenting him with might-have-beens.

Over and over again, his brain argued that she was his prisoner, a suspect in a murder, the sister of his sworn enemy.

But even as he repeated the thoughts to himself like a litany, he was unable to douse the primitive emotional desires that burned within him.

Did he really have the right to use her this way? As a pawn to trap her brother? Did he really believe that Clarence's duplicity had infected her too?

Damnit! He was losing his objectivity by even thinking such a thing. This woman was guilty—of how much, he was not yet sure. But she wasn't as innocent as she claimed.

And he would do well to remember that.

Revel-Ann and Pansy flattened against the wall as Augusta rushed past them. After several seconds of silence, Revel-Ann motioned for her companion to follow her down the corridor to the kitchen.

"We should be in bed," Pansy hissed as they burst through the swinging door and hurried to the cupboard next to the stove.

"We've got to get these things before those soldiers take it into their head to search the premises." She dragged a bundle free and handed it to Pansy.

"What's inside?"

"A pair of spare boots, some socks, and a shirt."

Pansy wrinkled her nose. "Why do we need their old clothes, anyhow?"

Revel-Ann shrugged. "I'm following orders."

She reached into the dark hole again, withdrawing a

small, pearl-handled derringer. Pansy's eyes grew even larger.

"Great Jehoshaphat, where'd you find that?"

Revel-Ann grinned. "Inside the major's greatcoat."

Pansy blinked. "He'll know it's gone by morning! You shouldn't have taken it, Revel-Ann. Not yet."

Revel-Ann shrugged. "He won't notice."

"What makes you so sure?"

"I took his greatcoat too. I hid it in the barn."

Pansy stared at her in disbelief. "You shouldn't have done that."

"Why not? I've got plans for tomorrow, Pansy. Plans." Then, gathering her nightdress around her, she crept out of the room, giggling softly to herself.

6

At the clang of the breakfast bell the next morning, Augusta threw open the bedroom door which she'd just been allowed to close for dressing purposes. Fully clothed in a black wool skirt, white broadcloth blouse, a voluminous apron, and her hair drawn back in a crocheted snood, she swept past Major Charles, hurrying downstairs to help serve the morning meal.

He didn't utter a word or try to stop her, but he might as well have done so for the way he watched her. She could feel his gaze upon her, so hot and hard and intense. His uneven gait tagged behind her, keeping time with her hurried steps.

As she entered the kitchen, Augusta clenched her fists in reaction to spending even such a short time alone in his presence. She gathered close to the other girls working around the stove, in a blatant attempt at putting a buffer of sorts between them. Such tactics were futile, she knew. It was only a matter of time before the next confrontation. The next kiss. As much as she might deny the possibility of such an action, it would happen, of that she was certain.

How could it not when their awareness of each other had become too tangible to ignore?

She made the mistake of looking his way. When their gazes locked, she could not ignore the surge of energy that ensued.

Turning back to the stove, she made a show of lifting lids and banging pots to appear busy. Her students gazed at her in confusion. Augusta was notorious for her bad cooking, and it was for that reason that she spent most of her time taking care of other chores—bookwork, gardening, teaching— doing her best to divert the major from speaking with Effie or searching for Elijah.

Even so, she continued with her playacting, praying that the major wouldn't sense her discomfort at being in the same room with him. She kept telling herself that she was behaving foolishly over a kiss, a simple kiss. But the sensations he'd inspired the night before had not eased. If anything, they'd grown stronger. She knew what to expect from this man if he touched her again. The anticipation was more than enough to drive her mad. Augusta could only hope she somehow found the will to resist her own inexplicable desires.

Her resolve strengthened, she abandoned the charade of cooking and took a seat at the table, glaring at the major. She couldn't get caught up with this man. Not because he meant to blame her for Senator Armiture's disappearance, but because he was everything that she had sworn she would avoid. A military man. One who was as thunderous and commanding as her father had been. Just looking at him made her understand how her mother must have felt all those years—feeling an overwhelming passion for a man she couldn't get along with.

Augusta had been in her teens when she'd decided for herself that her mother never should have married Lawrence McKendrick. In her opinion, her mother should have defied her parents when they proposed the arranged marriage. In the early years of their marriage there had been a real affection between them, but then, Lawrence had begun to develop a political career and he'd sought to mold her into the perfect diplomatic wife. Since she was headstrong, he'd sought to dominate her every word and deed. He'd forced her to follow him to Maryland for a time and to live like a Northerner, to outwardly adopt his own abolitionist views and to deny her Southern heritage. As a little girl, Augusta remembered the arguments that had ensued when her mother had dared to make a decision without consulting with her husband first. She'd grown to hate Lawrence McKendrick, even as their passion refused to die, becoming something base and cruel.

Augusta doubted that anyone else had guessed that facet of their relationship. She'd seen them once, her mother and father. By that time, her mother had run away from Lawrence's dominion and had returned to her Southern home under the guise of caring for her ailing parents. Within weeks, Lawrence had come to fetch her—how furious he'd been.

Augusta had only been fourteen at the time—barely aware of what was happening. Creeping up the stairs as her parents argued, she'd been less than a dozen yards away when her father pounded on her mother's bedroom door. She'd heard him demand the right to enter and spend the night. Her mother had refused. An argument had ensued. Then her father had pushed Vera McKendrick against the wall and kissed her until they'd both been gasping for breath. Augusta had nearly cried out when he'd ripped her mother's bodice and pushed her backward into the bedroom, slamming the door behind them. Augusta had wanted to leave, but she couldn't. Not when she heard the bed begin to squeak, the heavy breathing, the moans—her mother's, not of fear but of lovemaking. Just when she'd thought it would never end, her father made some sort of guttural victory cry and her mother had cried out in ecstasy.

Then a silence.

Whispers.

Coos of delight.

Augusta had crept back to her room then, frightened, anxious, and curiously angry at them both. She hadn't understood then as she did now that the raw emotion she'd seen was merely proof that a woman should never become involved with a man whose ideals were not her own.

Sweet heaven, was she doomed to follow her mother's mistakes? Was she cursed with an attraction to a man who was so different from her that they could only share a violent sort of passion?

No. Augusta did not intend to follow her parents' example. She planned to spend her life alone, become one of those eccentric maiden aunts who didn't give a damn about propriety and collected a menagerie of cats. Her skills as a teacher would allow her the freedom to move from job to job—perhaps even serve as a traveling companion. But she would not submit to a man.

Never.

If she ever bothered to take a lover, it would be *her* choice. Even then, she would see to it that he was allowed little more than her body. He would not be allowed into her everyday life.

Her emotions, her *soul,* were hers alone.

The remainder of the morning meal was a solemn, stifled affair. Usually, the young ladies giggled and talked and teased. But the presence of the three Union soldiers at their table made them nervous and quiet.

Too quiet and nervous, if that were possible, Augusta thought with sudden suspicion. On more than one occasion, she found them whispering softly to themselves, then staring at the men as if they were plotting something.

They'd better not be up to anything. The mere thought was enough to make her blood grow cold. During the years that this group had begun living together, they'd become as closely knit as any family—and as fiercely protective. She also knew that an anger burned deep in their hearts. One directed against anyone Northern—and after their families had been killed at the hands of the Yankees, who could blame them?

Seeing Buttercup mouthing something to her sister who sat opposite, Augusta tapped her leg under the table with her foot. When Buttercup eyed her quizzically, Augusta shook her head, praying that the girl would understand that they should remain out of this affair entirely. But Buttercup merely smiled and returned her attention to her food.

The girls were the first to finish eating. They consumed their bowls of porridge, then rose and began to help with the cleanup duties.

"Here, miss. Let me help you."

One of the soldiers—Boyd, she thought she'd heard him called—stood and offered to take the bucket of dishwater Thelma had been about to carry outside to empty.

She made a soft mewling sound, her eyes darting around the assembled group like a doe caught in a hunter's sights.

Seeing her predicament, Pansy rushed forward to grasp the girl's arm and Revel-Ann grabbed the bucket.

The clear evidence of Thelma's fear angered Augusta more than she would have anticipated. These girls had lived too long being scared. Why did it have to visit them again in the form of these men? If the army felt it necessary to punish Augusta for what they thought she'd done, why didn't they arrest her and take her away? Why couldn't the authorities allow Thelma and the other students to heal?

But before she could speak, Thelma was shaking herself free and donning a tremulous smile. "Of course, you may help us, Colonel."

"Sergeant."

Thelma looked at Pansy as if she were drowning, but the girl nudged her in the ribs. After a second's hesitation, Thelma batted her eyes—looking like she had soot in her eye. "You're only a puny ole sergeant? My, my, what naughty things have you done to earn such a low rank?"

Augusta was sure she could have been tipped over with a feather. Thelma Richter was playing the coquette?

Her smile growing more genuine and slightly victorious, Thelma led the man outdoors, her hips swaying in an exaggerated manner, her arms twined through one of his.

As soon as she'd disappeared, Revel-Ann stated baldly, "Pansy and I are doing the wash today, Major. If you and your men have anything you want cleaned, you'd better get it to me within the hour."

Revel-Ann was volunteering to do laundry? Blast it all, the girls *were* up to something. Something which could prove ultimately dangerous. And it was the major's fault. He was the one to put them in this position.

"Thank you, miss." He flashed Augusta a wry look, his brows arching as if he were wondering why *she* hadn't bothered to be so accommodating.

"Our laundry services will cost you a penny a piece, Major," Thelma said, planting herself in front of him, feet braced, her hands on her hips. "No exceptions."

"Isn't that price a bit steep?"

"Then take your things into town, I don't care." Her eyes narrowed. "But I don't think you'll find many folk willing to clean Yankee clothes," she said ominously.

Augusta prayed that the major wouldn't grow angry at the obvious affront. They couldn't afford to antagonize the man.

But she saw the corners of his mouth twitch and his shoulders shake ever so slightly. He was amused!

"Very well, miss. I'll have my men gather their things."

"I want the money up-front."

"Fine."

Revel-Ann's mouth slid into a self-congratulatory smirk. "Thank you for your business, Major."

It was as he was making his way to the table that

103

Major Charles pulled Augusta to one side. "You're training quite a pretty batch of extortionists, Miss McKendrick."

The remark stung, more than it should have. It implied that Augusta had failed miserably in molding them into proper young ladies—perhaps because he thought Augusta herself was far from proper.

By the time the soldiers finished eating, Augusta had worked herself into a finely honed fury, one which demanded some sort of outlet. Even though she knew she should avoid him, she turned to the major for her first outburst.

He tried to brush past her on his way to gather some of his things in the back bedroom, but Augusta planted herself firmly in the doorway, her arms crossed, the serving spoon brandished in one hand like a weapon.

"Well, Major?"

"Well what?"

"The supplies you promised. You said they would arrive today. I simply cannot continue to feed you and your men if I don't have the necessary foodstuffs. Our larder is far below what it should be."

"I'll send one of my men to check on the progress of your order. He should be back by late afternoon." His gaze was far more personal than it should have been, coursing from the tip of her head to her toes and back again. "Then we'll know if there will be any more delays."

The comment stole the wind from her argument before she'd even had the chance to get worked up.

"Oh."

He leaned close, causing her to flick a nervous

glance at her sister and the students gathered around the kettles they were heating on the stove.

"Good day, Miss McKendrick."

Then, as if sensing the female audience watching them both from the corners of their eyes, he touched her nose with the tip of his finger—the kind of endearing caress made by an adult to a child.

Or a man to his sweetheart.

Needing to save her pride in some small measure, she stated, "Good. I'll be watching for his return."

The major left her then—grinning widely—probably intent on his morning ablutions, or perhaps even to sleep. She was left in the care of the tall one, Frank. But that didn't allow her to relax. She expected the major to return at any time, kept *waiting* for him to return. But he didn't. Not while she helped Effie iron linens, or instructed her students in a review of table settings, or ushered them into the salon for their embroidery class. Finally, restless and edgy, she made her way to the parlor where she stood in front of the window and waited. For what, she wasn't sure.

But when she saw—not a wagon—but a whole platoon of soldiers, she froze.

No.

No!

This couldn't be happening.

Jackson awoke with a start to the sound of horses galloping down the drive. Swearing to himself, he swung to his feet and hurried out of the barn where he'd spread out his bedroll and attempted to get some rest. He'd been so sure that if he could get away from the school for a few hours and obtain some sleep—

some *real* sleep—he would feel more in control of a situation that was bound and determined to run from him.

But the instant he heard the horses, he knew something was wrong. He'd lived too long near the battlefield to not recognize the jingle of military-issue harnesses and men riding in formation.

A stab of pain in his thigh caused him to limp-run into the cold winter air. The instant he saw the man in the lead, he slowed.

General French veered his way, then drew to a halt, signaling for the soldiers behind him to do the same.

"Major."

"General."

French took the opportunity to remove the ever-present cigar from his pocket and light it. Then he studied the school grounds and asked, "Have you anything to report?"

Jackson shook his head. "Not yet, sir. The woman is proving to be . . . uncooperative in confessing."

French snorted beneath his huge whiskers, then squinted against the sun glinting off the snow. "I don't doubt that a bit. What about the brother?"

"No sign of him."

"Stay with it, boy. He's sure to show up." His expression grew ponderous. "Meantime, I've been thinking about the girl, the older one who was brought in for questioning once before. I want you to intensify your investigation of her." He sniffed in disdain. "I was there during the trial when she testified. Damnit all, everyone there knew she was lying. She'd been in contact with Clarence for months before her brother was caught. If I find a shred of evidence to point to the fact that she harmed Armiture, I'll have her locked up and hanged within a fortnight whether or not she confesses."

Jackson knew that French had been a poker buddy of Senator Armiture, so he didn't bother to speak. French would demand whatever justice he felt the situation warranted, even if others might find his methods unorthodox.

French leaned forward. "I'm trusting you, boy, trusting your instincts. But I can't give you much time. I'm catching the devil for not hauling that woman to prison right now. Do what you have to do and do it quickly. Make sure whatever you pull out of her is airtight. I want her to suffer in hell for what she's done, understand? Both of 'em. Her and her brother."

"Yes, sir."

The general straightened.

"I'll be checking with you again at the end of the week. See to it that you have something to tell me."

"Yes, sir." Jackson saluted and the general returned the gesture.

Then, as suddenly as he'd arrived, the general was gone, leaving an uneasiness in Jackson's soul that hadn't been there before he'd come.

But why? French hadn't said a thing that Jackson hadn't anticipated. The man was notorious for his impatience—and his reputation for seeing that justice was swiftly served.

So why did Jackson feel rushed? Pressured?

Shaking himself free from such thoughts, Jackson ran his fingers through his hair and brushed the last bits of straw from his pants. Then he made his way to the house for his next battle with Miss Augusta McKendrick.

She was waiting for him. Huddled against one of the porch supports by the front door, trying to ward off the bitter wind with nothing more than a meager shawl, she stood like a block of granite as he made his way toward her.

"What did he want?"

The fact that she blurted the question without any sort of conversation to lead up to it was more telling than she would have wished.

"He came to inquire about my progress."

She scanned the hazy winter skyline for one last glimpse of the troops, but the skeletal trees lining the road hid them from view.

Her chin tipped then, to that militant angle he was beginning to associate with this woman.

"I see. I suppose you were forced to tell him that there had been no confession as of yet because there was nothing out of the ordinary for me to confess."

He shook his head. "No, Miss McKendrick. I did not tell him that."

To his surprise, she did not try to reassert her innocence. It was as if she were beginning to accept the fact that he did not believe it—and would not believe it—unless he were confronted with some sort of cold, hard evidence.

"I've things to do," she said abruptly, whirling in the direction of the house.

He caught her before she could leave, not really knowing why he felt compelled to stop her, but doing so all the same. Unwittingly, his fingers slid beneath the cuff of her sleeve. Her skin was soft, so soft. And so cold.

"Come on." He pulled her into the house, past the

108

Browning girls, and inside her office. "Sit down by the fire."

He didn't give her a chance to resist—he knew she would, if only as a matter of principle. Pushing her into the chair, he took the fire poker and nudged one of the logs more directly into the blaze. A flare of warmth bathed his chest and thighs, seeping into his own icy limbs.

"Better?"

She didn't answer, but she was watching him. Steadily. Her bosom lifting in an irregular pattern of breaths.

The kiss.

The memory hung in the air with its own cloud of warmth. Expectancy.

Augusta was the first to speak.

"The cold must bother your leg."

The personal comment surprised him.

"Yes."

"Do you have other injuries?"

Again, her question gave him pause.

"I did. They've healed now."

"How were you wounded?"

He stared at her, but she appeared genuinely interested.

"I was in charge of a battery of cannon. Somehow, we received faulty supplies." He forced himself to remain still and to keep his words as general as possible. "When the cannon were fired, they exploded, killing my men and shattering my leg."

She looked truly horrified. "How awful."

"Yes, yes, it was awful." He wanted to say more, to ask her if Clarence had ever spoken of infiltrating

Jackson's platoon and playing him for a fool. Or how he'd exchanged the munitions he stole with inferior equipment, but he couldn't bring himself to do it. Not when she was gazing at him with wide, innocent eyes.

Innocent. The word reverberated in his head and he forcefully discarded it. She wasn't innocent. Not with a man like Clarence for a brother. Jackson had been fooled once by a McKendrick's wiles. He would not allow it to happen again.

Silence sifted between them like snow before she asked, "You fought for the North. Did you ever meet my father, General Lawrence McKendrick?"

He considered lying—she wanted so much for him to offer his assurances that he'd known her father. He could read that in her expression quite easily. But something about her, about those clear, dark eyes which held his own, kept him from prevaricating.

"No. I never knew him."

She sighed, her gaze becoming slightly unfocused as if she were peering inside herself. "My father never bothered to meet me, you know. Sometimes I had to travel hundreds of miles to reach his unit, but he always arranged for one of his aides to rendezvous with me."

Though she tried to hide it, he heard the hurt buried deep in her tone.

"There was a war going on, Augusta. He was constantly on the move."

She shrugged. "Too bad he didn't take the time to warn me."

He grew still. "Warn you?"

"That by coming to him for help, for medicine and food for his youngest daughter, I would be branded a criminal."

She stood then, ready to leave, but he blocked her way.

"Augusta, when—"

She held up an imperious hand.

"I don't want to talk about this anymore."

She didn't really have that luxury, but seeing the shadows under her eyes and the pinched quality of her features, he realized she was tired. As tired as he was.

"Sit down, Augusta."

"I will not."

"Sit down!"

He pushed her onto the settee. Although she sat stiff and proud, he arranged two pillows on the arm of a chair.

"Lie down with your head on these."

"Sit down, lie down, I'm not a lapdog to be ordered about."

"Do it!"

Sighing she leaned her head on the pillows, but she was as stiff as a poker.

"Put your legs up."

"No."

"Damnit, Augusta, don't argue with me. You're tired; I'm tired. We're calling a truce. One hour. One hour where we don't talk about what has happened, or what will happen."

"An hour?"

"Yes."

Bit by bit, she lifted her feet on the settee, reaching behind her to pull an afghan over her knees.

How small she appeared that way, small and defenseless.

Drawing one of the chairs close, he sank into its

depths and stared into the rollicking flames that were much too cheery and bright to exist in the tense expectancy of the room.

An hour.

Could they spend that much time in each other's company without arguing and probing?

Without wondering.

Unwillingly, he found himself drawn to the spot where her booted ankles peeked at him from beneath the covering of the lap robe. The tongue of her shoe had wriggled out of place, allowing him a peek of a stocking—cotton, to be sure—but pale pink. Not black, or brown, or gray, or any other practical color. Pink. So frivolous. So feminine.

That tiny insight bothered him more than he would have liked.

But he couldn't dwell on such ideas. He couldn't allow himself to acknowledge how he was drawn to her.

Damnit all to hell. She was so close.

So soft.

So real.

Closing his eyes, he rubbed at the ache beginning to gather at the center of his forehead. But that made things even worse. He could smell her scent, one reminiscent of spring—lilies of the valley, perhaps. It made him wonder where she'd obtained the perfume. Was it a gift from some old beau? Was she hoarding the last few drops of the precious stuff? If so, why had she worn it today when she knew she would see him?

He nearly laughed aloud at his own conceit. She wouldn't have worn perfume for *his* benefit. Not consciously.

But unconsciously?

He opened his eyes to discover she was watching him, appearing far from relaxed—as if she were somehow privy to the thoughts he'd been entertaining.

"You let me kiss you," he stated slowly, the words emerging before he'd known they'd been formed in his head. "Why?"

She didn't immediately answer, merely shifted so that she was lying on her back, staring up at the ceiling.

"I don't know."

The stark honesty of her reply affected him more than he cared to admit. He found himself magnetized by her presence, to the delicate color of her skin, to the lovely contours of her profile. His fingers twitched to touch her hair again, to see if it was soft and curly, twining around his hands like a lover's embrace.

"Do you ever wonder what life would have been like if not for the war?"

Her quiet rumination had the power of a knife plunging into his chest. If not for the war, he would have led a much tamer life. His future would have been mapped out to the finest degree.

Now he didn't know what life held in store for him.

Rather than answering, he asked, "Would you have stayed here at the school?"

"Yes. I think so. I like it here. I like the freedom it gives me."

"Freedom?"

"To be what I want to be. When you're a teacher of my ripe age, the populace begins to believe you've given up the idea of marriage. Therefore you're granted some leeway. In time, you're considered eccentric."

"*Have* you given up all thought of marriage?"

She appeared to be pondering the idea. "Yes. I believe so."

"Why?"

Her eyes filled with emotions that he couldn't begin to decipher.

"Because men, no matter how good they might be, have one goal where women are concerned."

"What is that?"

"Domination."

"Ahh."

"You don't think so?" She rolled to her side again, propping her head on her folded arm. In the process, she dislodged the afghan, exposing a good deal more of one leg, one shapely calf framed in petticoat ruffles and wool.

Jackson felt a familiar burning sensation begin deep in his stomach and pushed it away.

"It's true, isn't it?"

"What?" He had to force himself to concentrate on what she was saying.

"Men like to dominate."

"Some do."

"I think most of them do." She leaned closer. Again, the scent of lilies of the valley wafted toward him and at that instant, he knew that the perfume would be forever entwined with his memories of this woman.

"How do you think the average male would react should a woman decide to take control?"

"I am sure there are those who might object, but many men might find such a change invigorating."

She pondered that thought.

"Do you think so?"

"Yes."

She swung her legs to the floor, then, to his astonishment, she did not bother to return to the ladylike posture he'd been accustomed to seeing. Her skirts sagged between her legs and she slouched forward as much as her corseting would allow. Resting her hands on her knees, she bent near him.

"What about you, Major? How would you react?"

There was something about her pose, about her tough-edged attitude, that he was finding infinitely intriguing. He couldn't look away. He could scarcely believe that this woman with her curly hair drawn savagely into that awful snood was staring at him with the directness of an equal.

An equal.

A woman.

He grasped her wrist. "What are you playing at, Augusta?"

She wrenched free, and when she spoke, there was an edge of bitterness to her tone. "I want to show you what it's like to be on the other side of a seduction, Major. I want to show you how a man uses passion as a tool for domination. Perhaps then, you'll understand why you should leave me alone."

She stood then, her hands on her hips, circling his chair, studying him with the same cool manner of inspection that he was sure he'd used with his interrogation subjects hundreds of times.

After making the round, she reached out to tip up his chin. Her hands were warmer now, much warmer.

"You need to shave." Her thumb rubbed against the stubble on his jaw. "Your men have beards, but you . . ." She frowned, giving the matter some thought. ". . . you should remain clean-shaven. A beard only obscures your beauty."

"Beauty?" The word rasped from his throat.

"Surely you must know that you have a face, a form, that attracts women. You're so tall, so lean. And dark. You could have been the model for Heathcliff or Mr. Rochester. Women have a weakness for that sort of man, you know."

He swallowed against the sudden dryness of his throat. He knew she was purposely tormenting him— tit for tat. But as she moved, running her fingers across his jaw, his cheek, and into his hair, he found it difficult to remember anything but her scent, her warmth.

"Do you admire a woman in control, Major?" She leaned forward to whisper in his ear. "Or are you beginning to discover that you're no better than the rest of your sex? That without the power, you feel nothing?"

Nothing? She couldn't be farther from the truth. His blood was coursing through his veins, thick and charged and hot.

He could not prevent what was about to happen, what he knew would happen, any more than he could prevent his heart from beating. She was rounding the chair, still close, still leaning over him. When his arm wrapped around her neck, it took only the slightest pressure to pull her onto his lap.

And then, the kiss began. A hungry meshing of lips and crush of bodies. He couldn't get enough of her, the taste, the feel, the textures. His tongue immediately slipped into her mouth, exploring, delving. Her hesitance told him that she was not completely familiar with such intimacies, but all of his control fled. Especially when she began to return the caress, the embrace.

Dear heaven above, how long had it been since he'd been with a woman this way? Never? He couldn't ever remember having been so completely inundated with such passion.

He grasped her shoulders, ran his palms down her back, pressing her closer and closer until her head rested on his chest and he bent his head to allow the kiss to continue. Not content, he rubbed her arm, then strayed to her ribs, and up, up, up the ridges of whalebone he could feel through the layers of her clothing until he encountered her breast.

She gasped, arching away from him, her eyes opening. But she didn't push him away. Watching her, he rubbed a thumb across the nipple shrouded from view. Like a blind man, he felt it pucker and harden, and like a blind man, he imagined what it would look like free from its bindings, lying naked in the hollow of his hand.

Her eyes narrowed ever so slightly, and this time it was she who explored, stroking his neck, his shoulders, then down to where she could feel his own nipple erect and waiting for her caress, even through the fabric of his uniform.

He sucked in a breath, willing her to delve lower, much lower, but he knew by the sleepy languor of her eyes that she was content to continue mapping the area she had only now found.

Cursing his inability to stop and pull back, Jackson reached to pluck the pins from her hair and drag the snood away. He wanted to see the tresses down. He wanted to see them free.

Although she made a sound of distress, he didn't stop until the tawny waves plunged to her shoulders and beyond, burying his hands in her silken curls. Glorious. So thick and alive. A man could drown in such strands and be happy. So very happy.

Pulling her head down, he kissed her again, kissed her until the room faded. She clung to him, her arms wrapping around his shoulders so tightly that he found it difficult to breathe.

But he didn't care.

He truly didn't care.

Something was happening between them. Something he didn't wish to interpret or admit. But he would not will it away.

When at long last she drew free of him, her cheeks were flushed and her eyes sparkled. With passion.

With tears.

"Shh." He lifted a finger to erase a wayward drop, and she shook her head, trying to wriggle free. He hissed when the action aggravated a leg already throbbing.

"No!" Clasping her hands, he forced her to grow still again. "Sit for a minute."

But with each second that passed, he knew it was a mistake to keep her so close. When she jumped to her feet, he didn't stop her.

She went to the window, staring out at who knew what, keeping her back turned firmly in his direction. Bit by bit, he watched her arm herself, watched the stiffening of her spine and the tilt to her chin. Then she faced him, holding out her hands.

"My pins."

He gave them to her, aware for the first time that he clutched them in his fist.

She snatched them free, restoring her hair to its woven net in a matter of minutes.

"Your hour is up, Major," she stated tightly.

And as she marched out the door, he knew it would be a long time before he saw the woman who'd been in his arms again. *This* Augusta McKendrick, the one who stormed through the door on her way to—who knew where?—was bound to be as bristly and unapproachable as a bramble bush.

It took some doing, but the girls finally managed to gather around the boiling pot. As soon as she joined the group, Thelma was rewarded with several pats on the back and quick hugs.

"Well? Did I distract him long enough?" she asked eagerly.

Revel-Ann grinned. "You were wonderful."

"You didn't even faint," Pansy added, her eyes sparkling behind her spectacles.

"Did you get it?" Buttercup asked, looking over her shoulder to make sure they weren't being overheard.

"Yes, sweetie. I managed to steal six bullets," Revel-Ann stated proudly. "They were left in one of the belts that Boyd forgot to remove from his pile of clothing."

"Will they fit the derringer?"

"Nooo," Revel-Ann reluctantly drawled. The patent look of disappointment from the girls was quickly lightened when she said, "But I managed to sneak something else out of the larder to mix in with our soap."

She held up a crock and around her the girls stared in awe. The label on the front read quite clearly: quicklime.

Buttercup's eyes narrowed. "That's what Elijah used for whitewash."

"And to sprinkle on the compost heap when a rat dies there."

Revel-Ann chuckled. "Mix enough of it with water and it will dissolve granite. But if we put in a touch . . ."

"You are so wicked, Revel-Ann," Thelma whispered, half in envy, half in horror.

"I always knew she had it in her," Aster grumbled, but her mouth was split in a wide grin.

"Well? Should I do it?"

They exchanged furtive glances.

It was Buttercup who nodded. "Do it," she commanded. "Dump in a spoonful. With some luck, it will eat at their clothes like moths in a wool chest."

Revel-Ann snickered. "Aye, aye, Captain." Then she sprinkled a bit into the water and watched it hiss and bubble.

7

For the rest of that day and into the next, Jackson endured Augusta's icy glares, her frowns, and her silences. It should have been very irritating, but because he'd seen beyond the facade to the vulnerable woman hidden beneath the prickles, he found himself unaffected. In fact, it only made him watch her more closely, to see when the next crack in the dam appeared.

"Major Charles?"

The soft call scattered his thoughts. From his place in the back bedroom, Jackson looked up at the mirror hanging in front of him, seeing the rippling reflection of Augusta's younger sister. Effie.

Jackson had purposely avoided Effie. Not so much because Augusta had told him to do so, but because he'd known that he needed to work with her differently. If she knew something—which she probably did—she would only speak her piece if Augusta was in dire straits. Evidently, Effie didn't think Augusta's plight had developed that far yet. Nevertheless, he took it as a good sign that she'd come to speak with him personally.

She stood at the door, her face pale with worry, but radiating a certain genteel rebellion. Not wanting to startle her into leaving, he kept all motions slow and purposeful as he rinsed his razor in the bowl of warm water he'd been given for his shaving.

"Yes, ma'am?"

She hesitated, and he could see the way her hands clasped nervously in front of her.

"Frank sent me to get you."

"Frank?" Jackson was surprised that Effie would use his first name. Wiping his jaw with a towel, he dropped the razor into the water and turned to face her.

A creeping blush was beginning to climb up her neck. She must have felt it because she quickly added, "Yes. He said to tell you the supplies are here. He saw the wagon coming our way and asked me to come fetch you since he is currently guarding Augusta."

"Thank you, Miss Effie."

She backed up, but he stopped her before she could leave.

"You seem to feel more comfortable around Frank Conley than you do around me."

She started. "I-I suppose. We've talked a few times."

"He's a good man."

Again, the blush.

He opened his mouth, intent upon probing her for more information, but he stopped himself.

"Where is your sister?"

"The parlor."

He nodded, throwing the towel onto the dresser. "Thank you. Why don't you gather the other students in the kitchen area? They can help you put things away."

He was down the hall and taking the first few steps, when she called, "Major?"

She was watching him, her eyes so much like Augusta's, but softer, gentler. Even so, there was a determined glint in their depths.

"You mustn't hurt her."

He didn't know how to respond to that. If his investigation went well, he would be arresting Augusta. Quite soon. It didn't matter that he'd held her, kissed her, burned to deepen their embraces even further. It didn't matter that his emotions were becoming entangled in a web of deceit and desire. He had a job to do.

Not answering, he turned and made his way to the front parlor.

He would be coming to get her any second.

Augusta wrapped her arms around her torso, staring out at the hazy outline of a horse and wagon trundling down the main road. Within a matter of minutes, it would ease into the drive and wind its way over the narrow road before coming to a stop in front of the school. Then the major would come to fetch her. She had no doubts of it. No doubts at all.

She frowned. Since their encounter in the office the previous day, she'd been cool toward him. But it hadn't helped. She was drawn to him. It didn't matter that he could arrest her at the slightest provocation; it didn't matter that he could crush her future with a careless word. What she'd felt in his arms overshadowed her misgivings and she found herself longing for the next time, and the next.

What was she going to do?

Her eyes closed and her head bowed in defeat. She wanted to lay her head on someone else's shoulder and let them take charge for a while. She wanted to be comforted. She wanted to be pampered. She wanted . . .

Him?

No. Her eyes flew open. She might have enjoyed those moments of passion—she might even enjoy them again, but the man himself? No. He was not the only person who could inspire such sensations inside her. She would not allow it.

She must not.

The rattle of a wagon grew louder, then behind her, she sensed a presence.

"Frank, head outside with Boyd."

"Yes, sir."

Didn't that man ever make any noise when he entered a room?

Facing him, she dared him to chide her for their last encounter. But he didn't say a thing, he merely came close, causing a cool finger of anticipation to wriggle up her spine as she watched that uneven gait of his. Those broad shoulders. Lean hips.

"Let's go."

She didn't move.

He sighed in impatience, obviously thinking this was another of her games. He couldn't know that the deep tone of his voice had the ability to make her knees weak.

Taking her wrist, Major Charles dragged her from her place by the window. Throwing the front door open, he hauled her outside, abruptly stopping shy of the first step.

The momentum caused her to plow into the man. If not for the way she caught herself, her hands splaying against his waist, she would have tumbled headlong down the staircase. She knew she should pull back as if she'd been burned—as indeed she felt she had been. But she didn't. Seconds flashed by, minutes, and the only thing that penetrated the haze of her brain was the muscular physique she felt beneath her fingers. So firm. So finely honed.

So masculine.

"Get your hands off me, Augusta," he rasped, so low that only she could hear.

Only then did she manage to retreat. But not before she admitted that she was not the only one affected by the accidental contact. Although she had suspected as much, her actions during their previous encounter had unsettled him more than he would ever admit—and the knowledge pricked at her consciousness. Perhaps, she had been a fool to try to sway him with arguments. Perhaps, like her mother had done with Lawrence McKendrick, Augusta would obtain far better results by enticing him.

But as soon as the thought appeared, she abandoned it. There was too much danger in that course of action. A danger in her own emotions becoming even more involved.

"Everything you asked for is here—flour, sugar, yeast, salt, raisins—as well as those damned chickens and a cow!"

"A cow." The words left her lips in a reverent

whisper. The major could have handed her a pot of gold and it could not have appeared more wonderful.

"There's also some salted pork, dried beef, and a box of peppermint drops. Will that satisfy your sense of justice, Miss McKendrick?"

He whirled her to face him then, his hands gripping her arms with such force she knew they must be turning white at the knuckles.

"It's time for our midday meal, Miss McKendrick. And I believe that it should be *your* job to fix it."

"I don't cook."

He scowled.

"Well, I suppose I *could* cook," she added hastily when his expression grew thunderous, "but you probably wouldn't like the efforts."

"You said . . ."

"I said that *someone* would fix you a meal. I didn't say it would be me. Effie and the girls do most of that. They've managed to become excellent chefs by experimenting with our old cook's recipe books. Unfortunately, even with a recipe, I'm hopeless in the kitchen. Unlike the other girls who have attended this finishing school, I graduated long before the war forced a change in the curriculum and the girls started taking a hand in food preparation. In my day, it was not considered ladylike for a woman to concern herself with such things. She was taught to rule a bevy of servants in the cookhouse, not work there herself."

"Slaves, you mean."

"That depended entirely on each girl's particular household."

"What about yours, Miss McKendrick?"

"You claim to know so much about me. Surely you

were aware of the fact that my father did not allow slave labor."

"But your mother . . ."

She chose her words carefully before speaking. "My mother wasn't exactly an . . . abolitionist."

"So you grew up with slaves."

She didn't answer.

"A maid, a mammy?"

"Yes, Major Charles, I had servants of color. But that has no bearing on the fact that I have never learned to cook, will probably never learn to cook, and have no desire *ever* to learn to cook."

"She's right, Major." The hesitant comment came from the doorway where Effie stood, her eyes wide and focused on the way they stood too close together. "If your men will bring the things inside, I'll see to their meal."

"Effie—" Augusta tried to step free from the major, but he clamped a hand around her wrist.

Effie hushed Augusta's instinctive protest with a glance and Augusta realized her sister was probably right. There was no reason to further antagonize this man at this point in time. Not when he'd brought them the much needed supplies—and judging by the wagon, there were supplies for them all, not just his men. She should be thanking him, not bickering with him. But she couldn't help it. He'd put her immediately on edge—on guard. She fed off the energy their exchange had provided, doing her best to remain overtly calm.

"Boyd, Frank! Take the wagon around to the back and unload it."

Frank climbed onto the wagon bench beside his

companion. But when they rattled out of sight, Major Charles didn't release her. Augusta glared at him, but it was Effie who was the first to step away.

"Excuse me." The door eased shut behind her with the barest click of the latch.

Augusta waited one minute. Two. Then, when he made no move to drop her wrist, she ordered, "Let . . . me . . . go!"

Rather than loosening his hold, he jerked her against his chest, hard, tight. Her hands closed into fists at the contact, but he didn't allow his grip to ease, holding her wrists so tightly that she could feel each ridge and hollow of his chest beneath his shirt.

"No matter how many times I warn you, Augusta, you continue to tread on dangerous ground."

She didn't answer but cocked her chin at a rebellious angle.

"You don't seem to grasp the seriousness of your predicament. I am the man who will decide whether a trial is in order, or charges should be dropped. I am the man who will determine the length and breadth of the investigation. And I am the man to whom you should be showing a good deal more respect!"

As he spoke, Augusta was astounded to discover that his voice wasn't quite as forceful as it had been in the past. Instead, his tone grew more intimate, more . . . beseeching.

"Respect is something to be earned."

"As is your freedom."

The words altered her earlier thoughts. He wasn't trying to sway her from her current course—at least not out of any sort of personal concern.

"Are you trying to tell me, Major, that you are open to bribery?" She uttered a bitter laugh. "How typical of a man. Thinking that any woman in a precarious situation would be willing to bare herself, heart, soul, and body, in exchange for better treatment."

"Damn you!" he hissed. His hand tangled in her hair, pulling the pins free and dislodging the coiled plait. "I am *not* open to bribery—be it your body or anything else. I merely meant to remind you that everything you do and say forms an opinion. An opinion which may color my judgment if you aren't careful."

Augusta willed her fingers to relax from their fists.

"So does that mean . . ." she drawled, lowering her voice to a whisper, ". . . that in order to foster your good thoughts I should act the coy maid?"

She couldn't help herself. She had to push him to the limits one more time. She had to make him see that she would not bow to his wishes, and that if he pushed her into an emotional corner, she had a means of her own to fight back.

Augusta used a finger to draw a circle around one of his buttons. "Is that what you want, Major? After everything that occurred between us yesterday, have we finally uncovered the truth? What is it about a woman that really moves you? Evidently, you would like me to hang on your every word, to obey each command? Hmm?" The circle became wider. Instead of one finger, she used two, three, then an entire hand.

His grip had eased enough to allow such movements, but he did not release her, so she continued.

"Perhaps, you would like things to progress even further, Major. Perhaps you would like me to cuddle next to you and beg for protection." She stepped close, resting her cheek on his chest and wriggling, ever so slightly, so that her body fit more firmly against his. "Is that what you want, Major? A kitten-ish female who purrs in your arms?"

The hand in her hair grew tense. Then he jerked her head back, forcing her to look at him, forcing her to acknowledge the fire she'd lit in his eyes. Anger, frustration, and something more. Something baser. Something purely male.

"No more games, Augusta, no more ploys. You decide what you want *me* to be. A man who allows himself to look inside of you, share your emotions . . . or a soldier. Otherwise, I'll warn you now . . . you're playing with fire," he ground out through a tight jaw.

His hands framed her face, roughly, forcefully, holding her in such a way that she could not look away, no matter how much she tried. Then one thumb pressed against the corner of her mouth, slowly trac-ing the outline, parting her lips, grinding them against her teeth.

Sensual thoughts tumbled into her head. Inappro-priate thoughts she knew she shouldn't entertain. Now or ever. No matter how much she might want to do so.

He abruptly released her and strode in the direction of the barn. As she watched him go, she realized that she was indeed playing with fire. Because the moment that man's arms had fallen, she'd felt colder than ever before.

"Augusta?"

Augusta whirled to find her sister peering at her from the doorway. Barely disguised in the folds of her skirts was a tiny derringer—one Augusta had never seen before.

"Is he gone?"

Augusta nodded, then noted that—for the first time

in days—she'd been left momentarily unguarded. Hurrying to the door, Augusta pushed her sister inside before the major realized what he'd done and came in search of them both.

"Where in blazes did you get the gun?" she demanded.

"Buttercup."

"Buttercup?"

"They've been raiding the Yankees' supplies."

Augusta squeezed her eyes closed, praying for calm in light of that information, but her supplications were soon drowned by an even more potent concern.

"Effie, I need your help." She leaned as close as she could. "You've got to put something in their food."

"What?"

"I need some time. Alone."

"But—"

"I've got to check on Elijah and make sure he has the supplies he needs. Please. Do something with those herbs you've got. Please."

"Augusta!"

She started at the deep voice. The major had realized his error and come in the side entrance. He now waited for her, partway down the hall, a black scowl cloaking his features, his legs planted squarely apart, his hands on his hips.

"Get over here! If you're not going to cook, you can help unpack."

With one last squeeze of her sister's hand, Augusta said, "Please," then hurried to join him.

"It's time for an update on our plans," Buttercup said, pulling up a sack of potatoes and sitting on it as if it were a royal throne.

"How is the wash progressing?"

Revel-Ann grinned from her position as guard at the larder door. "We'll do the ironing tomorrow—make sure you wear your gloves, girls. We must have guessed right on the amount of quicklime to use because the clothes are as fragile as tissue paper, but they'll hold together for a time. At least long enough to give them a rash."

"Good!" Buttercup checked something off her list. "What about the seduction schemes?"

"Miss Effie seems to have taken a shining to Frank," Aster confided. "I haven't had to do much to distract him."

"Thank you, Miss Effie," Buttercup murmured, crossing off another item on her notes. "What about the other one? Boyd?"

"He's . . . uh, asked me to sit by him at breakfast," Thelma admitted.

"Marvelous. Keep at him, Thelma."

Thelma's cheeks tinged scarlet.

"What about our supplies?"

Aster hurried to a trunk in the corner. "We've managed to piece together a full uniform. Well . . . most of a uniform."

"Good. Miss Augusta will need it tonight."

The room was instantly silent.

"What?" Aster breathed.

"Miss Effie has informed me that we're to drug the men tonight so that Miss Augusta can check on Elijah."

"Oh, my," Pansy breathed.

Thelma reached for her smelling salts.

"So what other supplies do we have for her?"

"The derringer—"

"Which is useless without bullets."

"We've got bullets—"

"For a revolver, not a derringer."

"Ladies, ladies!" Revel-Ann interrupted. "You forgot I'm the 'wind.'" Grinning, she lifted her skirts and removed a long-barreled revolver from where she'd tucked it beneath the band of her garter and into her stockings. "More than that, while I was taking it, I heard the men talking. I managed to discover that Miss Augusta is only part of why they're here."

"I don't understand," Pansy whispered.

"They're hoping that by using Miss Augusta as bait, they can force her brother, Clarence, to make an appearance."

The news sent a wave of foreboding through their makeshift war room. Since they'd been at Billingsly when Augusta had first been investigated for harboring a spy, they knew what such news meant.

"Oh, dear," Pansy whispered.

Thelma whimpered and sank onto the bag of potatoes that Buttercup had just vacated.

"We'll have to pass the word to Miss Augusta somehow."

"What do we do in the meantime?"

"Exactly what we've been doing. We watch, we wait, we listen."

But as the silence of the larder settled around them, Buttercup knew that none of the girls were fooled. Despite the inroads they'd made in tormenting their captors, they were essentially helpless. And their meager attempts at subterfuge had gained them nothing more than a few pieces of clothing, a handful of bullets, and a couple of firearms. That was no real threat against the whole Union army.

"Please tell me you've found a way to subdue them for a few hours, Effie."

Under the guise of gathering the plates for the evening meal, Augusta was able to get close enough to her sister to utter the low comment.

"Yes," Effie whispered, her hands visibly shaking. "I wouldn't recommend the pudding for dessert."

With that, she was gone, bustling to set a platter of steamed potatoes in the center of the table.

"Miss Augusta?"

"Yes, Thelma."

The girl was especially pale tonight. In the past few days, she'd taken to wearing her smelling salts around her neck.

"Could I speak to you, please?"

She barely managed to get the question out.

Augusta glanced at the pudding on the stove, the men gathering around the table, then back to the young girl. She was tempted to put off any sort of conversation, but something about Thelma's wide eyes convinced her otherwise.

"Very well."

"Privately."

Augusta didn't know what the major would say to that request, but she nodded. "I'll try."

Taking her hat and scarf from the peg, she approached the major.

"One of my girls has a problem. I would like your permission to talk to her outside. Alone."

He shook his head. "No."

She tapped her toe in irritation, plopping her hands

on her hips. "Why not? I'm not about to send smoke signals or light a distress fire. I'd simply like your permission to walk with her as far as the pump—you can stand on the portico and watch us if you'd like."

He regarded her closely, then eyed Thelma in such a way that she clung to the counter as if ill.

"What's wrong with her?"

"Female trouble," Augusta whispered, knowing that the mere mention of such a thing would usually shut up anyone of the masculine persuasion. To her delight, the tactic worked on the major as well.

"Fine. But the pump is as far as you go."

Motioning to Thelma to follow her, Augusta took a pail from one of the hooks by the door—as if she'd always planned to go for water. In fact, she hoped that by filling the bucket from the pump outside, she could disguise their conversation from the major.

The weather outside was bitter—feeling more like January than November. She and Thelma picked their way over the icy path to the pump.

"What's wrong, Thelma? Have you and Aster had another tiff about—"

"No, Miss Augusta." The girl grabbed her arm with both hands, her grip surprisingly strong. "We managed to piece a uniform together from the wash. It's hidden in the larder."

"Excellent!"

"There's more. Revel-Ann has discovered from one of the soldiers that they've put you under house arrest in order to trap Clarence."

"What?" she whispered, the cold of the evening seeping deep into her bones. She'd guessed as much, but it was shocking to have her suspicions put into words.

135

"They think that if he discovers you are under house arrest, he will come to help you."

Augusta worried her lower lip with her teeth.

"What do you want us to do, Miss Augusta?"

The jarring information she'd been given was quickly superseded by her concern for her students. "Don't do anything, do you hear? No matter what is said, what is done, I want you to remain *out* of the whole affair."

"But—"

"Please, Thelma. Tell the other girls to stay clear of the major and his men. They must not be given any reason to question you."

For some reason, this time Thelma looked positively sick. "Yes, ma'am."

"Augusta!" The shout came from the portico. From the major.

Augusta squeezed Thelma's hand. "Remember what I've said. Do nothing. Nothing!"

8

Augusta watched the soldiers eat and waited.
While the girls had dished up the rest of the meal, Effie managed to point to a bottle of laudanum and a crock of her own special concoction of sleeping herbs so that Augusta would know how the men had been drugged. Judging by the way Effie reacted to the medications, Augusta calculated that the effects should make a grown man sleep heavily for at least an hour.

One by one, the women of Billingsly refused an offer of dessert under the pretense that they were too full to eat another bite. And after the dinner of ham, boiled potatoes, biscuits, and milk gravy, who could blame them?

Certainly not the men. The men complimented Effie on her cooking, then moved to their assigned guard duties—Boyd to the rear door, Frank to the front foyer. As for the major, Augusta was determined that if her plan was to work, he would have to think he'd fallen asleep on duty. So, pleading exhaustion, she retired to her bedroom early. Gathering several books of poetry from her bureau, she settled in the rocking chair by her window, a blanket folded around her legs, and began to read.

Within a quarter hour, she could see the major fighting his drowsiness. Feeling deliciously wicked at outsmarting him, she compounded the effect by beginning to rock back and forth. The chair—one commonly referred to as a "Baby Tendah"—was built low to the ground and reclined noticeably. In her mother's day, such a contraption had been used by the women who served as wet nurses since the position of the chair allowed a larger lap space for feeding and cuddling the child. The chair was so old, it creaked as she rocked, providing a lullaby of sorts for the man positioned in the hall.

Squeak, creak.

Even from her vantage point, she could see the major's eyes begin to glaze over. Once, his chin dropped and the jarring motion caused his head to rear back, his eyes to flicker. Then he succumbed, his chin drooping to his chest.

Augusta waited another minute.

Squeak . . . creak . . . squeak . . . creak.

He didn't stir. His breathing had become slow and heavy.

"Major?"

He didn't answer, and she rose from the chair.

"Major?"

Again, no response, so she dropped her books to the floor.

Bam!

He offered a boyish sigh, but didn't awaken.

Tiptoeing forward, she poked him in the chest.

Nothing.

"Major?"

Nothing.

Not willing to waste another minute, she rushed down the back stairs. Boyd was there, sprawled on the floor. Revel-Ann was putting a quilt over him where he lay.

"What in the world?" Augusta asked, wondering how the man had come to be lying on the ground instead of the chair at his side.

Revel-Ann offered her a coy smile. "I must have slid the chair in the wrong direction when he started to sway."

"Wrong direction, mmm?"

"Well . . ."

"You and I will have a chat of our own when I get back," Augusta warned. Then she was dodging into the kitchen.

"It worked, Effie!" she whispered in delight.

"What exactly are you going to do?" Effie asked as Augusta dodged into the back bedroom where the soldiers had been taking turns sleeping.

"I'm going to see Elijah, make sure he's all right."

"But—"

"Trust me, Effie. I've developed a plan."

But when she emerged wearing the pilfered Yankee uniform, Effie gasped.

"You can't go out like *that!*"

"I can, and I will. It's the perfect disguise. No one would dare to stop me if I'm in Union blue."

"Elijah might greet you at the end of a revolver."

"I'll take off the jacket before I get to Elijah's shack. Now, come on, Effie. Help me. We haven't much time."

139

It took little more than a quarter of an hour to fill a flour sack with a few provisions for Elijah. She would see to it that he received more foodstuffs from their supply, but for now, she took only what she could carry.

Scraping her hair into a tighter braid, she covered it with her coat and a woolen muffler, then paused to kiss Effie on the cheek.

"I'll hurry."

"You'd better. I don't know when they'll wake up."

"Yes, ma'am. I'll go as fast as I can."

The chill air seeped beneath her trouser legs as soon as she left the building and Augusta shivered. In all honesty, she didn't understand how men endured the winter in such clothing. Compared to layers of petticoats and skirts, the trousers felt cold and drafty and barely shielded her from the elements.

Of course if she had a greatcoat such as the major had . . .

Why on earth was she thinking of him? Now? When she should be keeping her wits about her.

Slowly, carefully, mindful of making any sounds which might betray her, she tiptoed outside and made her way down the back path to the trees beyond. Each step of the way, she scanned the area, looking for the slightest shadow which might be out of place. She didn't entirely trust her footing on the icy trail, nor did she trust the fact that the major might not have assigned sentries to the perimeter of the property. For all she knew, the area could be crawling with Union soldiers.

If only the moon would come out and bathe the area in light.

But then, if the moon offered its light for her, it might also reveal her flight.

Her toes were growing icy, her fingers numb. Shoving her hands as deeply into the pockets of her jacket as she could, she tucked her face into the muffler wound around her neck and clambered over the sty which had been built to traverse a retaining wall erected next to the creek.

As soon as she left the cover provided by the solid brick barrier, she was immediately buffeted by the icy wind. It stung at her cheeks and nose, urging her to turn back. But she couldn't.

The sleet and snow which had fallen made walking difficult. Her shoes kept slipping and sliding as she hurried over the back meadow and scrambled over the fence. Once in the orchard, she wound her way through the trees, following a familiar path that the snow had all but obscured. Beyond that was a rutted road that led farther into the hills for a mile and a half.

By the time she topped the rise and saw the bulky shape of the abandoned overseer's cottage, she could barely feel her feet, they were so cold. Her lungs burned with the effort to breathe. She all but stumbled down the hill and collapsed against the door frame. But she was not so tired nor so stupid as to enter without issuing a secret series of knocks.

She waited, saw the draperies at the window part ever so slightly. Then there was a faint sound of footfalls and the grate of a key in the lock.

"Lawsie, Miz 'Kendrick. What are you doin' here dressed like that?"

Elijah dragged her inside, closing the door behind her.

Heat. Blessed heat. The tiny house felt nearly tropical after the squall she'd braved.

"I came to see how you were." The words were barely recognizable considering the chattering of her teeth.

"Me, Miz 'Kendrick?"

She touched his hand. "Of course, Elijah. It's been so cold and I didn't know if you had enough wood and stores."

He offered her a shy smile, one that should have been at odds with his hulking body, but merely made him seem more endearing.

"I's fine, Miz 'Kendrick. There's plenty o' wood in the orchard if I needs it."

"What about food?"

"I could use some supplies—the broth I got's just about gone an' I'll need to make some more—but I kin make do with bread and cheese fer a few days."

"Here, take this." She shoved the sack into his hands, then crept closer to the fire. "That will tide you over for a day or two. Then I'll see to it that some salt pork and bacon are brought as well as some beef."

"Beef?" His eyes widened, lighting up like a child's at Christmas, and she laughed.

"Yes, beef! We've had some trouble with soldiers at the house." Elijah's jaw became hard and she held up a hand. "There's nothing to worry about. They can't prove anything, I'm sure of it. But they've insisted on staying for a few days, so I turned the situation to our advantage and wangled some supplies from the major in charge. If there's anything else you need, you let me know."

The quiet seeped between them then.

"What did you do with the senator?"

"Won't nobody be findin' him, Miz 'Gusta."

She clasped her hands together to keep them from trembling. Images of that night crowded into her brain. The senator's hands clawing at her sister. Effie's screams. Elijah's shout of outrage. The girls' panic.

"I didn't mean to drag you into this, Elijah." Her tone wobbled no matter how hard she tried to sound strong. "It isn't fair."

"I don't 'member anybody tellin' me that life had t' be fair."

She sighed. "I suppose you're right." A little more relaxed now, she gazed around the room at the surprisingly homey touches Elijah had made. Where once the space had been bare of furniture and completely spartan, now there were hand-hewn chairs with woven cane seats, flour sack curtains, and a battered table with a tin of pinecones and kindling sticks in the center.

"Your place is very nice, Elijah."

He grinned. "I've been thinkin' 'bout addin' on."

"Adding on?"

"Yes'm. There's a gal in Russleville who I asked t' jump the broom with me. She said 'yes.'"

"Oh, Elijah! That's wonderful!" Suddenly, it made sense—the furniture, the feminine touches. She stood and threw her arms around his neck. "I am so happy for you."

"Thank you, Miz 'Kendrick."

But she immediately sobered when she remembered why she had come.

"I should have seen to it that you left Billingsly days before Senator Armiture arrived. I should have known you wouldn't remain an innocent bystander."

"Hush. Knowin' he was comin' I woulda been there

143

no matter what, just t' make sure he didn't bother you." He shook his head. "Friends help friends, Miz 'Kendrick."

"Yes, but they shouldn't have to continue to endanger themselves in the process—especially now that I know you're planning to get married."

He grinned. "I ain't in no danger. I'm jus' tendin' to the sick, that's all."

Tending to the sick. What a simple way of describing all he'd done for Clarence the past few days.

Her throat was tight and raspy as she asked, "May I see my brother?"

"'Course you can."

Elijah took a lamp, leading the way to a rear bedroom.

The figure in the bed was still, frail, his knees drawn to his chest like a baby's, his fist ground to his mouth.

"Has there been any change?"

"No, ma'am. I can get him to eat, long as it's soup or such. But other than that, he stays on the bed starin'. Just starin'."

"What about the wound?" she asked, her voice husky.

"I shaved de hair away round de wound so's I could keep it clean o' blood, but . . . Miz 'Kendrick, I'd say his skull's in a billion bitty pieces. There ain't no way t' help him now." Elijah pulled back the covers to show the recent, angry wound at the back of the man's head.

The quiet was ominous, thick, building in the room like storm clouds. Augusta sank to the bed, running her hands over his brow.

"Clarence?" she whispered, leaning close. "Clarence, it's me, Augusta."

But he didn't respond. Just as she feared he never would.

Sighing, she placed a kiss on his cheek and stood.

Seeing her distress, Elijah touched her shoulder. "Y' didn't need t' come here, Miz 'Kendrick. I would've sent word if he'd changed any."

"I know, Elijah. But now that you know about the soldiers, you mustn't come near the place no matter what."

But what lay unspoken between them was that she'd come because she'd known there would be *no* change in her brother's condition. Not now.

Not ever.

That was why she had to protect him. Otherwise, the Union army would simply assume his guilt and execute him.

But Augusta wouldn't let that happen. No matter what he had done or the mistakes he'd made, when she'd sent a telegram informing Clarence that Armiture was about to pay a visit, he'd come to confront Senator Armiture and drive him away from Billingsly. All because he'd felt that if Armiture had a grievance, he should confront the man responsible instead of threatening innocent women.

For that alone, her brother, her baby brother, deserved to die with dignity.

9

Augusta felt much like a thief as she crept back into the house, hoping, praying, that her absence had not been discovered and no one had seen where she'd gone.

The moment she appeared, Effie rushed to meet her, carrying a lamp high over her head. "Hurry! There's no time to lose!"

Augusta grew cold. "What's happened?"

"Nothing. Yet. But the men are beginning to rouse. You've got to get up to bed. Quickly!"

Augusta was whipping the Union uniform off, piece by piece, as she ran to the stairs. Shoving the clothes into Effie's hands she said, "Hide these somewhere safe!"

Tiptoeing down the hall, she padded past the major in his chair. As Effie had said, his sleep was growing restless.

Running into her room, she dropped her shoes at the foot of the bed and dragged a nightgown over her head. Her heart pounding, she slid into bed, pulling the covers up to her ears.

Within minutes, she heard the creak of the major's chair.

He was awake—or at least aware of his surroundings.

She could only pray that he wouldn't know he'd been drugged.

His boots thumped.

No. No.

Please, don't let him come any nearer.

Jackson cupped his head in his hands and groaned softly.

The dreams. The horrible, horrible dreams. He'd been in battle, positioned behind a line of cannon. The noise had grown incredible, the stench overwhelmingly real. Through it all, he'd urged his men to fire faster and faster. Then a wall of fire had leapt in front of him and he'd been thrown to his back.

Jackson shook his head to clear it of the images, then regretted the hasty action when it made his skull throb.

Rising, he ground the heels of his hands against his eyelids, damning the sluggishness of his brain and the way his limbs seemed unwilling to follow the commands he gave them.

Taking a pocket watch from his vest, he popped open the lid, then stared at it in surprise. How on earth had he managed to sleep for eighty minutes?

He squinted at the clock on Augusta's dresser, just to make sure, but the timepieces gave the same information, give or take a minute. He hadn't slept that soundly in years, let alone while he was on guard duty. In fact, he couldn't remember resting so completely since his leg had been injured and they'd dosed him with laudanum.

Laudanum.

That taste.

It lingered in his mouth.

Laudanum.

Damnit, what in hell had Augusta done to him? But moreover, what had she *done* while he was all but unconscious?

He walked into her bedroom, searching for anything out of place, and saw nothing. She lay huddled on her bed, the covers drawn up to her chin, her hair drawn back in a little-girl braid and fastened with a pink ribbon.

Was she aware how sweet such a pose made her look? How lovely? How innocent?

It was really too bad that he didn't believe her act. He knew deep in his soul of souls that she'd been up to no good while he'd been drugged into oblivion. How could he have dropped his guard? Why hadn't he sensed some inkling of deceit when she'd insisted on retiring and spending a quiet evening reading her books?

The anger rose inside him, growing hotter. She was aware of every move he made. He was sure that if he touched her, she would jump.

His fingers curled toward his palm and he stared at the outline of her thigh beneath the covers. He knew well enough that it would be better for all concerned if he waited until morning to confront her—allowing his temper to cool. But he was not in the mood to pretend that she was asleep.

"You're awake. You might as well admit it."

She didn't respond and for some reason, the fact that she would continue to play out a lie infuriated him, so he moved closer, grasping the post of her bed.

Augusta didn't move so much as a muscle to reveal that she'd heard him or that she knew he'd come closer. She kept her breathing shallow and slow—a very consummate performance. But he wasn't fooled. She was aware of him. So very aware.

Her bed was a four-poster affair, small, narrow, the sort a child would be more comfortable in using than a woman, but the fact worked to his advantage. He could see her feet pushing at the bedclothes.

Leaning one shoulder against the heavy wooden pole, he reached down, uncovering her legs bit by bit, inch by inch.

She refused to move, but he sensed a difference in her posture, a tension, an expectancy.

"You know, don't you," he murmured silkily, "that there are many tests of whether a woman is truly refined. There are her manners, of course, her talents, her abilities, her gentility, her breeding. But one of the measures of a *real* lady is her feet. They must be tiny. Dainty. Smooth."

Without warning, he clasped her foot in his hand, curling his fingers around the instep. He felt her jump, the hiss of her breath, and it pleased him to no end, causing his anger to evolve into another emotion. One that was as powerful, but far more sensual. It didn't matter to him a bit that she didn't open her eyes, or that she gripped her blankets as if she planned to continue pretending she was asleep. She was listening.

"You have very nice feet, Miss McKendrick. I hadn't noticed until now. You're always wearing those awful boots. But your skin is soft, pink, as if you tend to your feet with great care. As a lady should."

His fingers splayed wide and she jerked a little, as if he'd tickled her with his movements. Rubbing his palm down the length of her foot, he remarked, "You have such narrow feet, a high instep, a beautifully shaped arch . . ." He ran a finger over the pads of her toes. "Lovely. Quite lovely."

He could hear her breathing now. Not quite so evenly. Not quite so shallowly. He moved his hand upward, curving over her ankle, and moving steadily on.

"What pretty legs you have as well. So slim and lithe."

Up, up, up . . .

He was nearly to the hollow of her knee when Augusta jerked into a sitting position and thrust the blankets tightly around her limbs.

"Will you please mind what you're doing!"

He chuckled at her outraged expression. Would he ever tire of baiting her, of making her argue with him? Straightening, he returned to his chair, leaving her sitting in the middle of the bed, her chest heaving in outrage.

It was a glorious sight.

A glorious sight, indeed.

She had finally dispensed with sleeping in her clothes—and although the matronly flannel gown she wore could not be considered enticing in the least, the figure it attempted to conceal was nonetheless alluring. Quite shapely.

How long had it been since he'd allowed himself to look at any female in such an intimate way? Longer than he would care to admit.

"What are you staring at?"

He jerked at the demand. When he saw Augusta, her hair tumbled, her eyes blazing in irritation, he could only crook his mouth in a slight smile and answer, "You."

She huffed in indignation, gathering the covers even higher, tighter. This merely caused the blankets to bunch so that her feet peeked out at him. Tiny and pink and endearing.

"I will not have it, sir," she finally said in impatience. "I will report you to your superior if such treatment continues."

"My superior wanted me to lock you up days ago."

That comment managed to silence her, but only for an instant.

"You can go to blasted purgatory, Major!" she snapped, then rolled to her side and pulled the blanket over her head—leaving him with a quite delicious outline of her rump.

Jackson chuckled, but the amusement died when he saw the boots tucked under her bed. Only the tips were visible, but that sight was all he needed.

For even in the dim light, he could easily see the fresh mud clinging to the soles.

"Where have you been, Augusta?"

She didn't respond.

"What have you done?"

Silence.

"I'm not a fool, you know. I'm well aware that I've been drugged for nearly an hour and a half. I'm also not so naive as to think that you've spent the bulk of that time in bed or reading poetry."

She shifted, lowering the bedclothes enough to peer over the top. "I don't know what you mean."

He sighed in infinite weariness. "I see. Wait here, Augusta."

Standing, he made his way downstairs.

Frank was standing at the half-open door, breathing deeply of the frigid night air. Judging from his guilty start, he too had thought he'd been sleeping on the job.

"Keep a sharp eye out for anything out of the ordinary, Frank. We've been drugged."

The man's patent relief was enough to make Jackson lose a bit of his pique and grin. He'd never seen Frank discomfited before.

"Let's find Boyd. Then I want you to search the area. There's no telling what's been happening while we've been out cold."

"Clarence," Frank whispered.

"Exactly."

They found Boyd slumped on the floor near the back entrance, his chest covered with a pink and yellow crazy quilt.

The two men exchanged glances.

Frank nudged his companion with a toe. Boyd smiled, muttering something in his sleep, and stretched. "Kiss me . . . 'gain . . . honey."

Jackson and Frank snickered. Seeing Frank's silent bid for permission, Jackson nodded. Frank crouched close to the man, murmuring in return, "Sure, darlin'."

Boyd froze, blinked, then scrambled to his feet.

"Damnit, Frank! I told you not to do that again. Lots of people talk in their sleep. That doesn't mean you have to make a fool of 'em!"

Frank laughed, an honest-to-goodness belly laugh that was especially strange coming from a man who was usually so grave. "You'd best be watching what you say, Boyd. One of these days, you might not be sleeping alone—and I don't think a woman would take too kindly to hearing you call her by another female's name."

Boyd sputtered and grumbled, but no coherent phrases emerged.

Somehow, the entire exchange had dampened the immediacy of the situation. Maybe it was the fact that he'd slept—really slept—but Jackson didn't feel nearly as angry as he had a few minutes earlier. It had been nice to discover that there were things in life that could make a person laugh.

Chuckling again at Boyd's comical expression, Jackson said, "Frank, let him know what's happened."

He turned, intent upon retrieving his saddlebags from the back bedroom. He would get some answers from Augusta tonight even if it killed him—killed them both. "If you find any evidence of Clarence's having been here, come get me. If not, I'll talk to you both in the morning. I've got business to take care of upstairs."

"Yes, sir," Frank replied gravely.

"I hope to hell you find out why she did this to us, sir," Boyd grumbled.

"'She'?" Jackson retorted tightly. "I wouldn't be surprised if the whole damn school was involved in this escapade tonight."

Returning upstairs, Jackson became icy calm. As much as he might have enjoyed the reprieve his men had created downstairs, he had business to conduct.

Very serious business.

He moved steadily down the hall, the saddlebags

he'd collected from his room held tightly in one fist. Each step he took was slow and measured, each second crowded with a thousand thoughts and strategies.

Entering Augusta's bedroom, he found her just as he'd left her, huddled on the bed, her knees drawn up around her chest.

"I'm pleased to see you followed my instructions."

"I didn't have much of a choice."

"That's never stopped you before."

She shrugged, but her manner was more subdued than he'd seen it before—and the reaction was telling. It informed him immediately that whatever she'd done during the night had been important to her. Important enough to risk getting caught.

Walking to the bureau, he took a bottle from his saddlebags and a pair of tin cups, setting them on the crocheted runner. Then he moved back to the bed, dumping the checkerboard and pieces onto the covers.

"Set them up."

"It really isn't necessary to—"

"Set them up."

"Here?" she asked, gesturing to the rumpled covers.

"Yes."

She complied, sitting cross-legged with the blankets wrapped around her chest. He saw the way her fingers trembled as she completed the task.

As soon as the board had been adorned with the wooden discs, he drew a chair up to the foot of her bed and straddled it, leaning forward to begin the game. She stared at the black piece which stood out of line from the others and he knew she was on her guard. This time, she would not win so easily.

"It's your move, Augusta."

"What if I told you I didn't want to play?"

He didn't give her the option of quitting. "Your move, Augusta," he said more sternly.

She sighed, pushing a piece forward. "I would really rather rest, if you don't mind."

"I do mind. A great deal."

She waited for her turn, then offered a lilting bit of laughter. "The fact that you think I've drugged you is preposterous. It's hardly my fault that you and your men ate so much that—"

He halted whatever excuse she'd been about to give by reaching for her boots and throwing them on the bed. Mud streaked her blankets where they bounced against her knee, then fell into her lap.

She stared down at the boots for several long moments, then swept them aside so that they clattered to the floor.

"You really can't blame me, can you? I had to do something to fight back."

"Where have you been?"

She remained mulishly silent, folding her arms tightly under her chest.

"*Where,* Augusta?"

"Out. I went out." She pushed the covers aside, sending the checkers and board flying. By the time the last piece had clattered to a stop, she was as far from Jackson as she could manage, standing near the window in the far corner.

Jackson forced himself to ignore the way the lamplight pierced her worn gown as if it were of little more substance than a cloud.

"Tell me everything, Augusta."

"Why?" She offered a bitter laugh. "Even if I were to offer the truth, you would assume I was lying."

He stood, sensing a weakening in her resolve—the first time he had ever considered such a thing from her.

"I'll believe you, Augusta."

"How will you discern I'm telling you the truth?"

"I'll know."

She shook her head. "No."

He eased closer, knowing that he might never have this opportunity again—a time when she felt vulnerable enough to trust him.

Jackson didn't bother to analyze why such a trust was important. Nor did he bother to analyze why his professionalism had been doused by an inexplicable wave of tenderness.

She was afraid.

He'd never allowed himself to see such a thing before—or if he had, he'd ignored it.

"Why are you scared, Augusta?"

He wasn't even aware that he'd spoken out loud until he saw the way she started.

"Scared?"

He touched her cheek with one finger.

"I think you're terrified. But not of me, not of what could happen to you, not even of a possible hanging. You're scared to death of something else. What?"

She shook her head, refusing to speak, but this time it wasn't stubborn pride that caused her silence, it was the overriding emotion he'd accused her of. It was there in her eyes, in the pale cast of her features, in the way she'd unconsciously gripped his wrist.

"Please tell me," he whispered fiercely. "If you do, and it is within my power to help, I *will* help you."

"No." It was a choked whisper, barely recognizable as having come from her. "Go away, Jackson."

The fact that she'd called him by his name affected him like a mule kick to the gut.

"Leave here now before you push things farther than they were ever meant to go."

"I can't do that."

"Why?" she cried fiercely.

"A man has died."

"But you can't *prove* that he did."

"I have to prove it. That's my job."

She broke free from him, leaning her hands against the windowsill, but he pulled her to him, wrapping his arms around her waist and murmuring in her ear, "Tell me. Tell me what happened. Did you kill Senator Armiture?"

The room echoed in silence, fraught with some added tension that he could not identify.

Slowly, she turned in his arms, framing his face with her slender hands.

"I wish I knew more about you, about your motives and beliefs and ideals. If I did, I might know what to say to you. I might know how to appeal to you."

Her frustration mirrored his own.

"I'm so tired," she continued. "So tired of it all— fighting to provide for us, being the strong one, the person in charge. I don't want to do it anymore. I want to find some tiny corner of the world that is happy and peaceful and I want to lie down and sleep for a hundred years. I want to dream."

Her eyes briefly flickered shut as if the image she'd created had disappeared from her mind's eye.

"Have you ever felt that way, Jackson?" The fingers at his cheeks dug into his skin. *"Have* you?"

He could no more deny her the answer than stop breathing.

"Yes. Every day."

A tiny choked cry escaped her lips and she stood on tiptoe. "Kiss me. Please kiss me."

"Augusta—"

"Don't think about what brought us to this point or what will eventually take us beyond it. I'm so tired, so very tired, but when you kiss me, when you touch me, I feel alive—for the first time in years."

10

Augusta pressed her lips to Jackson's and he could not find the will to resist. She was warm and lithe and womanly, filled with a vibrancy that had been tempered by sacrifice.

His arms swept around her waist, taking her weight and drawing her tightly against him. So much so that he could feel her unbound breasts pressing into his chest, the shape of her thighs against his own.

Almighty hell, she felt good, so good. It was all he could do to remember to breathe as her tongue swept into his mouth, searching, exploring, driving him insane. When she clutched at him, tugging his shirt from his trousers, then slipping inside to caress the taut muscles of his back, a heat built in his soul and began to radiate inward, collecting in his loins . . . and in his heart.

He broke free, staring at her, at her hungry eyes and swollen lips. He shouldn't let this happen—with a traitor, a suspect. It would be madness to allow his own emotions to become involved with this woman.

All his arguments scattered into the darkness and he kissed her again, hungrily, intently, his own desperation rising within him.

She broke away long enough to whisper, "Close the door."

"What?"

"Close the door."

With that simple command, she gave tacit permission for the one thing he had never thought she would condone, let alone allow.

One glimmer of chivalry survived the burst of passion she'd inspired.

"No, it isn't—"

"Damnit, Major, close the door," she growled huskily, nipping at his chin, his jawline, then moving lower, her hands working impatiently at his buttons. "I'm tired of doing what's right, tired of doing what's expected. I want this. I want *you.*"

He barely managed to shut the panels before she was lifting the gown from her body, and her sudden nakedness caused him to gasp. She was more beautiful than he had ever dreamed, her body proportioned so exquisitely with firm, high breasts, a tiny waist, and hips flared in a manner that invited a man's hands to explore.

When he would have hesitated, some tiny voice of warning filling him with doubts, she rushed forward to kiss him, again and again and again. Then she was drawing him backward to the bed so that they tumbled onto the covers.

"Major! Major, come quick!"

The distant cry was followed by the stomping of boots on the steps.

Jackson yanked free, breathing heavily. Staring

down at Augusta, he was amazed at how far things had gone. They had been so close to making love—*making love,* damnit.

But even as he stood and struggled to put his clothing to rights, he couldn't find it in himself to accuse her of bribing him with her body, or softening his will to interrogate her. No, what had happened between them had been a mutual need. A fire which had been stoked but lay smoldering, waiting for the next opportunity to flare.

The attraction was not over.

Far from it.

Without another word, he turned and strode from the room, carefully shielding any view of Augusta with his body until the latch clicked shut.

He arrived on the landing in time to see Boyd running up the steps.

"Come quick, sir, Frank thinks he's found something."

Jackson pushed his own lingering thoughts of Augusta away and hurried to follow Boyd.

The younger man took him outside to the rear portico. Automatically, his eyes narrowed and he scanned the area, but he found nothing out of place.

"Major? I think you'd better come with me."

Jackson felt a shiver of unease trace down his spine. Slowly turning, he regarded Frank Conley as the man walked toward him from the side of the porch where the stacks of wood were kept. The man's cadaverous expression was even more so. Not a good sign.

"What have you got, Frank?"

The man hesitated before speaking. "I'd rather not say. I don't want to jump to any conclusions."

Jackson followed him to the woodpile where a pair

of pants, a shirt, and a jacket had been shoved beneath one of the logs. He immediately recognized the pants as his own, the shirt and jacket as Boyd's.

Tugging them partially free, Frank pointed to the dirt stains near the hems. "Near as I can tell, the trousers were too long for Miss McKendrick."

Jackson didn't bother to comment on the fact that Frank had assumed Augusta had been wearing them. It was something they'd both concluded.

"If you look here, Major, there's some clay ground into the hems." He glanced up. "I took the liberty of making a tour of the area. What with the cold weather we've been having lately, there's not many places free of snow and ice. It was easy enough to find her trail." His dark eyes glittered. "She went north of here to a narrow creek, leaving the property entirely. There's some slide marks in the ground—as if someone were trying to get up the bank. It's got some heavy clay for soil." He paused. "About a mile beyond that is a small house."

Jackson's hands tightened around the sodden fabric. "Why didn't we notice the place before?"

"We never looked that far. We concentrated our search on the school grounds."

"Anyone there?"

Frank nodded. "A black man—probably Elijah Ward."

"Anyone else?"

"Hard to say. But if my gut instinct is anything to go by, I'd be inclined to say there is."

A rock settled into the pit of Jackson's stomach.

"Saddle up the horses. It's time we took a closer look."

* * *

Mist rose from the surface of the creek as Jackson and Frank made their way to the cottage resting in the hollow of the rolling hills.

"That's it, sir." Frank pointed to a spot on the riverbank where the frozen remains of sliding footprints could be seen. "And that's where I think she tried to get across."

Jackson didn't bother to dismount. He didn't need to examine the tracks more thoroughly. He knew deep in his gut that what he was seeing was Augusta's trail to this house.

"Let's go."

They rode closer, easing forward as silently as they could. But in the stillness of winter, the splash of the horses' hooves in the creek seemed especially loud, the crunch of snow ominous.

Sure enough, long before they'd reached the front steps, the door opened, a yellow bar of light spilling onto the ground.

"Who's dere?"

Jackson exchanged glances with Frank.

"Elijah Ward?"

The black man squinted into the darkness, the rifle in his hand held higher.

"Yes. Dat's me."

Jackson swung down from his horse.

"I'm Major Jackson Charles."

The rifle lowered a bit, but not much.

"My men and I have been—"

"I know where y' been, sir, an' what you've been doin'."

Jackson offered him what he hoped was a quick grin. "I suppose Augusta explained everything to you earlier."

Elijah didn't confirm or reject such a statement. He merely stared at Jackson with quiet eyes.

"Mind if I come in?" Jackson gestured to the inside of the house.

Before he could take another step, the rifle lifted again. "Yes, sir. I do mind," Elijah said softly. "I's a free man. You got no argument with me."

"True. I was just hoping we could talk."

"We got nothin' t' talk 'bout."

Jackson grew impatient with the man's resistance. "Nothing, hmm? Not even Senator Armiture?"

"Don' know nobody by dat name."

Jackson eased closer. "She's told me all about it, you know. She sent me to get you."

But if he'd hoped for a confession, he was sadly disappointed.

"Don' know what you mean, sir." He nodded in the direction of the man and horse that waited. "It's mighty cold out here. I suppose you'll be ridin' on."

"Soon." Jackson purposely looked beyond the towering black man, studying what he could see of the interior through the open door. "Are you alone, Elijah?"

"Yes, sir. This is my home."

"Mind if I confirm what you've said for myself?"

"Yes, sir. I do." The rifle wavered, then lowered. "But if yer set on comin' in an' lookin' fer yerself, den I suppose you'd better do dat."

Jackson was instantly on his guard, but he didn't allow his suspicion to show. Instead, he stepped into the meager warmth of the building.

It was a small house—obviously intended as bachelor quarters from the looks of it. There was a cramped keeping room with a fire, a rocking chair and a table with what appeared to be the remains of Elijah's meal. Beyond that was a smaller room. Moving to the doorway, Jackson saw a dresser and a narrow bed, the covers rumpled and untidy, but completely empty.

"Satisfied?" Elijah said directly behind him.

No. He wasn't. There was something wrong here. Something Jackson couldn't immediately identify. But for now, he would have to concede that he'd found nothing out of the ordinary. Nothing except . . .

The smell. The very faint odor of laudanum and sickness. Jackson would never forget that scent. Never banish the memories that sickly stench brought with it.

Jackson's lips twitched. He could see that Elijah wasn't under the effects of the drug. He was far too clearheaded and alert. No, someone else had been here at one time. Someone who'd been wounded. Someone who'd had access to a medicine more precious than gold in the South.

"Thank you, Elijah."

The man's brows rose. "For what?"

This time, it was Jackson's turn to refuse to answer. He wasn't about to let on that the faint odor of laudanum could reveal so much. Touching a finger to his hat, he made his way to the door. Just before closing it, he paused to say, "I'll be sure to tell Miss Augusta that you are well."

Frank waited until they'd mounted again and were well out of earshot of the house.

"What do you think?"

"Clarence McKendrick was there." Jackson absorbed the disappointment he felt at such news. He'd found even more proof that Augusta had lied to him. "Furthermore, I'd say he's wounded."

He brought the horse he rode to a stop in a stand of trees, turned and looked. "I want you to ride into Wellsville, Frank. Locate the general and tell him that we need another pair of men to serve as round-the-clock guards for this place."

"Why not arrest Ward and search the area for Clarence? If he's wounded, he can't have gone far."

Jackson considered the point, then shook his head. "No, not yet. There's something going on here, something more than Clarence's nearness. Until I know what it is for sure, I want to keep all of the players involved unaware of what we've found out tonight. Meanwhile, I'll wait for reinforcements."

Frank touched his heels to his mount. "Yes, sir. I'll be back within the hour to relieve you."

An hour, Jackson thought wryly as his man rode away.

That might be enough for him to cool the feverish ache left in his body from the time spent with Augusta.

Jackson Charles stayed away from Augusta for the next two days. Emotionally, that was. He continued to dog her footsteps, to monitor her every chore, but he didn't touch her, didn't talk to her.

He mustn't.

She was guilty of the crimes she'd been accused of committing. The more he tried to deny the possibility, the more he knew there was no escaping the fact— no matter how much he might want to.

Never in his career had Jackson wanted to be wrong

more than he did now—and it was enough to shake every professional code he had ever followed as an interrogator. But then again, never had he grown so close to a subject—physically and emotionally. He kept thinking there was a logical explanation, somewhere, somehow, that could prove his softer feelings for Augusta were justified. But with each hour, the evidence was stacked more firmly against her.

He knew she'd drugged him and his men and gone to Elijah Ward's cottage. He knew that Elijah was aiding her somehow—probably by hiding her brother.

That fact could be enough to convict her of treason. She was harboring a known criminal. An assassin. She could be hanged for such a crime, alone. Add to that the disappearance of Senator Armiture and she didn't have a prayer.

She was guilty.

She had to be guilty.

Damnit! So why couldn't he content himself with the facts? Why did he feel bound to dig deeper? Was it due to her allure, the almost overwhelming need he had to touch her?

Or was there more? An emotion that surpassed passion.

Leaning one shoulder against a wall that had once been covered in gold watered silk, he watched as Augusta McKendrick began instructing her students in the proper way for a woman to waltz. He'd heard her explain to them that even though they would be spending the holiday at the school, that didn't mean that they wouldn't learn a few social skills.

It was sad. A half-dozen girls in a small, dusty ballroom, learning to waltz when the chances of such a skill proving necessary were remote. Any balls or social gatherings organized this soon after the war's end would not include invitations to Southern orphans who'd taken refuge in a boarding school. These girls, whether they knew it or not, were doomed to an uncertain future, just as he was. The war had disrupted their plans and had left them floundering for a place in a society that was still scarred and reeling. At best, they might provide for themselves as companions or governesses or teachers. Some might even marry, but they would probably not obtain matches as influential as they might have done before the war.

"One, two, three!" Augusta called, her voice echoing in the barren room. Effie valiantly tried to play a waltz at a hopelessly scarred and out-of-tune piano—the only piece of furniture in the room. There wasn't even a chair left for Jackson to use, he thought, rubbing the ache of his leg. It had been giving him fits lately, reminding him that he would never have the agility for the kind of life he craved, for hard work and manual labor, for riding and training horses, for controlling high-spirited stallions, or pulling a foal from its mare.

He knew the time of his own accounting was near. He still hadn't notified his family of his whereabouts or told them when he would return—he wasn't even sure if his brothers or the family plantation had survived the war intact. They wouldn't have been able to trace his whereabouts with his name change.

But as soon as this affair had ended, he would have to go back to Solitude. He would have to admit to Micah and Bram that he was of little practical use to the family stud farm. Then he would have to leave before he became the recipient of his brothers' charity and their pity. As a boy he might have been the object of their indulgent attitudes, but he could not bear it if he couldn't return as their equal.

Shaking such morbid thoughts away, Jackson focused intently on the dance floor. The girls had paired up, awkwardly waltzing with one another, taking turns at leading. But their dual roles only seemed to confuse them and Jackson feared that some day one of these young girls might actually take the floor in the arms of a man they hoped to impress, then insist on taking *his* waist.

Leaving, Jackson made his way down the hall to where Frank Conley was examining the account books in Augusta's office. Jackson had noted that Frank's zeal in his searching had dimmed as well—as if Frank were reluctant to find any more evidence to damn Augusta McKendrick. Jackson was sure Frank's budding friendship with Effie had something to do with that.

"Go get Boyd, Frank."

The man rose from behind the desk with his usual slow grace. "Is something wrong, sir?"

"No. But I need both of you in the ballroom."

Frank's eyebrows lifted, ever so slightly, but he didn't question him. "Yes, sir."

Jackson limped back to where he'd been standing only minutes before. By this time, Augusta was trying to help Effie by singing the melody to one of Strauss's waltzes while the girls awkwardly bumped and swayed to the rhythm.

When his men came into the room behind him, Jackson tipped his head in the direction of the girls stumbling over their feet.

"Can you two dance?"

"Yes, Major," they answered in unison.

"Go help them."

Frank and Boyd stared. Neither one really seemed the suave, ballroom-type gentleman. But they were *men.*

"Well? What are you waiting for? Go on and help them," he urged when they continued to hesitate.

Boyd was the first man to accept the command. Crossing the battered dance floor, he tapped Buttercup's shoulder. She and Pansy jumped apart as if they'd been shocked by a bolt of lightning. Murmuring softly, Boyd took Pansy by the waist and gestured for Buttercup to join Frank.

There was an out-of-key chord, a lull in the rhythm, as Effie and Augusta noticed what was happening, but then the dance lesson continued uninterrupted. If not for the glances that Augusta shot Jackson's way, every now and then, he would have thought his interference had escaped her notice.

Soon, the other girls were eagerly lining up for their turns to dance with the men. Real men. Real dancing. In time, they'd all been given a turn and were laughing and giggling and becoming more daring in their choreography.

At one point, Augusta stopped her clapping, allowing the girls to move to the rhythm of the music unaided. They had truly learned to waltz, Jackson realized. Perhaps they weren't entirely graceful or completely sure of themselves, but the concept had been mastered.

Although he kept his gaze purposely averted, Jackson knew the precise moment Augusta began to move toward him. He could hear her skirts whispering over the wood, sense her presence in the faint scent of lilies of the valley she sometimes wore.

"Thank you, Major."

"My men were due for a break."

"But they didn't have to come in and dance. I appreciate it."

For some reason, her gratitude made him uncomfortable. It didn't fit into the relationship he'd established with her. Her attempts to control him through passion and outrageous advances. Nor did it help him to forget that he'd seen this woman without her clothing, her skin as soft and velvety as a newborn rose.

"You could join them, if you like."

He cleared his throat and forced his wayward thoughts into line. "I don't grace a ballroom much anymore. Not with this leg."

"Oh."

She looked sincerely chagrined by her faux pas and it surprised him. Why should she care that he couldn't dance, couldn't run, couldn't lift and carry as well as he once had? It was of no concern to her. A traitor. A murderess.

But as he stared at her, he couldn't bring himself to believe such accusations. She had weakened his will to prosecute her. She had made him begin to believe that Clarence was guilty of his own sins and Jackson's grudge against him shouldn't be extended to his family.

To this woman.

Augusta.

They stood in silence for several minutes, watching the girls with their ankle-length skirts take turns swirling around the floor with two unkempt soldiers as partners.

"What about you, Augusta?"

"Me?"

"Do you dance?"

"I suppose. At least enough to get by. I haven't had that much practice in the last few years."

Again the quiet settled over them.

"Why did you stay?" he finally asked, driven to know.

"Stay?"

"Here at the school. Why did you stay here as their teacher? Why didn't you go somewhere where no one would know of your past, the trial?"

Something deep in her eyes flickered for a moment, seeming incredibly sad. Then she shrugged as if it were of no concern. "I have nowhere else to go. And I won't become an object for charity."

Her response echoed his own views so exactly that he was momentarily taken aback. He wondered what she would say if he agreed with her sentiment and added his own. Or if he admitted to her that his time in the military was limited and he was leery of returning home where his wounds might become a burden to anyone other than himself.

The woman at his side was watching him, her eyes filled with a wealth of understanding. He was entranced at how luminous her eyes had grown, how the winter light filtered through the riotous waves of her hair. She was so beautiful, so incredibly beautiful. Did she know that? Did she know what she did to him? What she had already done? How she'd weakened him?

The air around them grew much too thick and he turned to go. "Send my men to the office when you've finished with the lesson."

Before he could leave, she touched his arm. It was

no more than a feather weight of pressure against his sleeve, but he stopped as surely as if she'd barred his way.

"I need to talk to you . . . about the other night." Her words were low and troubled. "I need to know if—"

"No, Miss McKendrick," he interrupted firmly, realizing that he must get control of the situation. Of her. Of himself. "We have nothing to talk about—unless you wish to shed some light on the situation with Senator Armiture."

She withdrew her hand, and he felt chilled in its absence.

When she didn't reply, he said, "I've given you enough time to think about the repercussions of your actions in drugging us, Miss McKendrick. This evening we will resume our game of checkers. Then, it will be *your* turn to provide some answers."

As she watched him go, Augusta knew that what he'd said was right. She'd delayed giving him the information he sought as long as she could. Or at least as much as she dared give.

Sighing, she slowly returned to her place by the piano, but her heart was no longer involved in the work, or the fight against these men who had stormed into their home. Her heart, she realized with something of a shock, lay somewhere else. *With* someone else.

How such a change had happened, she wasn't sure. Why it had happened, she could not ken. But she knew that if the major had not been called away that night they'd nearly made love, she would have begged him to continue.

She tried to comfort herself with the thought that she was lonely, that her reactions were nothing more than the response any woman might make if she had been denied the romances of her youth.

But she knew it wasn't as simple as that.

It would never be as simple as that.

11

The study was dim and gloomy when she entered. If not for a small fire in the grate, she wouldn't have been able to see the chairs drawn face-to-face and the tea table laid with a game of checkers.

She saw no evidence of Major Charles, but she was not so naive as to think that he wasn't there. She could feel him watching her from somewhere in the darkness.

"Are you ready?"

The sound of his voice startled her. Because it came from close behind her. So very close.

"Ready for what, Major?" Her voice held a hint of its usual defiance, but the hairs at her neck prickled in overt awareness of his strength, his maleness.

"Our game." The smooth, rich voice was enough to cause her fingers to curl.

She turned, ever so slowly, to discover that he was incredibly near to her, near enough that her shoulder brushed against his chest. In a flash, she was reminded of everything that had happened between them the last time they'd been together. The kisses, the embraces, the wanton hunger. Her response to it. Her torment. Her own brazen behavior.

"Which game are you referring to? The checkers? Or the match of wits?"

He chuckled. A sound that she would not have expected from him this night. She wondered, inexplicably, what it would be like to hear this man laugh. Really laugh. To see his stern features light up with joy.

Mentally, she shook herself. Such thoughts were nonsense. Complete and utter nonsense. She must be overtired or racked with nerves, because she didn't normally think in such a manner. She was not usually so . . .

Weak. ·

"Sit down, Augusta."

She didn't comply.

"What if I'm not in a frame of mind to play games?"

"That isn't one of your options."

He took her by the elbow, his touch scorching her through the cotton shirtwaist she wore. Determinedly, he led her toward her chair and prodded her into taking a seat. Then he took his own.

The firelight burnished Major Charles's cheeks and jaw. It should have given him the appearance of being one of Lucifer's angels. Instead, it only complemented his beauty. A beauty often obscured by so much anger.

"Why don't we dispense with the checkers, Major? Why don't you ask your questions and be done with it? Then we both can get on with our lives."

He cocked his eyebrow at her bold statement.

"I'd have thought you would want an opportunity to make me work for the information I require."

She leaned her head against the back of the wing-back chair, her fingers curling loosely around the arms. No, she must give an appearance of calm, of having nothing to hide.

"To be honest, I've grown tired of having you and your men at our school, Major. I've finally realized that you will not leave until you determine there is nothing of a criminal nature here to find. Therefore, I will tell you whatever you want to know, provided you give me some information in return."

"About what?"

"My brother. You claim he is alive. I want to know what proof you have."

The major studied her for some time. Then he nodded. "Very well."

He leaned forward, resting his elbows on his knees. "Tell me first about July 1856."

A shock of alarm jolted her, but she shouldn't have been surprised. Not when she knew where such questions would lead.

"I suppose that you are referring to the summer Effie and I were sent here?"

"Yes."

She shrugged. "There's nothing to tell. My mother and father had begun to live separate lives long before that, but that summer Papa packed his belongings and moved to Washington. My mother refused to accompany him—even for appearance's sake. She asserted, quite adamantly, that she may have been forced to marry a Yankee due to her own father's pressurings, but she would not set foot on Northern soil."

"Did this change upset you?"

She sighed. "Effie and I would have gone with him, but he wouldn't hear of it. He'd sent my brother to military school and he said our education was just as important, but that we needed a woman's influence in our upbringing. But, when we began to display the normal flirtatiousness of adolescent girls, our mother decided to send us away for finishing."

"So you came to Billingsly."

"Not willingly. We tried to contact our father."

"You tried to run away," he corrected.

He knew so much.

"Yes. We were caught at the train station by my mother's driver. He escorted us to Billingsly where we were . . . chaperoned by school personnel until we accustomed ourselves to the routines here." She lifted a hand in a querying gesture. "I don't see why you bother to ask these questions, Major. It's apparent that you have the information you need in this area. Why demand it again?"

"To make sure what I know is the truth." His eyes became more intense. "Considering the fact that you were brought here against your will, you stayed. You even became a member of the staff. Why?"

She couldn't continue looking at him. Not now. Not when she knew his questions were about to become much more difficult to answer. So she looked into the fire instead, watching the flames as they flickered and danced.

"My mother wanted me to marry a wealthy planter. One whose land adjoined the plantation she had inherited upon the death of my grandfather. The man she chose for me was much older than I. It would have been his third marriage."

178

"What happened?"

"He came to meet me, to make the arrangements, and decided he wanted Effie instead. But she was too young for such a match so my father refused to give his permission. After that, Papa refused to give his permission to any of the matches my mother suggested."

"That must have infuriated her."

"A very calm and polite way of explaining her reaction, Major. She was enraged. She swore that my father would pay for interfering. She claimed he had no right to make such decisions since he hadn't even seen us in years."

"And Senator Armiture. How did you know him?"

The question came from out of the blue with the same force as a fist to the stomach. For a moment, she couldn't breathe.

"I-I don't understand."

"He couldn't have been a stranger to you. His aide said that the senator sent regular correspondence to you and received letters in return."

This man had been thorough, very thorough. She supposed that she should be grateful that he'd waited this long before confronting her.

She jumped to her feet.

"I think I've changed my mind. I've had enough honesty for the evening."

He rose to catch her.

"Damnit, Augusta!" His cry was one of frustration rather than anger. "You said you were ready to talk."

But she was afraid to continue. Afraid this man would read too much into her words.

"I've *changed* my *mind.*"

"Good hell, Almighty!" He took her elbows, shaking her. "What will it take to drive it through your thick skull that you have been accused of murder?"

"An accusation that—after so much time at Billingsly—you still can't prove!"

"I don't *have* to prove it!"

The room shuddered in silence. "Don't you see," he rasped in a strangely tight voice. "You have a history of trouble; you are considered a risk. After Lincoln's assassination, the country has become hysterical about the safety of its leaders. One whisper of circumstantial evidence and you'll be hanging from a noose."

"So hang me!"

It was the first time she'd seen him even the slightest bit shocked.

"If you're so eager to proclaim me a murderess, whether or not the facts will support your claim, then arrest me. Haul me into jail. Hang me."

When he didn't answer, she grew quiet, a sick dread settling into her stomach. Suddenly it all became so clear and simple.

"You *don't* think I killed him, do you? You think I'm guilty of conspiracy, of aiding and abetting a crime, but you don't think I killed him."

He didn't speak, thereby giving her accusation credence.

"You think Clarence is responsible." She wrenched free, taking a step back. "Of all the despicable, low-down, sneaky . . ." Her hands balled into fists. "You're waiting for Clarence to ride into Billingsly intent on saving his sister from the army's wrath. The moment he does, you'll swoop down on him like the hounds from hell."

"Your brother is a criminal," he said pointedly.

"Then he would be a fool to come here, wouldn't he?"

"You're his sister. It's his duty to protect you."

"He won't come back here to Billingsly, Major. You're wasting your time."

"Senator Armiture was one of his most fearsome adversaries. During the war, Clarence escaped execution during Armiture's watch."

"He also beat Clarence nearly to death."

"You seem to have quite a grudge against a man you say you've never met." He paused, bringing the conversation back full circle. "Why did he write to you, Miss McKendrick?"

"I believe the man sent some campaign materials to my sister and I."

"Over a dozen times? His aide said he mailed at least that many letters."

"I wouldn't know about that."

"Just as you didn't know that the man intended to come to Billingsly for a personal visit?"

"Yes, Major. I believe you're finally getting your facts straight." She drew to full height. "You have no proof that Senator Armiture was here, that he was murdered, or that I—or anyone else here—had a hand in his vanishing. You have even *less* proof that Clarence had any hand in the man's disappearance. Therefore, unless you find proof of a crime or a body, I insist that you leave this property by morning."

He clasped her wrist and whirled her to face him. "No, Augusta. I won't be going anywhere." Reaching into his pocket, he withdrew a crumpled letter.

She blanched as soon as she saw it. She didn't need to read it to know exactly what it contained.

"Armiture was one of your brother's former jailers.

181

You must have been very angry that night. Or perhaps you were frightened." He twisted her arm behind her back, forcing her closer and closer until their hips ground together. "We found several copies of the same draft on the back of an envelope in one of the drawers filled with accounts. The handwriting is shaky, but unmistakably yours."

Her eyes closed and she damned her carelessness. She'd forgotten about the letter. Ever since the war had made writing supplies dear, she'd been so concerned about saving every scrap of paper, she hadn't thought that this note might someday be found. That it would incriminate her.

"It appears to be a confirmation of the senator's request to visit Billingsly. It even gives the time and day he should arrive. The second of November. Eight o'clock."

12

Silence enveloped the room.

Jackson watched the color drain from her face. In all the time he'd been at Billingsly, watching and waiting for some sign of guilt, he'd never seen her react so strongly.

"The truth, Augusta," he warned when he feared that she might try to evade the issue yet another time. "Tell me what you know about Senator Armiture. Then tell me what you know of Clarence."

He didn't inform her yet that he suspected her brother was somewhere in the area, no doubt being protected by Elijah Ward. So far, the guards had found no evidence of anyone entering or leaving the black man's cottage, but Jackson knew it was only a matter of time before they had proof.

"Please," Augusta whispered. "Please just leave it alone."

Her eyes were wide and dark. A man could drown in those eyes. They were so innocent, so tragic, so frightened.

Yet, there was more to her gaze than that. Behind it all was a cautiousness, as if she were picking her way carefully through an emotional battlefield, exhibiting some hope that if she said the right things, did the right things, all would be well in the end.

"Tell me about Senator Armiture."

She inhaled, the breath shaky, a near-sob.

"I'd never met the man before," she admitted weakly.

She was prevaricating, responding only to the smallest part of his question. But for now, it was a start.

"You never met him. Yet, he wrote to you time and time again, and you answered."

"Yes."

She was trembling, so much so that even in the weak lamplight he could see it quite clearly. The sight tugged at his conscience—more than he would have ever thought possible. He found himself wanting to help her, shield her from the ugliness he knew he would have to unearth before the night was through.

The entire situation was astounding to Jackson, the way he'd become so involved. Yet from the start, Augusta McKendrick had waylaid him, sidetracked him, intrigued him, and tormented him. Despite everything, he found himself leaning closer, seeking the truth now before she could be hurt any more than she had.

"Tell me, Augusta," he said, scarcely believing the tone of his voice. Urgent, smooth, cajoling. "Tell me the rest."

"There is nothing more to tell. Armiture wrote saying he would come to inspect the school and I responded to his query by telling him most of our girls would be away on holiday so there was no sense in visiting us at this time."

"You're lying."

She flinched but he pressed on nonetheless.

"Armiture came here, didn't he? He came here, to this school. Did you see him then? Did you meet with him?"

Her lips trembled and she pressed them tightly together.

Jackson's eyes narrowed as he strove to interpret the slightest change of expression.

"Did Armiture *come* here?" he repeated when she didn't respond. Grasping her elbows, he shook her. "The truth."

She remained stubbornly silent.

"Damnit, Augusta. You must realize now that you can't go back to acting as if you know nothing at all about what happened that night. No one will believe you—no one has believed you yet. You have to tell me the rest." He paused before prodding gently, "Who are you trying to protect, Augusta? Yourself? Effie? One of the girls?" His fingers tightened. "Or someone else?"

He felt the tiny start she made, one so slight that if he hadn't been holding her arms, he might not have caught it.

"Clarence." The word passed through his lips in a near sigh. "You know where he is, don't you?"

She shook her head. "No!" But the word was barely audible and he didn't believe her.

"Where he is? Tell me where Clarence is hiding. Is he with Elijah Ward?"

Augusta blinked, focusing on him so slowly he knew he'd struck a nerve. In that instant he was sure that she knew exactly where Clarence was hiding.

Unable to help himself, Jackson stepped forward, closer and closer, framing her face in his hands. "Tell me the truth, damn you," he whispered fervently, knowing what lay ahead for her if she didn't cooperate. "Tell me so I can help you."

"Help me? Why in the name of heaven would you ever want to help me?"

How could she ask such a thing? She must have guessed how he'd grown to care for her.

Jackson opened his mouth to utter some sort of pat answer, but the panic he saw in her eyes, the submerged anger, the sadness, caused him to stop and think carefully before responding. He didn't know how to put his emotions into words. They were too new for him to examine completely.

"I don't know," he finally answered. "I honestly don't know."

She grasped one of his wrists as if to push him away, but the action was aborted and she clung to him instead, mute.

He offered his own sort of confession. "I've always taken my work quite seriously. Yet, with you, I've dragged my heels every step of the way." His thumb stroked her lip and he was struck again by her beauty. Her strength. "You accused me of setting a trap for Clarence, and that was true. But after the first few days, I shouldn't have kept you here—I could have flushed him out much better if I sent you to jail."

She shuddered against him, her eyes closing for a moment.

"You've bewitched me, Augusta. You've taken a bitter, hardened soldier, and made him doubt."

"Doubt?" she echoed, looking at him in confusion.

"Yes." His head bent ever so slightly. "By seeing how you interact with your sister and your students, you've made me doubt that the world is really as awful as I'd believed, and that the people who inhabit it are really so greedy."

"I never hid him here during the war—I swear to you!"

The words bolted from her mouth, taking a sudden twist from the subject he'd begun.

"After my father died so suddenly, Clarence realized that Effie would be without her medicine. Oftentimes, he would leave a package for me on the school grounds filled with food and laudanum, but I never saw him. If that can be considered aiding the enemy, then I am plainly guilty."

"And Clarence. Did you give him any information about troop activity in the area?"

She shook her head. "I didn't know he was serving as a spy until he was apprehended and put on trial."

"Did he come to you for help after he escaped?"

When she hesitated, he forced her to meet his gaze head-on. *"Tell me."*

"Yes." It was a bare whisper of sound. "Yes, he came to me—bloodied and broken. Armiture had nearly killed him. He'd beaten him with a nightstick." She took a quick jerky breath. "But I knew Clarence couldn't stay here. The authorities would find him. So I sent him away. Later, when I was told he'd been killed and they sent me his personal effects, I regretted the action." She gave a short, self-deprecating

187

laugh. "I felt guilty. *Guilty.* Can you imagine that? He would have surely been found had he stayed here, but I felt guilty that he hadn't done so. Nearly a year ago, when he contacted me and informed me he'd staged his own death, I was so relieved." She squeezed her eyes closed, gathering her emotions. "After that, we kept in contact, but he never again asked for my help. His only concern was whether Effie and I were safe."

"Where is he, Augusta?" Jackson waited tensely, the cold of the room seeping into his skin. "Where is your brother?"

An emotion that he couldn't quite fathom seeped into her expression. One that was infinitely sad. "He's gone. My brother is gone."

For the first time since he'd met her, Jackson's heart whispered to him that she was being completely honest, but he pushed the sensation away. It couldn't be true. Clarence was hiding somewhere nearby with the help of Elijah Ward—and he'd been in the area for longer than that. French had sent word with a new set of guards that half a dozen witnesses had seen the man in the past two months, but he always managed to slip away. By tracing his trail, it was easy to see that he'd been making his way to Billingsly weeks before Armiture arrived.

Choosing to ignore that portion of their discussion for the time being, Jackson asked, "What about Senator Armiture? Did he know you had been in contact with Clarence?"

"No."

Augusta broke free, making her way to the fire and holding out her hands to the blaze. When she spoke, her voice contained a barely perceptible tremor. "Senator Armiture had his own agendas. He was sure that Clarence had something that belonged to him, some papers that were stolen from the prison. He was certain that they would have been sent to me with Clarence's effects."

"What kinds of papers?"

"I don't know. But I doubt they even exist."

She paused and the room radiated with an electric tension.

"Then why would Armiture contact you?"

The silence grew thick and heavy before she said, "My brother kept a journal, Major. He never went anywhere without it, saying that someday he would be as famous as Thoreau and the world would want to read about his daily adventures during wartime. I think he wrote something about Armiture in that book, something that the senator didn't want to be made public."

"That's a good deal of supposition, don't you think?"

She didn't answer him, didn't move. Then, after several aching minutes had passed, she straightened away from the fire. "Come with me."

Taking one of the lamps, she led the way out of the study to the staircase. Jackson mutely followed, realizing after a time that she was leading the way to her bedroom.

At the door, she waited for him to enter, then closed it as much as the shattered lock would allow.

Walking to the bedside table, she set the lamp down and pulled one of the tiny drawers out. Jackson briefly noted the contents—old playbills, a handkerchief, stacks of gloves, and a jar of buttons—before she emptied it on the top of the bed. Underneath, a creased envelope had been glued to the wood.

"A few months ago, Senator Armiture tried a new tack. He contacted Effie and began to threaten her. He told her if she didn't cooperate with him, he would see that the charges against me were reopened." Ripping it free, she handed it to him. "I found out about it, of course. Effie never could hide her distress from me. I helped her draft a scathing reply, but he continued to write, each letter more caustic than the last."

Jackson opened the envelope, removing the creased pages. Scanning them one by one, he was disgusted by the language Armiture had used. He envisioned Effie, a sweet fragile woman who was too naive and gentle for her own good, reading each word, each epithet. How could any man harm such a delicate creature, let alone torture her in this manner?

"It was not until Armiture's letters became more and more upsetting and abusive that we both realized he would not be so easily discouraged."

"Why didn't you file charges against him?"

"Come now, Major," she said in a pitying tone. "Who would have won that argument? The distinguished United States senator or two women from a family in disgrace?"

"So when you refused to take his threats seriously, he notified you that he would be coming for a personal visit."

She nodded. "To see Effie. To 'speak' with her. The portion of the letter you found was my attempt to control at least a small part of that confrontation."

A silence filtered into the room. Finally, straightening, forcing himself to scrape up each thread of professionalism he could muster, Jackson inquired, "So what happened to Senator Armiture, Augusta?"

She stood still, silent, then finally responded.

"He came here."

"When?"

"At eight o'clock. Just as I'd requested."

"What happened?"

Her eyes blazed. "He came inside, demanding that we feed him and entertain him as if his call were some sort of a social occasion."

"What about your students?"

"There was a benefit quilting bee at the church in town. We knew they would be gone until quite late. That was why I was so specific in my letter about the time the senator should come."

"You sent the girls out alone?"

She shrugged. "I assigned Buttercup to be their leader for the evening and Mrs. Marble agreed to meet them once they arrived in town."

"What time did they return?"

"Nine-thirty or ten."

"What about the senator?"

"The entire evening was unspeakably horrid. What manners he managed to display the first few minutes of his visit were quickly discarded. Within twenty minutes, he'd become intolerable."

"In what way?"

"Can't you guess, Major? Do I have to explain it all?"

"I must hear it in your own words."

"Why?"

"I have to know the details."

"Sweet Mary! He tried to rape her!"

As soon as the words shot free, she covered her mouth with one hand as if regretting her hastiness, but Jackson could not afford to stop now.

"Where is he, Augusta?"

How many times had he asked that question? How many times had she refused to answer it?

"He's gone!"

He grasped her arms to hold her still, but she wrenched free.

"He's gone, do you hear? That man, that ugly, vile man, tried to rape my sister and everyone is more worried about his welfare than hers!"

"I didn't mean—"

"Oh, yes you did! You don't care what happened to her. You don't care what happened to either of us. You only care about finding the man, or proving our guilt, or hauling us off to jail! Well, I'm tired of it all—especially of the way you Union officers think that anyone from the South is automatically the enemy, or a woman struggling to survive must therefore be some sort of traitor!" She rushed toward him, beating her hands against his chest. "Well, *damn* you! Damn you all!"

She hit him again and again and Jackson found he didn't have the will to stop her. Not when she was looking so devastated.

"Shhh." His arms slipped around her waist and he drew her close. "Hush now, Augusta."

But her anger was not so easily dismissed. She gripped his shirt, shaking him, a feral, angry sound coming from her throat.

"Shh," he whispered again, splaying his hands wide. She was so tense, so taut, as if one wrong word would destroy her.

Ignoring the way she struggled, he pulled her closer and closer, pinning her against his chest, forcing her head onto his chest. Then he was rocking her, muttering those inconsequential phrases that were meant to soothe but that he feared would be far too ineffective now.

The fists which were balled against his chest moved, opened, sweeping around his back where she clutched at him, pulling closer and closer, shivering as if cold and seeking his heat.

Heat.

Even now, despite the circumstances of their embrace, he couldn't control the fire that surged through his veins.

But before he could draw the rein in on his wayward impulses, she stood on tiptoe, pressing anxious kisses to his jaw, his chin.

The entire effect was explosive. Never before had he thought that a woman could so enflame him. But time and time again, Augusta had wiped reason away and filled him with passion. Sheer, unadulterated passion.

He tried. He truly tried to back away. But he couldn't. Not when she made a whimpering cry against his cheek, not when her fingers laced through his hair, not when she brushed her lips to his.

In a moment, all control was lost. He was pulling her to him, taking her weight as much as his injured leg would allow. One hand managed to disengage itself long enough to roam the contours of her back, then slip lower and lower, until he was able to cup her buttocks and pull her higher and tighter against him.

Sweet heaven above! How she felt against him, so warm, lithe, and *feminine.*

Groaning, he thrust his tongue into her mouth, finding hers waiting, toying, dueling. His legs began to tremble, from the impact of the embrace as well as the effort of holding her, and he backed her toward the bed, settling her onto the mattress.

She didn't protest. In fact, she pulled him down on top of her. He nearly gasped aloud as her thighs shifted, rubbing against him, against his arousal.

"No!" he whispered violently, trying one last time to draw away.

But she wouldn't allow it. She clutched him to her, her kisses growing more frantic, more feverish. She reached for the placket of his shirt, ripping it open, sending the buttons popping and bouncing onto the floor.

He gasped as she stroked the flesh she had so hastily revealed. She'd grown so wanton, so needy, and it inspired the same response in him. It had been so long since he'd felt such a wild storm of sensation—and indeed, he was sure that he had never felt like this before. So when her hand burrowed between them, working at the buttons of his trousers, he didn't stop her. He couldn't have stopped her.

Tugging the shirtwaist from her skirt, he began his own investigation. But he was thwarted in his efforts when he encountered the trappings of her undergarments instead of smooth, bare flesh.

Groaning, he tugged at her skirts instead, pulling them up to her knees, her waist, then sliding his hand down the length of her leg. But even then, he was to be denied. Stockings, pantalets, ruffles, they all managed to get in his way.

She was gripping his arms now, urging him on with incoherent, breathy whispers. Sliding a hand up her knee, up her thigh, he sought the split of her pantalets and there, finally, he encountered bare skin. Soft, velvety, womanly skin.

He moaned, overwhelmed, inundated, all clear thought racing from his head. He had only one goal. Pleasure.

His.

Hers.

Especially hers. Later, when this was over, when she remembered all that had happened, he could not let her regret it. It would kill him if she did.

So he began to stroke her, intimately, sweetly, purposefully.

She writhed against him, moaning, releasing him to fling her arms over her head so that she could grip the rungs of the bed.

So lovely. With her hair coming loose and spilling over the pillows, her skin flushed and glistening, her lips parted and swollen. It took every ounce of strength he possessed to tarry over his ministrations, to coax and tease and torment her. Then, when he heard the rhythm of her breath increasing, felt the ever-tightening tension of her muscles, he slid between her legs. Pulling aside the last few pieces of his clothing that separated them, he touched her again, intimately, lovingly. Then he positioned himself above her, and pushed deep inside her.

He was not prepared for the gasp of pain, or the way she became suddenly rigid, pushing against his shoulders.

"Good hell, Almighty," he whispered, staring down at her.

A virgin.

She'd been a virgin.

The moment the thought raced through his head, he didn't know why he'd been so surprised. She had responded to him with fervor, yes, with hunger, yes, but not a great deal of experience. Instead, her actions had been greedy, fumbling, hasty.

Resting on one elbow, he pushed the hair from her face.

"You should have warned me."

"Warned you?" There was no disguising the wounded tinge to her voice.

"You've never made love before," he said.

She was pushing against him now. Pushing him away.

He knew he should refuse her silent command. He knew that he should finish what they'd begun, that he should show her there could be pleasure, not just pain. But there was something in her eyes, some deep private anguish that she could not disguise and he could not ignore.

Rolling away from her, he sat on the side of the bed, gripping the mattress, praying he would say the right thing and not make things worse between them.

He heard the rustling of her clothing behind him, then felt the shifting of the bed as she sat on the other side, facing the opposite wall.

"I think you should go."

"Augusta—"

"No," she interrupted when he tried to soothe her. "No. Don't try to explain what happened, don't try to minimize what's occurred. I need to be alone. Please leave me alone."

He sighed, an ache settling in his chest. And the guilt. What heavy, overwhelming guilt.

"I want you to know I didn't plan for this to occur," he said finally.

It was her turn to sigh. "I know."

But that was all she said.

In time, the silence grew too painful. So Jackson stood, refastened as many of his buttons as remained, and left the room.

Augusta sat stiffly on the bed, hearing the squeak of the hinges as he tried to close the door behind him, then the creak of the floorboards as he made his way downstairs.

A laugh, one that was nearly hysterical in its absurdity, threatened to escape her throat. She remembered it all, the way Major Charles had broken her door so long ago and the way she'd baited him ever since.

No.

Not *Major* Charles.

Jackson.

Jackson Charles.

Suddenly cold, she crawled beneath the blankets. Later, she would find the energy to wash, to change, to move. But for now, she could only huddle beneath the covers, shivering. Rolling to her side, she clutched her pillow to her cheek, willing the world to melt away into the numbing blackness of slumber. She didn't want to think about the disappointment he'd expressed when he'd found her a virgin, the shock, the hint of anger. She wanted to melt away on a tide of forgetfulness and pretend that the whole event had never happened. If she could only dream.

But she didn't sleep.

Not for a long, long time.

Because Major Jackson Charles took his position in his chair outside her door and guarded her.

Through it all, she prayed that she hadn't said too much.

Prayed that she hadn't given too much.

Because she might allow this man to break her silence, or even break her pride . . .

But she must never let him break her heart.

From the far end of the hall, Revel-Ann shrank into the shadows, knowing that she had seen too much. Heard too much.

Unlike the other girls at Billingsly, Revel-Ann had not led a completely sheltered life. Her parents had been avid followers of the transcendental movement and had insisted that their daughter be exposed to life in all forms. She knew about sex, passion, and love—and how she should guard against the differences in each. When she'd seen Miss Augusta leading the major to her room, she'd sensed that some sort of turning point had been about to occur, so she'd stayed in her hiding place by the linen closet.

Little had she known what she was destined to witness by lingering. The murmurs of desire, then the muted conversation, and the major's withdrawal.

Revel-Ann hadn't moved, even after the major abandoned his post in the hall and went downstairs. She'd been given a piece of knowledge that she knew she shouldn't have, and she wasn't sure what she should do with it. Not yet.

But one thing was for certain. The major must be watched. Now more than ever.

13

Jackson returned to his post in the hallway nearly an hour later, but it was dawn before he heard Augusta's shallow breathing and knew she'd fallen asleep. Rising from the chair where he'd spent most of the night, waiting for any sign of regret or panic, he scooped a copy of *Gulliver's Travels* from where he'd dropped it on the floor, and made his way downstairs. He needed to change. His men would only have to look at him to know what had occurred, and he couldn't allow that—he *wouldn't* allow that. He must not let Augusta's reputation be damaged due to his own carelessness.

She was innocent of Senator Armiture's murder. She *had* to be innocent. After all that she'd told him, he felt that fact deep in his soul.

But if that were the case, what had really happened to Senator Armiture?

Stepping onto the braided rug of the foyer, he turned to make his way down the hall, then paused.

No. He wasn't ready to confront his men or anyone else. He needed time to himself.

Shunning the back bedrooms where he and his men kept their things, he made his way to the study, returning the book he'd borrowed in an attempt to keep himself from thinking about his and Augusta's aborted lovemaking. As he slid the panel doors wide, he examined the cool interior.

Why was he continually drawn back to this place? This room? It had become a ritual to him, to spend at least a portion of each day here. In the quiet. The solitude.

Stepping inside, Jackson slid the doors closed behind him.

He'd almost made love with her. He'd been completely under her spell.

Jackson would rather be shot than admit to anyone how quickly Augusta had worked her way into his heart. Even now, he could not deny that he felt more alive than he had in months. More in control. Because he was needed. He could help this woman—he knew he could. And he was probably the only man alive who would bother to try.

But the awakening of that intimate, possessive part of his mind and soul was not entirely pleasant. Like a limb which had fallen asleep and was returning to full awareness with stabbing thoroughness.

How? How had she managed to inspire such a reaction? If it weren't for the fact that Jackson had hoped to trap her brother, he would have thrown her in jail long ago for her holier-than-thou attitude. He would have had her locked up for attempted murder without a second thought. But lately, the idea of Augusta in a prison cell had become repugnant.

Unthinkable.

So how had this woman tamed him? How had she made him think of things which could never be? After all that had occurred, why was he suddenly imagining what it would be like to have a real place to stay? Not just a cot, but a room of his own—maybe even a whole house. And what if he had some land—raised some horses. The idea appealed to him more than he would have ever guessed. A new country would be emerging from the ashes and it would require an equally new line of horseflesh to see to its needs. He'd seen enough combat to know what gave an animal heart. Strength. He could do it. He knew he could.

Stop it!

Slamming a fist against the mantel, Jackson leaned forward, staring into the glowing embers. A future. He couldn't even begin to think of a future. Such a thing would be impossible—at least until Clarence Mc-Kendrick had been found and this whole mess with Armiture was settled.

And what about Senator Armiture? Was the man dead as those who searched for him supposed? If so, how had it happened? Had it occurred before or after his visit to Billingsly? The same blood that ran through Clarence's veins ran through Augusta's as well. If the senator had tried to rape Effie, Jackson knew that Augusta would have reacted like a lioness with her cub. But could Augusta succumb to the darker side of her nature? Could she kill?

No.

It wasn't possible.

Deep down, she was as gentle as Effie, as easily hurt. She might cloak her emotions in vinegar. She might bluster and bully and annoy. But she could not murder a man.

She wasn't capable of such a thing.

Then what about Effie? Had *she* killed the senator?

Again he shook his head. Not because he didn't think Effie capable of defending herself, but because Jackson knew that she wouldn't have been able to hide her guilt. Not for this long.

But that led him back to the maddening crux of the situation. What had happened to Senator Armiture? And where was he now?

Damn it all, *where?*

Turning, Jackson surveyed his surroundings with narrowed eyes. The answers were all here, somewhere. He could feel them, just out of his grasp. If only he could clear his head enough to pull it all together.

Sighing, he collapsed on the settee, flinging an arm over his brow and squinting into the darkness. As the seconds ticked by, his vision coalesced, focused, and tuned to a spot over his head. A tinkling, shimmering crystal which hung from the chandelier.

His stomach clenched and a sick dread settled into his chest.

"Good hell, Almighty," he whispered aloud to the room, to himself.

Blood.

The crystal was spattered with blood.

"Frank!"

Jackson stormed from the room, the crystal held tightly in his grip.

Frank ran from the back of the house, swiping a towel across his chin to relieve it of the shaving lather.

"Yes, sir!"

"Go get Elijah Ward. Now!"

"Yes, sir!"

"Then I want the guards French sent to search the place. If they find any evidence of Clarence McKendrick, they're to bring it—or the man himself—here immediately. Understood?"

"Yes, sir!"

If Frank had any questions about the unusual nature of Jackson's attire, he didn't ask them. In less than five minutes, Jackson heard the clatter of a horse disappearing down the back path.

"Boyd!"

The other soldier had been drawn into the hall on the heels of his companion and automatically drew to attention.

"Round up the women. I want them assembled in the front parlor in ten minutes."

"Yes, sir!"

Then Jackson was taking the stairs, the crystal nestled in his hand. Augusta McKendrick owed him the rest of the story. He had to know, damnit. He had to know how deeply she was involved.

Striding into her room, Jackson sat on the edge of the bed, waiting for her to awaken. As soon as he detected the first hint of stirring, the slight flickering of her lashes, he held the crystal over her face, in her direct line of sight.

The weather was to his advantage. He couldn't have planned it better had he tried. After days of overcast skies and intermittent snowfall, the sun streamed from a brittle sky, glittering against the frost collected at the edges of the windows, and catching the facets of the crystal. Multicolored rainbows danced on the wall and over her head, their perfection marred by the blotches spattered on the surface.

He knew the moment she focused. She became still, rigid, her breath coming quickly and harshly.

"You failed to look up when you cleaned the room, Augusta."

In all his years of interrogation, he had never seen anyone react so quickly, so nakedly, then cover the emotions so completely it was as if they had never existed.

She was afraid.

Very afraid.

The quiet of the room became deafening. She blinked. Once, twice. And looked away.

When she opened her mouth to speak, he interrupted her with, "Don't. Don't lie to me. Don't tell me it's paint or punch, or a hundred and one other excuses." The need in his voice could not be denied, and he didn't try. She had to know that after the intimacies they'd shared, she was no longer just a subject to be interrogated. She was more, so much more. She was a woman he cared about. So deeply, it frightened him to put a name to it.

She held his gaze—far longer than felt comfortable. Then she took a deep breath, covering her face with her hands and grinding the heels of her hands into her eyes as if they ached.

"Can I get dressed before we talk?"

Augusta's voice was thin, weak, something he was not used to encountering from her. The reaction affected him far more than anger might have done.

"Of course."

He stood, laying the crystal on her bedside table.

Then he left the room, closing the door all but a crack behind him.

He'd only been in the hall for a few seconds when he became aware of being watched. Looking up, he saw Effie standing at the far end. How long she'd been there, how much she might have overheard, he could only guess.

"She didn't do it."

The words were so soft, he thought he might have imagined them. But when he saw the way Effie gripped her hands, her knuckles turning white, he knew they'd been real.

"She didn't kill that man. I did."

Jackson was shaking his head in disbelief, but before he could deny such a statement, Augusta cried, "Effie!"

Behind him, Augusta threw open the bedroom door. She was fastening the buttons to her day dress.

"She's lying, Jackson. She's trying to protect me. Effie hasn't done anything."

"I have so!"

"Effie! You can't lie about this. You'll only get into trouble if you do."

"Then I deserve it. I killed him. I shot him with the derringer. This derringer." She withdrew the gun from her pocket, waving it wildly in the air. Jackson's eyes widened as he recognized it as his own, and he knew in an instant that she was lying again.

"I shot him in the head, and I'm *glad!* He was a horrible man. A horrible, *horrible* man!"

"Effie!"

Augusta rushed forward to fold her sister in her arms, glaring at Jackson. "Now look what you've done."

"I've done!"

"Hush, Effie."

The whisper of skirts and the clatter of footsteps heralded the arrival of the students.

"You can't possibly be confessing," Buttercup exclaimed.

"I did it!" Aster cried.

Buttercup glared at her. "What utter rubbish. *I* did it!"

"No, I killed him!"

"I did." *"I* did!" two more shouted in unison.

"I—"

"Quiet!" Jackson bellowed, his patience snapping.

Effie sobbed against Augusta's shoulder, clutching her sister as if she were her lifeline to sanity.

"I think you should leave us alone for a while, Major," Augusta suggested quickly.

He had to steel himself against the sight, against the two women who were so pale, shaken, and obviously frightened, as well as the young girls who were openly lying, but were willing to put their own lives on the line for their teachers. He wanted to shield them all— even though he wasn't quite sure what he was supposed to shield them *from.* There was just a feeling, a certainty, that nothing was as it appeared, and it nagged at him, eating at his conscience. All the while, no one was inclined to step forward and offer the truth!

"Major!"

"What!" he shouted, his frustration bursting free as he whirled to face Boyd Peterman.

The man seemed taken aback by the violent tone of his voice, and saluted out of pure reflex. "Sir! General French and a dozen of his men are approaching, *sir!"*

Jackson swore bitterly under his breath, rushing to a window at the far end of the hall and pushing back the curtain. Just as reported, a dozen men were galloping down the drive. At the head of the group was the imposing figure of General French.

"Damnit!" The general was hell-bent on getting a confession—a *proper* confession—from someone in this group. One which Jackson felt he was a hairsbreadth away from obtaining. But knowing the general's flair for bluntness which tended to offend all who crossed his path, Jackson saw the opportunity slipping through his grasp.

"Augusta, take your sister to her room. I want you to stay with her until I call for you."

"But—"

"Do it!" His tone was just savage enough to make her obey—although he was sure it galled her to no end. "The rest of you downstairs, in the kitchen. Now!"

The girls rushed away in a whisper of skirts, all but dragging Thelma who had become rooted to the floor and was staring disbelievingly into space at the turn of events.

As soon as the door closed behind them, Jackson turned to Boyd. "Lock Augusta and her sister in Effie's room, then join me downstairs."

"Yes, sir!"

Jackson took the time to make a detour by way of the back bedroom where he and his men had left their belongings. Snatching up his last clean shirt, he swiftly changed, combed his hair with his fingers, and grasped his blouse.

He was buckling his gunbelt around his waist as he joined Boyd in the hall.

"What do you think he's here for, Major?"

"The general has obviously decided to make a surprise visit. He'll probably want to speak to the McKendrick women. Under no circumstances is he to be given that opportunity."

The soldier's jaw dropped.

"Anything else, sir?" he asked weakly.

"Yes. Cover my back if the man flies into a temper," Jackson muttered as he made his way to the front door.

"What are they doing, Gus?"

Augusta moved closer to the window, pushing the edge of the lace curtain aside with her finger and peering into the yard below.

"They seem to be arguing."

"Who?"

"The major and the general."

"Oh, dear."

Augusta leaned as close to the pane as she dared, trying to hear the muffled conversation.

"The general is impatient with the slow progress . . . he wants an arrest to be made . . . he wants to take . . . me."

"No!"

"Hush, Effie, I can't hear."

But it was too late anyway. The major and the general had moved onto the porch and their voices became too muffled for her to catch the thrust of their conversation.

"What are we going to do, Augusta?"

Augusta sighed, pressing a finger to each of her aching temples. "You really shouldn't have told the major that you were responsible for the senator's death."

"I had to do something."

"But not *that!* I had everything under control."

Effie uttered a snort of disbelief. "You might think so, but personally, I don't see why you've been behaving the way you have—arguing with the major, antagonizing him, all but making him your enemy, then confessing to the man. Have you gone completely mad? I thought our whole intent was to make him believe that nothing happened and then persuade him to go."

"I tried that," she said wearily.

"Not very convincingly."

"Damnit, Effie! I tried!" As soon as the outburst blurted from her lips, Augusta wished she could call it back. But it was too late. Effie was blinking back tears.

"I'm sorry." Augusta rushed to hug her, but Effie shrank backward.

"Don't you dare cosset me."

Her unaccustomed defiance caused Augusta to stop in her tracks, her hands dropping to her sides.

"I think you're wrong, Augusta. I think you've gone about this all wrong—and now it's too late. Don't you see? You're in *trouble,* you're in serious *trouble.*"

"I know that, Effie," she whispered. "But I didn't know what else to do."

Effie grasped her wrists. "The major will help you if you ask."

Augusta doubted such a thing. Not after last night. Not after she'd sent him away.

"He wouldn't do a thing for me now, Effie."

"He would. I've seen the way he looks at you, how

he follows you with his eyes. He's changed from the man who first came to us, Augusta. I think that he and his men have come to care for us."

There was much more to what her sister was saying than lay on the surface.

"Oh, Effie." She sighed. She'd seen Effie's tentative responses to Frank and she worried that her sister might be hurt. Not physically, but emotionally. "You've fallen for Frank, haven't you?"

Effie's lip trembled. "Do you think . . . do you think he could learn to forgive me for what I almost let Armiture do to me?"

"Forgive?" Augusta echoed, pulling her close. "There is nothing to forgive, Effie. Any wrongs committed were done *against* you. If he's any sort of man at all, Frank will understand that."

"You're sure?"

"Yes. I'm sure."

Her sister gripped her in a tight hug as if she were trying to absorb some of Augusta's strength. And with each second that passed, she convinced Augusta that there would be no turning back from the course ahead of her. No turning back at all.

Augusta would have to trust the major not to expose them now when they were all at their most vulnerable state.

"Major, I want a report. Now." French shifted uneasily in his saddle. "I told you I'd give you some time to get this woman's confession. But when the guards I sent your way explained to me that you thought Clarence McKendrick was in the area, I expected an update long before now."

"Yes, sir." Jackson saluted, then stepped from the

front portico onto the pea-gravel drive below. "Wouldn't you rather come inside where it's more comfortable?"

"Comfortable! Damnit, man, this isn't a time for socializing. I sent you to do a job—and by thunder, it should have been done already. I want the person responsible for Armiture's disappearance to be arrested!" He slammed his hand against the pommel of his saddle. "If the girl did it, I want Augusta McKendrick tried for her crimes; otherwise, bring me her brother so he can be hanged for the outstanding charges against him. Was there something about that order you didn't understand?"

"No, sir." He stepped closer, lowering his voice, knowing instinctively that Augusta was standing at the window above them. He wasn't sure how much she could make out, but he knew he had to prevent her from hearing any more.

"I would be more than happy to give you a progress report, sir. But I would prefer to do it inside."

French frowned.

"You're growing soft, man."

Jackson bit back his own urge to swear. "Not at all, sir," he stated slowly. "I would merely like to ensure our privacy."

He flicked a glance at the window overhead. The twitch of a lace curtain was confirmation enough that what he said was true.

Huffing as if supremely put upon, General French hefted his girth from the saddle and swung one leg free.

As General French dismounted, Jackson crooked a finger at Boyd and murmured, "Take the girls away from here—the pond, the carriage house, anywhere you like. I don't want them eavesdropping on the general and telling tales to Miss McKendrick."

Boyd nodded and hurried back to the house.

"Well, man, let's get on with this."

Jackson gritted his teeth. "Yes, sir."

He ushered the general into Augusta's office and carefully closed the door.

"Before we begin, sir, is there anything you need? A meal? A—"

"A good, stiff drink would hit the spot. It's blasted cold outside, you know."

Jackson nodded, anticipating such a request.

A soft knock interrupted Jackson before he could make any response. Opening the door, he stepped forward in such a way that Boyd's slighter frame would be all but hidden from the general's view.

"Yes?"

"I can't find them, sir," Boyd murmured softly.

"You can't *find* them?"

"No, sir. They were in the kitchen when the general appeared. Now I can't locate them."

"Any of them?"

"Well, sir, I found the oldest one. Thelma."

"Well?"

"She's . . . er . . . fainted, sir. On the floor. Dead to the world."

"Damn." His eyes were drawn to the "spy glass" overhead. The tiniest whisper of movement gave the girls away.

"Check the upstairs dormitory hall."

"Major!" General French bellowed.

"Get the general some whiskey, Boyd. Now."

Boyd grinned. "Yes, sir."

As soon as Boyd had returned with a bottle, Jackson closed the door. Pouring a healthy measure of whiskey into the man's glass, he waited for him to drink and grow somewhat calmer.

"Has she confessed?" the man demanded.

Jackson hesitated, then, not really knowing why, said, "No."

"You're slipping, Major."

"No, sir. I've simply discovered that the same tactics used on a man don't often work on a woman."

The general's scowl grew even blacker. "Don't be mollycoddling her. She's a killer, you know." He waved the glass in front of him in emphasis, then held it out to be refilled. "You know what she's done, don't you?" he asked after a sip.

"Done, sir?"

"She drew Armiture right into her lair. She wrote to her brother explaining he would be coming, begging for help." He took another gulp of the fiery liquid. "Clarence had a soft spot for the girl. I'm sure he couldn't stay away, couldn't resist his sister's calls for help. Armiture should have listened to me."

"*You,* sir?"

It was the first time that Jackson had been aware that the general knew in advance that Armiture planned to visit Billingsly.

"We were poker buddies." French's eyes narrowed. "I told you that already, boy."

Jackson let him talk.

"I told him he was a fool to meet with Clarence's sisters. They didn't have his journal or he would have heard from them long ago."

"His journal?" Jackson asked casually.

French emptied his glass and held it out for anoth-er. "It's all there, you know. Every plot, plan, and contact. We believe that Clarence masterminded his own death—even went so far as to plant his belongings on a dead soldier. When his personal effects were returned to his family, his journal was listed as being present. These effects were then sent to his sister. If we could only discover where the diary is. It's all there!"

Jackson froze.

"What's all there?"

General French became suddenly silent, frowned, and drained the glass. Slamming it onto the desk with more force than necessary, he jammed his hat onto his head. "One more week. I'll give you one more week to wrap this up. If not, I'll haul the whole lot to prison. Understood?"

"Yes, sir."

The general whipped open the door, but Jackson had one last question to ask.

"General, when Clarence was originally apprehended for treason, why didn't the army make an effort to uncover his contacts behind Union lines?"

"We tried, Major."

"There's no record of an investigation in the transcripts I've studied. But there must have been someone supplying him with information as well as the munitions he exchanged for stolen cannon. From all our reports, those flawed cannon had markings from a Northern manufacturer."

General French didn't so much as twitch. Even so, Jackson had the impression that the man knew more than he was willing to confess.

The tick of the hall clock punctuated the silence, then the general said, "I've heard that theory before.

But if such a person existed, why haven't we found any record of those kinds of activities?"

Within minutes he and his entourage had left, the muddy, churned-up snow on the drive the only sign that they'd ever been there.

That and the empty glass in the office.

Jackson took the glass and stared at it as if it were a crystal ball.

French knew that Clarence McKendrick had written a journal.

A journal Armiture had gone to such lengths to recover.

So where was the book now?

A chill settled into his bones as Jackson grew aware of the significance of such a book. If it existed as everyone claimed, and if it held all the information Armiture had said it did, it could prove Clarence had contacts in the Union army that were supplying him with information and equipment.

It might also prove that Clarence had merely been a pawn in a bigger, deadlier game.

Buttercup herded the rest of the girls into her room and slammed the door. But even as she did so, they could hear Boyd running up the stairs to apprehend them.

"What are we going to do?" Aster cried.

Buttercup's lips pursed. "We'll have to divert attention from Miss Augusta."

"The major won't hurt her," Revel-Ann insisted.

"What makes you think that?" Buttercup demanded, hands on hips.

Revel-Ann smiled knowingly. "He's sweet on her."

"Nonsense," Pansy said dismissingly.

Boyd had begun pounding on the door.

"Drat!" Buttercup hissed. "We haven't had time to make up a story."

"I told you," Revel-Ann insisted again. "The major will help Miss Augusta."

"What makes you say that?" Thelma whispered.

"Because I saw them—" She snapped her mouth shut.

"Saw them what?" Buttercup asked.

The pounding grew worse. "Ladies! Come out now."

"I saw them . . . mooning over one another," Revel-Ann answered hesitantly.

Buttercup knew there was more to the explanation than Revel-Ann was telling them, but with Boyd ready to break down the door, there wasn't time to pry the information loose.

"Very well, ladies. Revel-Ann thinks they're fond of each other, but I say we stick to our own backup plan just in case?"

"What plan is that?" Thelma asked weakly.

"Do all you can to confuse him so he won't uncover the real story."

14

B oyd!" Jackson yanked open the door of the office to discover that Boyd was in the foyer, the students of Billingsly in tow.

Jackson pointed a finger at them. "In the parlor," he ordered curtly and they scurried to obey. Then he turned to Boyd. "I want you to find Frank. I sent him to get Elijah Ward. Tell him I want them both here. Now!"

Boyd clicked his heels and saluted smartly, then all but ran from the building.

Ignoring the pounding from above which could only be Augusta kicking at the door of Effie's room, he slipped into the parlor.

"Now, ladies," Jackson said warmly, throwing them what he hoped was a disarming smile. "Suppose we have a talk."

A pair of elbows jabbed Buttercup in the ribs and she stood, looking far from indomitable in her girlish day dress, her hair drawn into a single braid.

"I've been elected spokeswoman of the group."

"Fine, fine—although I don't think that will prove necessary."

Again, he smiled.

It had no noticeable effect.

"Are you going to interrogate us?" Pansy blurted before being shushed by her sisters.

"No. I just thought we'd chat."

After casting a quelling glance at her companions, Buttercup asked, "About what?"

"About what really happened the night Senator Armiture came here."

"Why should we tell you anything?" Aster snapped.

Thelma paled and grabbed for her salts.

Jackson bit back a sigh of impatience. "You all know I've been sent here in an official capacity—"

"You just want someone to blame!" Revel-Ann snapped.

"Stop it!" Buttercup shot them a scathing glance. "I was the one voted as spokeswoman. If you can't be quiet, then I'll have to insist you leave so that the major and I can talk rationally."

Not a bad idea, Jackson thought, considering his thinning patience.

"Aster, take the rest of the girls into the hall. I want to talk to Buttercup alone."

"But—"

"Go! I'll call the rest of you in one by one when I'm ready to speak with you."

The girls protested vociferously, but they soon disappeared into the corridor, leaving Buttercup in the room with him.

"Now, Buttercup," he said purposefully.

It was obvious that he'd shaken her bravado a bit

because she sank onto the settee, her hands twining together. "Continue with the inquest, Major."

He drew one of the leather chairs close and settled into it with overt ease—at least he hoped he appeared at ease. It had been so long since he'd been required to be kind. So very long. It was like wearing a shirt two sizes too small.

"So, Buttercup—it is Buttercup, isn't it?"

She nodded, unusually quiet.

"Does it make you nervous that the other girls are gone?"

That comment made her stiffen.

"Not at all, sir. Since I've confessed to the crime, I don't see that there's anything more I can worry about."

"Hmm." He steepled his fingers and peered over the tops in much the same way he'd done with Augusta on numerous occasions. "Tell me what happened that night."

"The man came, he made me angry, I shot him."

"Suppose you tell me everything in more detail." He leaned forward ever so slightly. "What time did Senator Armiture arrive?"

"Eight o'clock."

"Why had he come here?"

"He wanted to visit with Miss Augusta and Miss Effie—or so he said. In my opinion, the man was here for far more nefarious reasons."

"Such as?"

"He came with the intent to seduce me."

One of Jackson's brows rose.

"Seduce *you?*"

"Do you find that so surprising?" It was obvious she was insulted by his reaction.

"Not at all. It's merely in direct opposition from what Miss McKendrick told me."

"Which Miss McKendrick?"

"Does it matter?"

She shrugged. "I suppose not. You see, they're only trying to protect me."

"Why would they want to do that? You're just a student here."

She sniffed. "It's clear that you don't understand." Her hands tightened. "My family is from Vicksburg, Major."

"I'm well aware—"

"No, I don't think you are. My sisters and I haven't spent the war at *Billingsly.* We went home to our grandmother soon after Sumter was fired upon. But when everything we knew—every*one* we knew—was decimated . . ."

Jackson grew still.

"We came back here, Major. It was the only place we could think of where we would be relatively safe— and we're not accepting charity, either. We do our own share of the work, help with the cooking and the cleaning and the ironing. We're studying to be teachers ourselves. As soon as testing resumes in the spring, Aster and I will be earning our certificates."

"If you aren't in jail."

The statement reminded her that she'd confessed to a murder. "Of course."

"You didn't really do it, did you, Buttercup?"

She didn't even blink. "Yes. I did."

"Do you realize that such a confession could result in your being hanged?"

"Yes, sir. I do."

"And you have nothing you want to add?"

A pounding pressure was beginning to thud against his temples. Where was Frank, damnit?

"No, sir. I don't."

"Then go out in the hall and send in Aster."

During the next twenty minutes, the rest of the girls were interviewed individually. By the time he'd spoken to all of them, five confessions had been given—or rather, four. Thelma managed to offer little more than her name and the time of Senator Armiture's arrival before she fainted dead away.

So far, he had the senator arriving at seven, eight, and eleven in the evening. Armiture's reasons for coming included an inspection of the school, Buttercup's and Aster's being seduced, Pansy's summoning him here on official business concerning her father, Revel-Ann having sent him threatening letters, and Thelma . . .

Well, who knew with Thelma.

By the time he'd sent the girls away, his head was aching and he had the sudden urge to escape from this place himself.

"I take it that the afternoon did not go as you had planned."

He hadn't heard Augusta come in. As a soldier, that fact was even more disturbing. He was a man who'd always been on his guard. A man who'd always been cautious.

But looking at her now, seeing the way the sunlight stroked her hair and feathered over her cheeks, he couldn't credit how much he'd changed. How much she'd changed him.

"Who let you out?"

"Pansy."

He should have known one of the students would sneak upstairs to release her.

Rising, he rubbed at the ache of his head. "I came to this school for one suspect, hoping for one confession. I now have seven suspects and seven confessions."

She leaned against the door, her hands behind her, clasping the knob. "You should never have come here."

"I'm beginning to see that." He sighed, knowing that the time had come for confessing of his own. "I came looking for something that wasn't here."

This time it was her turn to frown. "I don't understand."

He shrugged. "I came looking for vengeance. Retribution."

"From whom?"

"Your brother."

She sucked in her breath. "So you were looking for him too."

He rubbed at the back of his neck. "I meant to avenge myself for something he did long ago."

"And now?"

"Now I'm beginning to realize that desperate men do desperate things in wartime." He moved toward her, needing to be near her. Touching her face, her hair, he bent close, resting his nose against her cheek. She smelled so fresh, so lovely. So feminine. "How can I blame a man for doing what he thought was necessary to win his own cause. Especially when— after all he's done—he's willing to risk being caught in order to protect his sisters. I can't fault him for that."

Jackson took a deep breath, wondering if his words made any sense.

"I didn't mean to hurt you last night," he whispered.

She shuddered against him, gripping his waist.

"You didn't."

"You should have told me you were a virgin."

"Why would you think otherwise?"

He cleared his throat. "So many women were . . . hurt during the war." He waited a beat, then asked again, "Why didn't you tell me?"

"You would have stopped."

"It would have been the right thing to do."

"No, it wouldn't have." Then she was rising on tiptoe, kissing him.

"Upstairs," he murmured when the passion flared, knowing he couldn't stop, but acknowledging they should have a proper bed.

"No," she said firmly. "Here. Now. I want you, Jackson. I need you."

With that, he was undone. Pressing her against the wall, he reached for her skirts, bunching them madly with his hands to get to the soft skin he knew waited beneath.

"Yes, yes . . ."

The panting cries urged him on, spurred him into action. Damning the pain that shot through his leg like lightning, he lifted her, carrying her to the brocade swooning couch in front of the fireplace.

Lifting to her elbows, she panted, "The windows."

It took less than a minute to lower the shades and draw the curtains. When he faced her again, it was to discover that she had unbuttoned her blouse and her skirt and stood in front of the fire dressed in little more than her undergarments.

"You didn't kill Senator Armiture, did you, Augusta?"

He had to know. He had to know *now.*

"If I told you I was the one responsible, would it matter?"

"Hell, yes," he muttered. But long before the statement left his lips, it lost all conviction. No. It didn't matter. Not at this moment in time. She could tell him she'd killed President Lincoln and he would want her so much it ached.

He went to her, cupping her face in his hands. She must have read the answer in his eyes, because she said softly, laughing, "You don't know what to think, do you, Major?" She purposely melted against him, taking one of his hands and kissing his palm. "So don't think. Just *feel.*"

"Damn you!" he whispered fiercely, drawing her to him.

"What's the matter, Jackson?" she murmured next to his skin. "Do I frighten you? Do my supposed crimes frighten you?"

Her fingers began to explore the muscles and sinews of his arm as if she were blind, working their way up to his shoulder.

"No. You don't frighten me, Augusta. But your bravado does. You're like a train heading down a dangerous track. You refuse to see that disaster awaits you. A kind of hell you couldn't imagine."

She merely shrugged. "I've seen many kinds of hell, Major. Another variety fails to scare me."

"It should terrify you."

"But it doesn't." She drew on tiptoe. "The only thing which could frighten me now is if you told me this meant nothing to you. That it was all a game. I want to be something important to you—even if we have no future beyond this moment." She became suddenly vulnerable. "Please tell me this is special to you. Even if it isn't, tell me it is."

Jackson forced her to look at him. "I would never lie about such a thing."

When she continued to watch him with haunted eyes, he hastened to reassure her. "I have never felt this way about a woman before. Ever."

"I want to believe you."

"Then do, because it's true." He stroked her cheek with his thumb. "If you are bound and determined to charge full-force toward disaster, I suppose you'll be taking me with you."

Then he was pushing her backward until her calves met the edge of the swooning couch. He kissed her, long and slow and deep, absorbing each nuance, each wonderful texture and skin-tingling sensation.

When he drew away, she smiled at him like a temptress—the temptress she was. One who had seen that his heart was all but destroyed and had taunted it into caring again. Caring about her, about her sister, her students, their predicament.

"The door is locked," she whispered, unfastening the first petticoat, the second, the third.

"You're sure?" He could barely speak as the layers fell from her body piece by piece.

"Yes. I'm sure." Her hands reached for the hooks of her corset, releasing them one by one, and dropping the garment to the floor so that she stood in the faint covering of her pantalets and camisole. "No one will disturb us." She untied the ribbon at the center of her breasts with tantalizing slowness, then the one at her waist, until the garment draped, allowing him to see her breasts. Her beautiful pink breasts.

"They wouldn't dare," he grumbled, then wrapped his arms around her waist, taking her down to the couch and settling over her.

She gasped, and for the first time, he noticed an angry welt which stretched from her shoulder to her back.

"What's this?"

She shook her head. "A burn. It doesn't matter."

"It does matter. What happened?"

"Later. I'll tell you later."

Although he wanted to press her into explaining, there was no time for talk. Their kisses were heated and intense, but indulgently slow. Jackson leisurely explored every inch of her body in the way he'd dreamed of doing. He caressed the gentle indentation of her waist, the thrust of her hips, the strength of her thighs. There was a spot behind her knee where she was ticklish, a point near her ankle that made her sigh.

Soon, her own hands had slipped the clothing from his body and they lay together, chest to chest, their legs intimately twined. With each moment that passed, Jackson's hunger for this woman grew more intense, more powerful. But he held back, needing to know that she was ready for him and that he'd given her pleasure.

So he suckled at her breasts, causing her to gasp and her hands to tighten in his hair. Then, reaching low between their bodies, he began to rub her intimately, stroking the moist recesses that only he had been allowed to caress in such a manner.

When she began to moan, writhing against him, her eyes closing, he allowed himself a small surge of self-congratulations. Soon, even that was forgotten as he lost himself in her reactions, in the way she reached above her to grip the pillows. He heard her breathing coming in quick gasps—and sensing her release was at hand, he settled over her, his manhood nudging the velvety warmth he had claimed once before.

Then there was no more time to think at all. He could only react, thrusting inside her, plunging deep. She made a small cry, gripping his shoulders and tipping her hips toward him.

"Let it come, Augusta," he whispered against her when she seemed to be fighting the ultimate burst of pleasure. "Let it come!"

And then he felt the tremors deep inside her, felt them squeezing him, heard her gasp of pleasure, her cry of relief. Unable to control his own instinctive reaction any longer, he gave one last thrust, closed his eyes, and felt the blinding passion swamp him in ever increasing waves, over and over again.

Some moments later, he collapsed against her and felt her pushing the hair from his brow.

"Thank you, Jackson," she whispered. "If you can't give me anything else, thank you for this. I will always remember being close to you this way."

He shifted from her then, pulling her against his side and holding her close.

"You make that sound as if it will never happen again."

She didn't answer and when he tried to press her for some sort of response, she wriggled away from him, beginning to dress.

He caught her hand. "What are you doing?" he asked.

Her gaze flicked to the door. "They'll be knocking soon to see if I'm all right."

He knew she meant the students.

"I'd rather face them with my clothes on."

Again, he held her still. "Do you regret what has happened, Augusta?"

She smiled at him, radiating such a mixture of joy and sorrow, he could scarcely credit the combination of emotions.

"No," she said simply. "Not now. Not ever."

But what lay unspoken between them was the question of how many such opportunities they might have to enjoy each other's company in the future.

15

Jackson waited ten minutes before leaving the parlor. During that time, he'd heard Augusta shepherd her students away and comfort them with an "Everything's all right, ladies."

It wasn't the truth.

But at this point, what else could she say?

"Sir?"

He looked up to find Frank standing hesitantly in the doorway.

"Thank goodness it's you, Conley."

Frank's brows creased in confusion but he didn't speak.

"Where's Elijah Ward?"

"He . . . isn't here, sir." Again, he hesitated. "I think you'd better come with me."

A sick feeling of dread settled into Jackson's stomach when he followed Frank outside and found that there were two horses saddled and waiting.

Quickly mounting, he followed Frank through the back fields, retracing the same route they'd taken once before to Elijah's cottage. Yards before reaching it, however, he saw the two men lying facedown in the snow, pinkish stains leading trails away from their heads.

"Donnelley and Abernathy, two of General French's men. Both of them were killed instantly. We found them twenty minutes ago, then rushed to get you. We're making a cursory examination of the area, but the bodies haven't been touched."

Jackson noted the abandoned air to the house.

"Elijah Ward was responsible, I suppose?"

"I don't think so."

Frank's low answer caused Jackson to bring his mount to a halt. "What do you mean?"

"Come with me, Major, and I'll show you."

Jackson trailed Frank into the cottage. As soon as he stepped inside, he began to see how Frank had formed such a conclusion.

"Judging by the blood of the guards, they couldn't have been dead for more than an hour—two at most."

"But there's no heat in here."

"From what I can tell by the ashes in the grate, there hasn't been a fire in more than a day. There's also a distinct lack of food, clothing, supplies— anything normally used on a regular basis."

"So you think Ward left here some time ago."

"Yes, sir."

"But how? He was guarded around the clock."

A twinkle appeared in Frank's eyes. "Come and look at this."

He ushered Jackson into the smaller room. There, the bed had been pulled away from the wall and tipped on its side to allow access to a trapdoor in the floor.

"I'll be damned," Jackson murmured. Crouching as much as his leg would allow, he lifted the planks to expose a yawning black hole. Behind him, Frank held a lantern overhead.

"It's a tunnel, sir, not just a cellar. I'd say it was probably one of the stops used by the Underground Railroad before the war."

"Did you follow it to see where it goes?"

"As far as I could, but about ten yards south of here, the passageway has been purposely collapsed."

"Probably by Elijah Ward."

"Or Clarence McKendrick."

"That's why we didn't find Clarence here the first time we came to search the place."

"Ward must have seen us and hidden him down here, then covered the trap with the bed."

Jackson straightened, wincing when the movement was sharply protested by his leg.

Slamming the trap closed he stood with his hands on his hips, glaring at a spot in the floor.

"So if Elijah left here—probably days ago . . ." He met Frank's gaze. "Then who's responsible for killing those men?"

Frank had no answers. "Should I notify the general?"

Jackson opened his mouth to give his assent, but something stopped the words before they could be spoken. A whisper of warning. A sense of danger.

"No. Is Boyd in the area?"

"He's combing the woods for clues."

"Have him bring the men in here and wrap them in a quilt. For now."

Frank didn't question the unusual request, but he hurried to do as he was told.

Leaving Jackson to wonder why he felt he was missing something—something important. But if so, what?

What?

"Frank, I want you to ride back into town. Get ahold of Armiture's aide and have him tell you again every place the senator planned to visit, every report he made. Then I want you to search his room—go through the hotel staff rather than any of the Union officers present."

"What am I looking for?" Frank asked.

"I don't know. Anything out of the ordinary— letters, telegrams . . ." A thought raced through his head. "Anything that mentions a journal."

Frank rushed into the cold.

Sighing, Jackson went outside to the two figures lying in the snow. Boyd was about to roll them over, but Jackson stopped him.

"Go get the blankets first," he said.

When the man disappeared, he knelt, ignoring the stabbing pain of his thigh. Reaching out, he pushed aside the hair matted by the bullet hole located beneath the left ear. Shifting, he saw that the second guard had the same sort of wound.

In the same place.

A chill shuddered down Jackson's spine as a tiny piece of the puzzle clicked into place. This was no random act of violence, no wild shoot-out, no hasty reaction.

These men had been executed.

* * *

Augusta was restless. Not so much because of all that had happened with Jackson. She'd resigned herself to the girls' reactions. She'd also managed to push a good deal of her body's aches and twinges aside—or at least refuse to think of them. Her anxiousness had a different source. It was more because . . . because . . .

Jackson wasn't watching her.

The thought brought her up short and she turned in a slow circle. Jackson wasn't guarding her.

She'd grown so used to having him dog her steps, it was nerve-racking to have him gone.

She began to pace the office, her hands nervously tucking a curtain back into place, fluffing a pillow on the settee, swiping at a speck of dust. But even those commonplace routines didn't have the ability to calm her. Unaccountably, she kept thinking of Jackson, wondering where he could possibly be, why he hadn't arranged for a guard. She even found herself wondering if she should go and find him.

Go and find her captor?

No, not her captor. Her lover.

Where was that man?

Pivoting in midstride, she went to find him, cursing herself the entire way for being a fool—for seeking out trouble when it had seen fit to leave her alone.

Moving down the hall, she was able to avoid the worst of the creaking floorboards—something she'd learned to do from years of practice. This situation must be an oversight on his part. Perhaps their lovemaking had managed to scatter his wits.

Her lips twitched in the tiniest self-congratulatory smile. Yes, she liked that idea. Liked the thrill of power it gave her.

She looked in the kitchen first, the hall, the rear classrooms, the parlor, even the ballroom. But he wasn't there. Nor was he in the larder or the back portico.

Drat it all, where could he be? Surely he wouldn't have abandoned her completely. She'd never known the man to be careless—and she doubted that was a character trait he often displayed. He had to be somewhere nearby, perhaps watching her, waiting to see her reaction to his absence.

So where could he be?

Returning to the foyer, she gazed around her in confusion. She was about to open the front door when she felt a prickling at her nape. It was a sensation to which she was growing accustomed. One which told her that the man she sought was near. Very near.

Looking over her shoulder, she gazed up, until she saw the infinitesimal shadow behind the curtains of the window the girls referred to as the "spy glass."

Major Charles was there.

He'd been watching her the whole time, watching her fruitless search.

She could have withered beneath a wave of embarrassment. Her actions had been so telling. Without saying a word she had shown him how aware she had grown of him, and how she'd been just as keenly aware of his absence. Such an awareness had increased one-hundredfold since he'd held her, caressed her.

The shadow wavered and disappeared, but she didn't move. He was coming to her. She knew it without listening for the betraying squeaks and groans made by the old building.

When he materialized at the top of the staircase,

she faced him, feeling breathless, anxious as a hundred memories rushed to the fore. The way he'd touched her. How he'd tasted. His scent. The texture of his skin.

Just as warily, Jackson stopped halfway down the staircase, sinking onto the treads. Resting his elbows on his knees, he studied her silently for several minutes.

"You didn't do it, did you, Augusta?"

She remained silent.

"You didn't kill Senator Armiture, but you're willing to take the blame for it. Why?"

Again, she remained silent, but her heart was pounding thunderously in her breast.

"Is it because Effie is responsible? Are you trying to protect her?"

"You know my sister is innocent."

He sighed, stretching his injured leg out. The hall clock ticked loudly in the silence. "So what am I supposed to do, Augusta? I've worked with General French long enough to know that he doesn't make idle threats. He will see that someone is punished for the crime. He wants the whole scandal to go away. He wants to prove that the provisional government will not tolerate anarchy. So far, you are the most likely candidate for such retribution."

He waited, but she did not respond. What could she say? What did he want her to say?

"This would have been so much easier a few days ago."

"Why?" She could barely force the word from her lips.

"I would not have known you so well then."

"Do you know me so well now?"

"Not entirely." He thoughtfully rubbed at his leg. "But when I first came here, you were a name in a file. It was so easy to be objective then. So easy to place blame." Grasping the banister he pulled himself to his feet and took each stair, tread by tread, as he spoke.

Approaching her, he rubbed a strand of hair between his finger and thumb. "I've touched you, I've loved you, I've delved into some of your innermost secrets, both emotionally and physically. I find it very hard to be objective at all."

"You could leave."

"No. I don't think I can."

He came even closer, so near that she could feel his breath on her cheek, the warmth of his body being absorbed into her own.

"Why have you done this to me?" he whispered.

"What? What have I done?"

"Augusta, you've made me feel pity, passion, humor, joy—everything but the anger and bitterness the war inspired. Those are emotions I didn't think I would ever feel again."

How was it possible that a few simple words were able to wring her very heart?

He cupped her cheek with his hands, those strong, masculine hands, and she leaned into the embrace, needing the warmth it gave her, the elemental sense of security.

"It's wrong, you know."

"What is?" she whispered, unable to think clearly, to string his words into some logical framework.

"The way I've become personally involved with you."

"Involved."

"I don't want it to be this way."

His expression grew intent. Fierce. She could not look away.

"But this is how it has to be, because I don't have the strength or the will to stop it." Then he pulled her into his arms, kissing her, blindly, heedlessly.

She wrapped her arms around his waist.

When he retreated, they were both breathless.

"Tell me you didn't do it," he said fiercely, forcing her to look at him. "Tell me, and I'll believe you."

"I didn't do it."

"We've got to get you out of this."

"I know."

"I won't see you hanged."

Her laugh was choked and filled with emotions that she could not express in words.

"I really would prefer that option."

"We'll find some way of seeing this through, of making everything turn out all right."

"Yes, yes."

"I won't lose you. Now that I've found you, I won't lose you. You're mine, do you hear. You're mine."

She felt a twinge of unease at his pronouncement, but she pushed it aside. Jackson Charles wasn't like the other men she'd known. He wouldn't dominate her. He couldn't. It was not something she would allow.

But then he was kissing her again, driving all coherent thought from her brain. There was room for little more than sensation, primitive, basic sensation. She could not get close enough to him.

He wrenched free, cupping her face in his hands. "You've got to trust me, Augusta."

"Yes."

"You've got to tell me the truth."

"Anything, anything."

"Where is your brother?"

She bit her lip, knowing there was no turning back. She must trust him, or deny any hope of a future together.

"Elijah Ward has a cottage just past the bluff of the river. Clarence is with him."

"They're gone."

The words sank into her brain by degrees. First, it registered that he'd been there. Next, that he knew Clarence was with Elijah. And last, that they weren't there.

"What?"

"You weren't very careful about covering your tracks that night you drugged us. Frank and I confronted Elijah soon after—but even though there was evidence that your brother had been in the cottage and was probably wounded, we didn't find him."

"He has a head injury."

Jackson continued without pause. "I asked General French to assign a couple of men to guard the place 'round the clock. Today, those men were found dead."

"What!"

"Naturally, Elijah and your brother were our first suspects, but they appear to have been gone for some time."

"The tunnel. Elijah would have used it as soon as he'd discovered he was being watched."

"Where are they?"

"I don't know. The tunnel leads to an abandoned church on the other side of the knoll, but it wouldn't provide enough shelter for them to stay there."

Jackson held her shoulders so tightly, she feared her skin might show the marks later on.

"I don't want to hurt you, Augusta. But you've got to know that if I find your brother, I will have to question him about the murders of those guards as well as the disappearance of Senator Armiture."

"He didn't do it."

"Damnit, Augusta! How can you be so naive? Your brother was a spy for the Confederate army. He would do anything for a price—blockade running, gathering information, even murder."

"But he didn't kill Armiture!"

"How can I believe you?" He shook her as if he could rattle some sense into her head.

She yanked free. "Because my brother is all-but-dead!"

Her shout echoed through the foyer, causing Jackson's eyes to narrow.

"Weren't you listening? My brother suffered a *head* injury! A very serious one! He can't speak, he can't walk, he can't even take care of himself—and he won't be able to go on like that for much longer. It's only a matter of time before his body will fail him as completely as his mind."

16

The night was black and icy, filled with a thousand secrets.

Jackson leaned one hand against the window frame and stared out past the drifts, past the haze lingering over the hills. Over and over again, he kept hearing Augusta's words.

"Weren't you listening? My brother suffered a head injury! A very serious one! He can't speak, he can't walk, he can't even take care of himself—and he won't be able to go on like that for much longer. It's only a matter of time before his body will fail him as completely as his mind."

His eyes closed and he sighed, praying that he could make some sense out of this mess he found himself in. Three men had been killed—Armiture and two guards. Yet, no matter how hard he tried, he couldn't piece together the truth, even though he sensed the murders were inexorably linked.

The muted rumble of the pocket doors to the study alerted him that he was no longer alone and he stiffened, not bothering to face the intruder. He knew who it was.

"You're going to have to tell me who killed Armiture, Augusta," he said softly.

The doors closed. "No."

He sighed in impatience. "You didn't do it. We both know that. You're protecting someone—someone here in this school. I can only help you if you let me know here—now—who that person is."

There was no response. Only silence.

When he turned and saw the resolve shining from her eyes as well as an insurmountable sadness, he knew that there would be no explanation. Not from her.

"You realize that I can't protect you without the facts. If the true culprit isn't caught, French will railroad you into paying for the crime."

"Yes. I know."

"And you're willing to protect this person?"

She nodded.

Suddenly angry, he strode across the room, hauling her into his arms and forcing her to look at him. "Why do you have to be so damned stubborn? Why can't you just trust me?"

"Trust?" She shook her head in amazement. "How can I trust you when I don't trust myself around you?"

Her words had the power to soften the anger building in him.

"Don't you see? Mere years ago, you and your kind were my enemy. I fought against your army for years, struggled to keep them from taking what was mine." The breath she took was more of a sob. "But now, I find myself *giving* away those things I thought no man would ever have. My body. My control. My emotions. My passion." The words were nearly torn from her throat, proving just as painful to hear. "How can I trust you when you have changed me so completely?"

Unable to bear it any longer, he held her close, rocked her, feeling her anguish keenly because it equaled his own. His confusion. His uncertainty.

Then he was drawing her down to the settee, intent upon doing little more than holding her. But when she clutched at his clothing and began slipping the buttons free, he found his control sorely tested. When she began kissing his chin, his throat, his breastbone, he was lost.

He could only pray that somehow he could find a way to unravel this affair. Quickly. Cleanly. Without hurting Augusta any more than he had.

The next morning, Augusta surprised even herself. She woke in her room, in Jackson's arms, wearing nothing but his shirt, and she wasn't embarrassed. Wasn't distressed.

To the contrary. She wanted more. So much more. Whatever the fates would allow her.

So she sent Effie and the girls away on a wild errand, insisting that they needed greenery and pinecones to decorate the school for the holidays.

The excuse was flimsy at best, but it gave her at least two hours. Two hours with the man who had tormented her, taunted her, goaded her, and threatened her.

And now intrigued her more than life itself.

To her delight, Jackson must have sensed her purpose because he sent his men with the rest of the girls under the pretext of keeping an eye on them. They didn't question the instructions, there was no need. It was completely plausible and aboveboard.

As well as entirely selfish to their own needs.

They stood on opposite sides of the verandah, offering their own sets of instructions, until the wagon was loaded with women and baskets and gardening shears. Then, taking charge of the team, Frank called to the horses, and they were lumbering down the rutted drive.

"How long?"

She didn't need more explanation to Jackson's inquiry.

"Two hours. Maybe longer."

He looked at her then. "It will have to do."

They went to her bedroom, where he undressed her piece by piece. Then it was time to touch, caress, unveil, until they were both nude and fervently aware.

Their lovemaking was quick, heated, passionate, the empty house giving them the courage to indulge in their wildest fantasies. When the explosions of pleasure consumed them, they both cried out.

Later, much later, they curled back-to-front, spoon fashion. Tickling his forearm, Augusta was the first to speak.

"Tell me what you remember about your childhood, Major Charles."

"Don't you think you could bring yourself to call me Jackson? You have before."

"I don't know . . ." She'd abandoned calling him "The Major" in her head, but it seemed strange to call him anything else out loud.

"It wouldn't be proper," she whispered, the training of a lifetime giving one last gasp of protest.

"Nothing we've done could be considered 'proper,' Augusta."

She looked at their hands, lacing their fingers together. He was right. How much more intimate could they be?

"Then tell me, Jackson. Tell me all about you."

She could feel the tension that gathered inside him. It was there in the line of his body at her back and in the arm that lay over her waist.

"I've told you about my family."

"Your brothers . . . what are they like?"

He thought for an instant. "Micah is strong and implacable, a man of few words. Bram, on the other hand, has a lightning temper and sharp wit."

"What are they doing now?"

There was a beat of silence and he took a breath. "I don't know."

She peered up at him. "You don't know?" she repeated incredulously.

"I haven't contacted them yet."

Her mouth gaped. "Whyever not?"

He didn't immediately answer, but when he did, his expression had grown grave and his eyes dark. "I swore I wouldn't go home until I'd avenged my men."

Augusta's brow creased. "Your men."

He nodded, watching her carefully, and she knew at that instant that whatever future they might have, however fleeting, would rest on her reaction to all he meant to tell her.

"I told you I was in charge of a battery squad once, do you remember?"

"Yes."

"That squad was decimated when the cannon we were using backfired. Later, it was discovered that those munitions were not the originals sent to us by the quartermaster. They were substitutes exchanged by your brother after he waylaid a supply train."

A sick dread filled Augusta's chest. Of course. That was why Jackson had once told her that his interest in her was "personal." He too was looking for Clarence.

"I see." It was all she could manage to whisper.

"No, you don't." He cupped her cheeks, preventing her from looking away. "I hated Clarence, hated what he did to my men, to me."

She squeezed her eyes closed, not wishing to see his anger, his recriminations.

"But all those emotions are gone, Augusta."

His whispered confession opened her eyes. "I don't know how it happened, I don't know why. But I'm tired of hating, tired of looking for revenge. It doesn't solve anything in the end. It only creates more grief." He stroked her lips with his thumb. "I don't know that I'll ever forgive Clarence for being a part of that portion of my life, but I no longer want to punish him. Especially not"—he pulled her to him—"when such an attitude could alienate me in his family's affections. One sister in particular."

Affections.

The word echoed in her head, growing stronger and stronger.

Jackson cared for her. In a way that went beyond passion. But, how did she feel about him? For so many years, she had convinced herself that there was more to life than the sentimental nonsense she'd been taught to aspire to as a girl. She'd grown content at the lack of gentlemanly companionship. She'd made a name for herself—a professional niche, of sorts. Having a schoolful of students had even assuaged her own instinctive needs for nurturing and tutoring children of her own.

Then she'd met Jackson Charles. He'd shown her so many facets of her life she hadn't even admitted were missing. He'd offered her more, so much more. But everything she'd learned, everything she'd experienced, could be snatched back at any time.

"What are you thinking?" Jackson asked against her ear, so quietly, so gently.

"That I shouldn't have allowed this."

"We didn't plan it."

"We didn't prevent it."

"Do you regret that we've made love?"

She shook her head, unable to lie. "How could I? But it would have been easier if it had never happened."

"Yes." His answer was slow. Careful. "But life isn't always easy. Some of the greatest joys come after hardship."

She clutched his wrist, praying it were true, praying that something good would come from these past weeks.

By the time the other women returned, there was no evidence of their hours of passion. Augusta was dressed and working on the books in her office; Jackson waited on the porch for his men. When the sleigh drew to a stop, he helped unload the pine boughs and fragrant cones and took them into the foyer.

Only once did he look Augusta's way.

Catch her eye.

Read the submerged passion.

Then he busied himself with the matter at hand,

knowing that acting on such thoughts would have to wait until dark.

They were never given that chance.

The sudden clatter of horses up the drive alerted them all. Dropping the bundles in the hall, Jackson hurried outside in time to see French and his men riding pell-mell for the school.

"I am here to relieve you of your duties, Charles," French exclaimed, signaling for his men to come to a halt.

Jackson didn't move, so stunned was he by the announcement. "You said you'd give me some time to resolve the situation and obtain her confession. What are you doing here so soon?"

French shifted in his saddle, deftly sliding his cigar from one corner of his mouth to the other.

"I've reason to believe that you've lost your objectivity in this case."

"I assure you, sir—"

"Don't bother to argue. I've assigned a man to ride by the house and check in on you now and then. This afternoon he returned to give me a report that you were seen embracing our dear Miss McKendrick."

Jackson didn't bother to refute the accusation. How could he when her scent clung to his skin?

"You are discharged, Major Charles."

He nodded. "I'll go back to headquarters and oversee the—"

"You misunderstand me, Charles. You are *discharged.*"

The men on either side of him gaped.

"From the army?" Jackson asked.

"Yes, Mr. Charles. You are hereby relieved of your

duties. How you leave will determine whether you are discharged honorably or without your stripes."

Jackson didn't respond—didn't really wish to. He'd seen French in moods like this before, completely unapproachable, reacting from emotion rather than reason. It was the one trait which had moved him from a battlefield command to the less volatile interrogation offices.

French gestured to the men who surrounded her. "Take the girl." He looked at Augusta then. "Miss Augusta McKendrick. You are hereby charged with the disappearance of Senator Armiture. From this point on, you will be housed in Mannington Prison."

"No! You can't take her!"

Effie rushed forward then, but Augusta caught her and held her back, whispering something in her ear. Although Effie trembled, she didn't make another outburst.

Two soldiers swung from their horses. One quickly manacled Augusta's wrists, the other her ankles. Then, lifting her onto the horse of another soldier, they resumed their places.

"An hour," French said, pointing one finger at Jackson. "You and your men have one hour to leave the premises. This case is closed."

With a wave of one glove-covered hand, he motioned for his men to follow him from the property.

Behind them, they left an eerie silence.

Jackson was the first to move. He automatically took a step forward, but drew to a halt again. Augusta was gone. Gone.

Damnit all to hell, what was he going to do?

His hands clenched into tight fists, growing white in the cold. He stood still, braced against the newel support, staring at that spot where he'd last seen her, overcome with an emotion that he hadn't felt in years.

Panic.

The war had taught him what it meant to fear, what it meant to want. But it had also taught him that if a man were prepared for any contingency, such emotions could be blunted.

Nothing he'd experienced before could have prepared him for this. Until he'd seen her struggling against the manacles, turning her face back to him for help, he hadn't realized how much he'd grown to . . .

Care for her?

No. It was so much more than that.

He loved her. Body and soul.

The realization washed over him in a cool wave. He *did* care for her. As strange as it may seem considering their relationship: interrogator and prisoner, captor and captive.

Man and woman.

Lovers.

Damnit! What was he going to do?

"Major?"

He whirled to find Effie looking at him with wide eyes.

"They just want to question her further, don't they?" she pleaded. "Don't they . . ."

Jackson shook his head, unwilling to lie to her, to cause her further pain down the road. "No, Effie. They mean to hang her." He touched her cheek. "But we will stop them. We have to stop them."

Brushing past her, he strode into the house, intent on finding something, anything, which would help him to prove that Augusta was innocent.

It was nearly an hour later when he found the

packet of belongings tucked beneath a silk petticoat in the bottom drawer of her highboy.

There was a faded uniform, a frayed Confederate flag, some banknotes, and a pocket watch. Beneath that was a bundle of envelopes which were crisp and new and nearly untouched. They were addressed to Augusta, but looking at them, Jackson surmised they'd never been mailed. She probably hadn't read them when they'd been returned with Clarence's belongings. At that point, she'd believed him dead and it must have been too painful for her to delve into the messages they contained. He would not have given them much attention if not for the fact that he wasn't really sure what he was looking for.

But when he unfolded the first missive, he paused, a prickling sensation washing over him. He became chilled, his heart growing sluggish in his breast.

They were from Clarence, but they weren't letters. They were journal entries, detailing day by day, hour by hour, exactly who he had talked to, what campaigns he organized.

His stomach lurched as if he'd been punched in the gut and he sank onto the bed, quickly pulling the pages free, leafing to that date so long ago when his life had ended and begun.

It was so easy. The supply train stopped just where R. said it would be. We rode up on the guards, clubbed them into unconsciousness and took the munitions supplies. We cleaned out the whole boxcar! I would have loved to have seen those Yanks' faces when they saw it empty . . .

Empty.

Jackson reread the passage, but it was the last page to be included in this envelope.

Empty. The boxcar had been empty when Clarence had left it? Then who had supplied the faulty cannon? *Who?*

Images began crowding into his brain. The squeal of dying horses, the thunder of battle. And the smells: gunpowder, mud, death.

The journal entries slid from his lap to the floor, spreading out on the rug. Bending, he scrambled to pick up the letters, tearing them open, then throwing them to the ground when they weren't the ones he wanted. Finally, he saw the heading he sought and read the rest of the sentence.

. . . 'course the car won't be empty once it reaches its destination. R. has made a deal with a Northern munitions factory that came under scrutiny after their cannon failed in battle. The manufacturer was willing to pay R. a fortune if he'd hide the report and allow him to send the last questionable shipment to the front lines.

"Major?"

He jerked, the papers crushing in his grip.

"Effie." Her name was a sigh of surprise. He'd been so intent upon his own thoughts that he hadn't heard her join him.

She stood beside him, gazing at the fallen papers, her hands gripping each other until her knuckles gleamed white.

"I fear the time has come for me to break a confidence."

Still stunned by his own discoveries, Jackson didn't absorb the gravity of Effie's statement. But as her nervousness, her intensity, increased, he set the notes aside.

"What is it, Effie?"

"I promised that I wouldn't tell, but I have to. I have to do it." She shuddered as if chilled to the bone. "If you would be so kind as to harness the sleigh, Major, I will take you to Senator Armiture's murderer."

"How lovely you look, my dear."

Augusta whirled from where she'd been staring out the barred window. Hugging her shawl closer, she stared at the man responsible for bringing her here.

"What do you want?"

He allowed himself a small smile. "Such spirit. Amazing from a woman so deep in trouble."

She tilted her chin, unwilling to show this man that he alarmed her. "State your business, French."

"General French."

She refused to acknowledge his title or his position of authority.

"Why did you do it, my dear?"

"What?"

"Kill Senator Armiture."

"He tried to attack my sister. So I shot him."

French made a *tsk*ing sound with his tongue. "Is it really that simple?"

"What else could it be?"

He gave a short bark of laughter. "Come now. It's past time to be coy." He began to move closer, his steps so slow and deliberately menacing that she had to brace herself to keep from retreating.

"Where is it, my dear?"

" 'It'?"

"The diary."

"I don't know what you mean."

"But you do." His voice had grown low and gruff. "I want it, and I want it now."

She dared to give a slight toss of her head. "Even if I knew of the existence of such a thing, why on earth would I give it to you?"

"Because, my dear"—he stroked her cheek with his knuckle—"if you do, I will let you choose the method of your death. Quick and painless, or very slow, and very torturous." He sighed. "Because you see, madam, even as pretty as you might be, you must be killed."

"Why?"

"Because you've read the journal."

"I assure you, I have not."

"It doesn't really matter. I don't believe you. And I'm not about to let you live to tell your tales. I'm not about to let either of you live."

"Either?" she breathed. "Effie hasn't seen the journal. She doesn't know anything about it."

"I'm not talking about your sister, Miss McKendrick. I'm quite sure that she has no knowledge of the book—Armiture assured me of that. And the stories of your protectiveness of her are well-known. You wouldn't have been foolish enough to make her privy to the information you carry."

"Then which one of the girls—"

"Not the girls, Miss McKendrick. Your lover."

"Jackson?" When he nodded she hastened to explain, "But he doesn't know where it is."

"Probably not. But he's a smart man. If he manages to find the journal, it will only take a short time for him to realize that Armiture and I were two of your brother's contacts within the Union."

"What?"

"Don't look so surprised. It was a very profitable exchange. We sold him information and supplies and he brought us Confederate gold."

"But you were one of the men who apprehended him."

He shrugged. "Once his funding began to dwindle, we had no more use for him." His lips twitched in a small smile. "So I gathered enough evidence against him to bring him to trial and arrange his execution." He chuckled. "I lured him into a trap and once he was jailed I kept promising him that Armiture and I would arrange an escape. Naturally, he believed us."

"Until Armiture beat him."

"An unfortunate occurrence, but you see, he finally caught on to our game and threatened to divulge our association with him. Armiture attempted to . . . silence him."

She backed away from him then, truly frightened by the gleam she saw in his eyes. Greed. Hate. Power.

He clasped her neck, bringing her retreat to a halt, his fingers biting into her skin. "How much did your brother tell you?"

Augusta couldn't talk. She could only shake her head.

"Come now, he must have said something? Must have told you about how the three of us met."

"No." The word was barely audible.

"Then would you like to hear it, hmm? Would you like to know the way he approached Armiture about selling munitions to the South?" He made a scoffing sound. "As if Armiture could help him, the old fool. He might have had the connections during the war, but he didn't have the brains to get away with it. So Armiture brought me into his circle of traitors."

He laughed softly. "It was so easy, really. We made a fortune with Clarence's help, and no one would have ever known if he'd died as he was supposed to do. It wasn't until Clarence had disappeared that Armiture informed me about your brother's damned journal. He saw him writing in it once." He sneered. "Armiture thought he knew how to get hold of it, but obviously he wasn't successful, was he, my dear?"

He sniffed, getting control of himself bit by bit. "But that's neither here nor there. I intend to force your brother out of hiding once and for all. Then, I will have that journal and I will have your brother's life too."

He pushed her roughly against the stone wall and strode to the door. Augusta didn't know how she found the courage, but she called after him, "Just how do you intend to do that, General?"

He eyed her with open disdain. "If your brother had one weakness, it was you and your sister. He doted on you two. You were all he talked about." French brightened ever so slightly. "As soon as he hears you're about to be executed, he'll come running."

"When?" Augusta breathed.

He answered with great satisfaction, "The day after tomorrow there will be a firing squad assembled in your honor. Since your arrest hasn't flushed him out, maybe your death will. If not"—he shrugged, taking a cigar from his pocket and clamping it in his teeth— "at least I'll have one less witness to deal with."

"What about Jackson?"

"Charles?" He *harrumph*ed with evident humor. "I'll see to him myself. Some night when he's riding down a darkened road. Then he'll be as dead as you."

17

The building was modest, even when compared to Elijah's simple cottage. It was a shack, really. One small room, a single cramped window, and a metal stovepipe with a waft of smoke drifting from the top.

"Who's staying here, Effie?" Jackson asked, his voice sounding too loud to his own ears in the winter stillness.

She didn't answer but brought the sleigh to a halt near the front door.

Jackson saw the way a crack of light grew wider. As the lamplight spilled into the snow, he recognized Elijah Ward's powerful frame.

When the black man drew his rifle up, sighting down the barrel, Effie jumped from the sleigh, holding up her hands in a bid for restraint.

"It's all right, Elijah. *I* brought him here."

Elijah didn't move. The gun didn't waver.

"Please, Elijah." Effie sighed in supplication. "Augusta's been arrested."

The man's frame sagged against the door, and Jackson caught the honest grief reflected in Elijah's face.

Rushing forward, Effie touched his arm. "It's not Major Charles's fault. He had no choice in the matter. In fact, he was relieved from his duties when he tried to help Augusta."

"Den what's he doin' here?"

Effie's attention bounced from man to man. "I think it's time we asked for some help."

Elijah stood still as stone.

"Please, Elijah. We don't have any other choice."

The man scowled at Jackson, clearly wishing he could bash him into the snow, but at long last he relented, nodded, and backed into the shack.

Effie followed, then Jackson.

There was barely enough room for the three of them to stand in the small space that remained to the side of a metal cot and an iron stove.

Jackson's eyes were immediately drawn to the figure on the bed and he had to steel himself to keep from shuddering. A portion of Clarence's hair had been shaved away to reveal an open, angry gash. Matted blood caked the area, but could not hide the crimson streaks radiating from the wound. Nor could it hide the stench.

"Gangrene."

Elijah's head dipped. "Yes'ah. I put de creams on it dat Miss Augusta give me, but . . ."

But nothing could cure gangrene. Especially not in a man who was all but dead.

Jackson felt a wave of sadness, an inestimable sense of waste. Augusta had been right. Even without the wounds, the sight of this man would have been grim. The way his eyes were open, staring sightlessly. He'd curled into a fetal position, his mouth open, spittle running from the corner of his mouth to the towel Elijah had placed on his pillow.

"How long has he been this way?"

Effie and Elijah exchanged glances. At Ward's imperceptible nod, Effie volunteered, "Since the night Senator Armiture was killed."

She bit her lip.

"It's my fault, you know. He'd come to Billingsly to see me. He wanted me to . . . that is, he tried to . . ."

Jackson touched her shoulder. "Augusta told me that he tried to rape you."

She bit her lip, obviously embarrassed.

"What happened then, Effie?" Jackson urged. "What happened after he tried to force himself on you?"

"Augusta had sent word to Clarence, and he agreed to meet her at the abandoned church. She didn't want to leave me alone, but I convinced her I'd be all right." Her chin wobbled. "They almost didn't make it back i-in time." She took a shuddering breath.

"Armiture had just pushed me onto the couch when Augusta stormed into the room, Clarence fast on her heels. Armiture was enraged the moment he saw my brother. He picked up the fire poker . . . they struggled . . . and Armiture struck him over the head."

When she couldn't continue, Elijah took up the narrative. "Miss 'Gusta, she took de poker from him, but he grabbed a branch from de fire."

"The burns . . ."

"Yes'ah. He struck her on de shoulder, an' was about to hit her 'gain with de stick when . . ."

"You shot him," Jackson supplied understandingly, knowing everything now, the whole twisted scheme.

"Yes'ah."

"The girls were just returning from town. They ran into the study in an effort to help. The house was in an uproar," Effie whispered.

"So Elijah took Clarence away to his cottage first," Jackson guessed.

Elijah nodded.

"I hid him in de cottage and came back fo' Armiture."

"By that time, Augusta had shooed the girls away and was ready to clean things up," Effie whispered.

"So you took the body away," Jackson surmised out loud, "and then you waited to see what would happen, hoping that no one would guess that Armiture had met with a bad end."

Effie grasped his wrist. "No one came for weeks! We thought we were safe."

"But when Augusta was put under house arrest, none of you came forward."

"She wouldn't let us. She knew that if it was discovered that Elijah was responsible, he would be lynched long before any sort of trial."

A sad but true fact. In the South, race relations were far from amiable.

"Augusta was sure that there wouldn't be enough evidence for her to be brought to trial, that being a woman would lessen any threat of retaliation. She wouldn't turn in Elijah. Not after all he did to help us survive the war."

Jackson lifted his hands to his face, running his fingers through his hair. "So what do we do now?"

Elijah became stiff and proud. "I's goin' to confess."

"No, Elijah!" Effie gasped. "Augusta would never forgive any of us if we let you do that. There has to be another way."

Jackson looked at the man on the bed, knowing that they could somehow frame Clarence for the deed, but even as desperate as he was, he knew he couldn't do that. As Augusta had once said, her brother deserved the opportunity to die among the company of those who cared for him.

"Where did you hide Armiture's body, Elijah?"

"In de woods. I dug a grave in one of de caves dere and collapsed de hole. All I brought back was his coat an' his gun."

He reached beneath the mattress to retrieve the items. Clarence didn't stir even after being so rudely jostled.

Elijah handed the things to Jackson. "What will you do with 'em? Can you find some way t' help us all?"

Jackson opened his mouth, but the platitudes didn't come. "I don't know, Elijah. I don't know."

This time, it was Jackson who took the reins. Once they'd arrived at Billingsly, he helped Effie from the sleigh, then took the horse and conveyance to the carriage house.

Slowly, thoughtfully, he removed the traces and bedded the animal down—the motions familiar and comforting, bringing memories he'd been without for so long. They'd had a sleigh at Solitude too. One big enough for three strapping boys, his father and mother.

Sighing, he retrieved the coat and revolver from the seat, no longer able to avoid the question thrumming through his brain.

What was he going to do?

His steps were heavy as he entered the school and made his way upstairs to Augusta's room. Sinking onto the bed, he threw the coat onto the chair and braced his hand on either side of him. In doing so, he came in contact with Clarence's old uniform. It made a rustling noise like crumpled paper as it slid to the floor.

Damn. What was . . . he . . .

Frowning, he grasped the ragged blouse, searching the pockets. But they were empty. He was about to throw it down when he heard the sound again. It didn't come from the pockets, but the coat itself.

Clenching great handfuls of fabric now, he found the spot in the back hem which was stiffer to the touch. Taking his knife from his boot, he slit the fabric open and reached between the lining and outer material.

Paper. Only three sheets, but paper, nonetheless.

Drawing them free, he sank onto the settee again, holding them to the light.

But he didn't need to read them.

He recognized the initials and names for what they were. A key to all of the codes Clarence had used in his journal. A roster of traitors. And right at the top was General Robert Siddington French.

As Jackson strode into the telegraph office, he wasn't sure what he should write. Grasping the tiny stub of a pencil, he hesitated.

Were his brothers even alive? If they were, would this telegraph manage to reach them?

He was taking a chance, he knew, counting on things that might no longer exist. But he had to do something. He needed help. And these were the only two men he could trust.

"Sir?" The clerk looked up at him expectantly. "Is there something wrong?"

"Yes," Jackson said softly, scrawling the only message he could compose. "Send this as quickly as you can."

The sentiment the paper contained was blunt and to the point—as was its signature. For the first time in years, he used the name his family was accustomed to seeing, and not the identity he had employed after he'd been wounded.

Need help. Please. J.B. St. Charles.

"Augusta?"

She didn't even turn when she heard Jackson whispering to her from the other side of the jail door. She was staring out the window, looking at the sergeant who was carefully sweeping the cobbled yard below. The yard where she would be shot at dawn.

She didn't know how Jackson had managed to sneak into the prison, but it took all the will she possessed to keep the length of the cell between them. She mustn't go to him. She mustn't let him see her worry. There was no help for her own situation, not anymore. But she had to see to it that Jackson was left unharmed. Alive.

Would he take care of Effie after she was gone?

Would he offer his protection to the girls?

Please, dear God, please. If ever she had done

something worthy of a shred of compassion, please let Jackson live to carry on with those duties.

"Augusta?"

She resisted the entreaty in his voice, resisted the come-hither quality she'd grown to love.

Love?

Yes. Love.

"It's my own fault, you know," she said softly. "I didn't think it would be this difficult to face a firing squad." She offered a bitter laugh. "Not a hanging as we feared, but a firing squad."

She turned in time to see Jackson reaching for her through the bars. "It doesn't have to happen. I know how to help you now."

She faced him fully then, her face shiny with the tears she hadn't even felt until that moment. "How? How can you help me?"

"Effie has taken me to Clarence—"

"No!" She swiped at the moisture on her cheeks. Forgetting her resolution, she stormed toward him. "No, I won't let you blame this on my brother!"

Jackson caught her and held her tight.

"No, you've misunderstood. I won't turn him in, Augusta. You were right. You can't help him now. You can only give him the peace he needs to die."

Her eyes filled with more tears and she damned herself for the weakness. "He's worse?"

"Gangrene."

A choking sound came from her throat.

"Hush, sweetheart," Jackson said, stroking her face, her hair. "I doubt if he's in any real pain. His body may not know it yet, but his mind is gone."

She cried then, reaching through the bars to hold Jackson as close as she could. Just one more time.

Jackson let her sob, even though he knew his time was limited. The corporal who'd let him into the jail cell would insist on his leaving again before word of his visit reached French. He held her, soothed her, loved her, all the while praying that she would trust him. Trust him with her very life.

When he heard the distant sound of footsteps on the stairs, he tipped her head up. "Listen to me, Augusta. I don't have time to explain, but I've found a way to help you. I'm going to force French to make a trade."

"What?"

The footsteps were on the other side of the outer door.

"I can't explain now. Just trust me. No matter what happens, trust me. Can you do that?"

She nodded, her cheeks moist with tears.

"But—"

"Trust me, Augusta. I love you, do you hear? I won't fail you. Not while we have our whole lives ahead of us." He lowered his head to the bars, kissing her through the small space. "Trust me."

Then he was gone.

Leaving her with that tiny word which allowed her to hope.

Love.

Jackson waited impatiently on the railway platform, clutching a telegram of confirmation in his pocket.

Both of us arriving on six a.m. train. Be there, damnit.

Micah and Bram

Jackson was filled with uncertainty, wondering what his brothers would think of him for waiting so long to contact them. What with the war and all, they might not even be hale and hearty enough to help him.

No. He mustn't even consider such a thing. No matter their physical condition, the three St. Charles brothers had always been close. They'd banded together during countless scuffles at school, done their drinking and their philandering together, and shared every goal, every impossible dream.

They would find a way to help him.

From far away, he heard the shrill call of a whistle, then the rumbling, the panting. The train had come.

Straightening from the beam which supported the station overhang, Jackson tried to deny the nervousness which gripped him. He was about to be reunited with Micah and Bram. It shouldn't worry him. He should be delighted.

But the emotions didn't fade. Indeed, they intensified as the brakes squealed and the train rasped to a stop in front of him.

Tugging his hat more securely over his brow, he straightened, damning the cold as it made his limp more pronounced. A cripple. *You're a cripple.* The words raced through his head. The images of how he and his brothers had been as boys—running, running. Always running. What would they think of him now?

The engine came to a complete stop and rested eerily on the rails, panting softly to itself. The porter stepped from the only passenger car, aligning a set of wooden steps on the platform.

A woman dressed in rough homespun was the first to alight. She turned to help a small boy from the train, then took his hand and led him into the warmth of the building. After that was an old man, a boy of about fourteen, and a toddler—all of whom seemed to be traveling together.

Then the nighttime blackness grew grim.

The tension he'd felt began to drain free, leaving Jackson exhausted. They hadn't come. Despite the telegram, they hadn't been able to come.

Jackson tried to reassure himself that they'd missed the train or their connections en route, but his heart was too tired, too disappointed, to heed such attempts.

Rubbing at the ache in his thigh, he forced himself to move. He would have to find some other means to help Augusta. There wasn't enough time to send another plea to his brothers.

"Damnit, Micah, this animal of yours has got to be the ugliest, stupidest mount alive."

The faint comment caused Jackson to pause, his breath to lock in his chest.

"Well, I haven't had the time to buy anything else, so shut your trap. It eats, it runs, it breathes. As far as I'm concerned, that should be enough to see me through."

The voices were coming from farther down the track. From the boxcars.

Turning, he saw one of the heavy doors slide free and a man jump to the ground.

"Slide that ramp out. I'm frozen clear through to the bone."

"Jackson will have whiskey waiting for us."

"He'd better. What possessed you to take a cattle car instead of booking us passage in a regular car?"

"I didn't think it wise to leave our cargo unguarded."

"What in the world made you bring Jackson's share of the family fortune with us?"

"Why don't you talk louder and inform the whole county of what's hidden in those crates, Bram?"

"Damnit all to hell, only a fool would try to steal that heavy crate in this kind of weather."

"The world is full of fools, haven't you noticed?"

"Mmm."

The grousing was so familiar, Jackson felt transported through time. His throat tightened and he found himself staring at the two dim shapes in the darkness. Then he was moving toward them, slowly at first, then faster and faster.

They were here, hale and hearty.

"Where is he, anyway?"

"Jackson?"

"Of course, Jackson. Who'd you think I meant? You sent a cable for him to meet us, didn't you?"

"I've told you a hundred times that I—"

"I'm here."

Never had any words tasted sweeter on his tongue. Nor had he ever experienced the joy he felt when the men faced him and the lamplight from the station flooded over their faces.

Micah, strong, giant Micah. He was the first to move, jumping from the boxcar to be on the same level as the others.

"Dear God, Jackson."

Then, he was wrapping his big hand around Jackson's neck, pulling him into a bone-crushing hug.

Jackson gripped his older brother tightly, inhaling the scents of the earth that had always seemed to cling to Micah—woodsmoke and damp ground and crushed autumn leaves.

"Move over, Micah, I want to see the rascal."

Micah released him and Jackson faced the second brother. Abraham. Bram. Always the thinker, the planner, Bram looked older, harsher, but so familiar. It made Jackson wonder if he was so different from the rapscallion he'd once been.

"You," Bram said, pointing an accusing finger at Jackson, "have scared us both half to death. Next time you enlist, leave a forwarding address, do you hear?"

Then Jackson was being pulled close for another hearty hug and a clap on the shoulders.

"So, where's the whiskey?" Bram finally said, pulling away and patting Jackson playfully on the cheek much as he'd done when they were small. It was a gesture that used to annoy Jackson to no end, but now caused his chest to ache in pleasure.

"I've got you booked in a hotel. I would have taken you to Billingsly, but I was afraid you'd startle the girls."

"Girls," Micah repeated slowly.

"We should have known," Bram added. "We should have guessed his disappearance had something to do with a woman."

"Or *women*, as the case may be."

Jackson opened his mouth to explain, but Micah

gestured to the boxcar behind them. "Help us get the horses and wagon unloaded."

"Wagon?"

Bram clapped him on the shoulder, leading him forward. "We'll explain it later. After we've had a bite to eat."

18

Jackson and his brothers were ensconced in the hotel room in Wellsville, a fire roaring in the grate, the remains of the soup and thick beef sandwiches they'd consumed for dinner mixed with the crumbs of cake scattered on the small table.

"Well, Jackson, let's have it," Micah prompted as soon as their hunger had been satisfied and their bodies warmed.

"I was injured during the war."

"We guessed that much," Bram said dismissingly, waving a negligent hand in the direction of Jackson's leg. "Did you think it would matter to us?"

Jackson detected the fact that Bram was a bit offended.

"I wondered."

"Idiot," Micah chided in a familiar manner.

"I suppose I should have contacted you, but my injuries occurred under peculiar circumstances involving a Southern spy. I was sure that if I altered my name, I could track him down without anyone questioning my motives."

"Did you find him?" Bram queried.

"Only recently. But at the same time, I uncovered proof of the fact that he was only a pawn in a much larger game. One orchestrated by a Union general."

"Who?" Micah asked, his gaze steely.

"General Robert Siddington French, the man I've been serving under."

"So what do you want us to do now?" Micah asked. "That box we hauled all the way from Virginia has enough gold to take care of whatever needs you might have."

"Gold!"

"Your share of the St. Charles treasure gathered by our illustrious ancestor and then hidden for times of need. Bram and I have determined that the St. Charles men are more than in need of some capital to rebuild."

"But—"

"Don't argue with him," Bram supplied smoothly. "It won't work. I tried. Besides, a healthy portion has been put aside for future generations. What's in that crate is yours."

Jackson was flabbergasted, realizing that he had just been handed his future. No doubt his leg would continue to plague him—there was no avoiding that. But with his share of the St. Charles fortune, he had the means to circumvent such an obstacle and hire experts to help him. But right now, that was of minor concern compared to the challenges he must face in the next few hours—challenges that no amount of money would alter.

He needed help. His brothers' help.

Jackson took a deep breath, knowing that what he was about to suggest would be dangerous—some would even say foolhardy. But he also knew that he wouldn't have to ask his brothers to participate. They were here for him, angry and spoiling for a fight as older brothers were wont to be.

"I say we make a trade. What I have for what he has."

"Get that woman out here! Now!"

Augusta was wrenched from her uneasy sleep by the shout that reverberated through the stone prison chamber. Scrambling to free herself from the meager blanket she'd wrapped around her body, she was barely standing when her cell door flew open and a pair of armed guards entered.

"What's happening? No one was supposed to come for me until dawn," she gasped when she saw that one of them held a black scarf which she had assumed would be her blindfold for the execution.

"Shut up," one of the men growled. The other held her tightly as the fabric was stretched taut over her face and knotted.

"No," she whispered, a dank terror filling her breast. "No, you aren't supposed to come until dawn!"

But her cries were ignored and she was being lifted and thrown over a man's shoulder and carried away.

She tried to tell herself this was a mistake. She tried to think of Jackson. She trusted him to help her. During the long hours of the night, she'd convinced herself she wouldn't die, that the execution would be canceled. She hadn't even considered that French might have his own plans.

No! She couldn't let this happen.

But when she tried to fight, the guards held her that much more tightly. She was jounced against an unmovable shoulder as their pace increased.

"Good," she heard a voice saying from far away. French. It had to be French. "Let's go."

There was a cold rush of air, the icy penetration of a breeze, and she knew she was being taken outside. Then her hands and feet were roughly tied and she was thrown onto a hard wooden surface.

Moments later, as she heard the snuffle of horses and a muted "hiyahh!" she realized she'd been put into a wagon. Her panic grew tenfold. They couldn't take her away! They mustn't! Jackson wouldn't know where to find her. He wouldn't know how to help her.

It seemed like eons passed, each second drowned out by the thunderous beating of her heart, before the wagon creaked to a halt and callused hands reached for her, all but dragging her to the ground, a knife slicing through her bindings.

Stumbling, she quickly caught her balance, praying that if they let her walk under her own power she might have a chance to run, to hide, to do something.

She didn't want to die. Not now. Not after she'd found so much to live for. Her work, her family. And Jackson. Jackson most of all. Hadn't the war taken enough from them both? Didn't they deserve a chance? A future?

"Give her to me. Then stay here by the wagon. I don't want you approaching us no matter what you hear."

She recognized French's voice, so near to her now that she knew it was his hand that took her elbow.

"Understood?"

"Yes, sir," the guards mumbled as she was dragged forward over an uneven surface.

Stumbling, she tried to keep up to French's pace until he brought her to an abrupt halt again. The blindfold was ripped from her face and she gasped, realizing in an instant that she was not positioned in front of a brick wall, but at a solitary spur of railroad track. One she recognized as being little more than a half-dozen miles away from Billingsly.

From a hundred yards down the track, a locomotive sputtered and hissed as it slowly ground its way forward, foot by foot, inch by inch, until it came to a stop at the platform in front of them.

Soot and steam flooded the air and coiled around their feet, causing her to blink against the stinging of her eyes. When the shapes appeared in the hazy mist, she squinted, wondering if what she saw actually existed, or if they were merely figments of her imagination.

There were three men, three tall and powerful men dressed in dusters, the brims of their hats pulled low over their eyes. One, large and bearded, lifted a rifle and sighted down the barrel. Another, slim and dark, held one revolver primed and aimed, a second weapon at the ready in the fist at his side.

And Jackson in the center, his eyes searching hers, offering her strength and reassuring her that the men he'd brought with him would see she was freed.

French must have come to the same conclusion, because she heard him swear under his breath.

Augusta's eyes clung to Jackson, one last time, needing to memorize everything about him. Because she knew that even though he had come to rescue her, she wouldn't be allowed to leave here alive. She would be shot in the back before French would allow her to go. She knew far too much about him.

"Let her go, French!" Jackson called over the distance that separated them.

"Where's McKendrick?" French countered, his grip growing so tight, Augusta nearly cried out. "The message you sent to me stated that he would be here too."

There was a slight pause. Jackson sought Augusta's gaze. "Dead. He died last night from the head wound he suffered grappling with Armiture."

A small cry escaped from her lips, but she squelched it immediately. She couldn't think about her brother now. She had to keep her wits about her.

"Hand over the girl, French."

"Not until I have what I've come for," the general growled.

"The journal pages?" Aiming his pistol, Jackson used his free hand to reach into the pocket of his duster. "Is this what you want?" he asked, holding the papers high.

The wind gusted bitter-cold around them.

"Yes."

"You know that you have more than a written record as a witness now, don't you, French?"

The man grunted. "I'm not a fool. I knew that if you found them, you'd read them."

"Quite a dangerous game you've been playing for the past few years."

"Dangerous, but very lucrative."

"You sacrificed your own men. You even shot your own two guards so that you could blame their executions on Clarence. That way, if you failed to find him, the army would intensify their search. But those murders are nothing to the hundreds of your soldiers you killed during the war."

French laughed. *"My* soldiers? I didn't care about the conflict. As far as I was concerned it was merely another way to further my own ends. I would have fought for the South if I'd thought they were capable of winning."

"Did Clarence know about your bizarre sense of allegiance?"

"Clarence didn't give a hoot what I did as long as I gave him the information and supplies he requested."

"It wasn't until later that you discovered he'd left a legacy behind him to incriminate you and Armiture."

"I underestimated him—and I must admit it has been the cause of some concern. But thanks to you, I don't have to worry about the journal popping up at an inopportune time."

His lips tipped in a feral smile. "Now, if the man is dead, as you claim, then I have only you to contend with. You and the men you so foolishly brought with you. Then I will take care of this woman."

"You're amassing a list of victims, General," the bearded man commented.

"All part of the casualties of war. You see, I've been taught to look ahead. I've seen to it that there's a fire at Billingsly."

"No!" Augusta tried to wrench free, filled with horror.

But the general wrenched her closer, placing the tip of his revolver against her temple.

"The papers, Major Charles."

There was a long silence. Then, eyes growing fierce with anger, Jackson stated, "If you want them, you're going to have to find them yourself."

His fingers relaxed. The papers crackled. Then tossing them into the air, he allowed the wind to carry them helter-skelter into the winter darkness.

"Damnit!" French shouted, the click of the hammer being drawn into place loud in Augusta's ear. "She'll die for that. You'll die for that."

"I don' think so. *Sir.*"

The growl was low, and mean, coming from behind them.

Before French could react, a fist flew out, striking the general on the jaw and sending him sprawling.

Momentarily stunned, Augusta was rooted to the ground as Elijah scooped up the general's revolver and pointed it at the man's head. His finger wrapped around the trigger with deliberate purpose. "I'd be more'n happy t' kill you now, sir. All you got t' do is move."

Augusta wilted in relief. Then she was running to Jackson, being scooped into his strong arms and held there tightly, so tightly.

"I love you," she whispered against his ear, knowing that now was neither the time nor place for such a confession, but needing to make it nonetheless.

"I know, I know," he whispered back to her, kissing her quickly, desperately.

"Billingsly," she gasped, breaking away.

Jackson swore, pulling her in the direction of the

train and boxcar. "Micah, Bram, get those horses unloaded. We've got to warn the girls at the school!"

Micah jumped to obey while the slimmer one, Bram, she assumed, crouched close to French murmuring, "Do you know what's going to happen to you, old man? You tangled with the wrong family."

His expression grew fierce. "You see, the government owes that one there"—he pointed to his older brother—"more favors than you could care to count. Me? They owe the courtesy of making my present life as comfortable as possible for serving in their Secret Service. And Jackson? I suppose you could say that they owe him a future for what he's done to uncover a bed of vipers. Any way you look at it, you'll be swinging by the end of the week."

"Bram?" Jackson called, tugging the man's horse free from the cargo car along with his own.

"Go ahead. I'll stay here with Elijah and see to this bastard."

Augusta, afraid they had delayed too long, grasped the reins in Jackson's hands and swung onto the mount, urging it into a gallop.

"Damnit, woman!" she heard Jackson call, but she didn't stop, didn't pause. She had to warn Effie. She had to help the girls.

She was only a mile away from Billingsly when she saw the first tinge of color on the horizon. One that was too rich and red to be the gentle peekings of dawn.

A huge invisible hand clamped around her throat, making breathing all but impossible. It couldn't be happening. Not after so much had been taken from her—and so much had been given in return. God couldn't possibly want more. He mustn't take what was left of her family.

The horse was galloping as fast as it could, but she urged it on, bending low over its neck. She could hear the noise of more hooves behind her, but she didn't alter her headlong pace.

The moment she crested the knoll leading to Billingsly, she saw the flames leaping into the sky, greedily coming from the windows.

"Effie!" she screamed. "Effie, get out!"

There was no reply, only the hungry snap and roar of the fire.

"Pansy! Buttercup! Aster!"

The horse skidded to a halt and she was running the last few yards. "Thelma! Revel-Ann! Somebody please answer me!"

The heat was intense, searing her, causing her to falter and cover her face with her arms, then continue more hesitantly. "Please answer! Someone . . . any-one . . . please."

Strong arms snapped around her waist, pulling her away. She fought against them, knowing that if she didn't stop him, Jackson would prevent her from helping those inside. Scratching, clawing, kicking, she struggled to get free.

"Stop it! Stop!"

He pinned her arms to her sides.

"Augusta, stop!"

Behind them there was a huge crash and she looked back, aghast, as the roof collapsed into the house. Beneath that the first floor crumpled, then the second, and slowly, agonizingly, the walls wobbled and fell inward in a heap.

Augusta felt the gorge rising within her, the strength leaving her body so that she sank to her knees sobbing.

"Ef-fie!" she cried out, leaning toward the school, expecting someone to emerge from the flames.

But no one did.

Jackson dropped beside her, holding her as she sobbed, absorbing her pain into his body. But as much as she loved him, as much as she needed him, it wasn't enough.

"I've lost them." She sobbed into his shoulder. "I've lost them all."

Dawn had come and gone, the fire had burned to the ground before Jackson had been able to convince Augusta to leave this place.

By that time, her face was streaked with ashes and tears, but he could tell that the skin beneath held a sickly pallor.

Scooping her into his arms, he carried her to the carriage house. Once there, he laid her in the seat of the empty sleigh. He would leave her here, out of the bitter wind, and fetch the horses. Then they would meet his brothers in town.

His brothers. The elder *St.* Charleses. She marveled that the two men who had come to the station to help her were Jackson's brothers and that Jackson had hidden from them for so long in order to find justice for what had happened to his men. That trail for vengeance had led him here in search of Clarence but had ultimately uncovered a much greater foe.

"Micah? Is he here?"

He shook his head. "When he saw he wouldn't be of

any help here, he went to tell Bram what had happened."

She squeezed her eyes closed, and Jackson knew she was unable to believe it yet. That so many vibrant, gentle lives could be extinguished so quickly. So finally.

"Take me away from here," she at last whispered.

"Yes," Jackson answered, stroking her cheek. "Just let me hitch up the horses and we'll go to town."

"No." Her grip grew tighter, fiercer. "Take me from this place, from Wellsville, from this state. Take me somewhere where I won't be reminded, where the green of the grass in spring, the breezes of summer, the cool of autumn, won't bring it back."

His throat grew tight with emotion and he climbed into the sleigh, drawing her snugly against his chest, knowing instinctively that there was no place on earth that would make her forget Effie's gentle charm, Buttercup's glum humor, Aster's energy, Pansy's inquisitiveness, Revel-Ann's bravado . . . and Thelma's fits of vapors at the slightest provocation.

But sensing that she needed something to distract her, he whispered, "Shall I take you to Solitude, hmm? That's my home. Bram says there was some trouble there, but a new house is being built, and it's to be mine. Mine and yours." He cleared his throat when his voice grew gruff. "You'll love it there. Rolling hills sweep down from the woods where my brothers and I used to play. There's a swimming hole nearby, and a meandering stream. Come summertime, we'll fill the meadows with broodmares and a stud or two. In time, we'll have colts frisking about, and maybe even a child or two of our own."

She gripped his shirt, burying her face against him, sobbing as if her heart were broken. He didn't need to ask why. It wasn't because she was offended by his assumptions, but because it was what she wanted, what she'd never allowed herself to dream could be possible. Now that it was being handed to her—a home, a husband, and children of her own—the price seemed so dear. So very dear.

From far away, he heard the muted clatter of hooves and guessed that his brothers had come to find him. To find *them*.

He tipped her head up. "It isn't enough, I know. But I promise you that I will love you more each day, each breath I take. I promise that I will make you happy. I promise that the two of us will grow old together. Somehow, we'll find a way to put the past to rest. If only you'll continue to love me as I do you."

He bent for her kiss. A kiss that went on and on, tinged with sadness and a hope for the future. A future together.

"Spring," she said brokenly when at last she drew away. "I would like to be married in the spring." Then they were kissing again, holding onto each other as drowning men held to lifelines.

"Damnit to hell, Jackson!"

The two of them sprang apart when the main door slid open and Bram and Micah glared at them both from a patch of morning sunlight.

"I told you the two of them would be holed up in here," Micah said, folding his arms over his chest.

"It would serve them right if we left."

Micah nodded.

Jackson rose, about to rebuke his brothers for their

callous remarks, but a distant noise alerted him. Voices. Feminine voices.

"Look, Jackson," Bram grumbled. "When you asked for our help, you didn't say we'd be spending the night with your women, for hell's sake. That Revel-Ann kept coming up behind me and staring at me like I was some sort of bug. Then she kept going on and on about how we had to warn the major and his men about the clothes. They mustn't wear the clothes."

"You too?" Micah demanded, glowering. "Did you know they boiled them in quicklime?"

"*Quicklime?* Why, that would eat the hair off a hide."

"What about that pale one?" Micah added.

"The fainter."

"I hate that quality in a woman."

"Then there's that nosy one."

"And who the hell in their right mind would name a passel of girls after flowers? *Flowers!*"

There was a gasp from Augusta. Then she was scrambling from the sleigh.

Jackson jumped to the dirt right behind her, but Bram snagged one elbow and Micah the other. He was held immobile as Augusta slipped and skidded her way to the gaggle of girls surveying the remains of the fire.

"She thought they'd died," he murmured.

"Well, if you'd come to town, you would have discovered that Frank and Boyd followed them there earlier that evening when they insisted on trying to see Augusta in prison."

Frank and Boyd. In his efforts to comfort Augusta,

he'd forgotten all about his men. It was merely another sign of how much this woman had begun to color every aspect of his life.

"When they discovered that Augusta had been taken away, the women planted themselves in French's office and refused to leave until they had an explanation. They were sitting there bold as brass when we hauled the general in to be locked up."

Micah chuckled. "You should have seen the look on French's face when he saw them."

"Then, you should have seen the look on his face when Effie jabbed him with a hat pin."

"A hat pin?" Jackson asked weakly, taking in the women who were hugging and squealing and talking all at once.

"She's got a temper, that one."

"A hat pin," he said again, grinning. Then he was laughing, patting his brothers on the back and pulling them close.

Bram and Micah withstood it for little more than a minute, then drew away, eyeing him with concern. "You've been around these girls too long," Micah commented under his breath, tugging his vest into place.

"Good hell, Jackson," Bram added, tugging his hat over his brow. "Don't tell me they'll be coming with you to Solitude?"

Jackson didn't give it a second thought. "Yes. Yes, they will."

Micah grinned. "I'll be damned—what an irony. Then I suppose you'll be using your share of the St. Charles treasure to convert Solitude into some kind of girls' school."

Jackson liked the idea. Liked it a lot. It would be

just what Augusta needed. She wasn't the homemaker type. She needed action, life, her students.

"Yes, yes, I suppose I will."

"Damn," Micah muttered. "I guess that means we hauled the gold all this way for nothing."

"Not quite. I think on the way home, I'll visit some stud farms along the way."

"You were always good with the horses as a kid, Jackson," Bram said, clapping him on the shoulder and leading him forward. "I think that's a grand idea."

"Even after buying the stock you need, there should be enough of your share of the treasure to get a school started," Micah commented.

"My wife, Marguerite, would be pleased to help, I'm sure. She and her family are tailor-made for such an enterprise." Bram's eyes twinkled. "Why, that might be enough to blast Nanny Edna out of living in my house. I'm sure she'd like to stay with you."

"Don't forget that Joliet fellow."

"Oh, yes. The artist. He'd be delighted to teach, I'm sure."

Jackson wasn't really sure whom his brothers were referring to. But as he was led into the morning air, he decided it didn't matter. It didn't matter at all. He had all the time in the world to get caught up on what had happened to his family in his absence.

His eyes clung to Augusta, seeing her bright smiles, her gay features, and he sent a prayer of gratitude skyward.

They both had all the time in the world.

Epilogue

Virginia, 1866

Flowers. There were flowers everywhere. Tulips and lilacs and hyacinths, buttercups and bluebonnets. Long ago, as a child, she'd dreamed of having a wedding on a day like today. One filled with sunshine and happiness and anticipation.

"You look beautiful, Gus. Just beautiful."

She grinned as Effie's reflection joined her own in the cheval mirror. Although most of Solitude was in a state of restoration, Jackson had seen to it that her own chambers had been finished first. There was painting to be done, a bit of woodwork, but the floors had been waxed to a high sheen, curtains draped over ornate rods.

And a bed.

Her wedding bed.

Effie's eyes twinkled as if she'd guessed the nature of her thoughts—for Effie had married Frank only a few days after Billingsly had been burned. She was so much stronger now. So happy. She hadn't been able to understand why Augusta had insisted on waiting for the spring to be married.

"Let me pin this a little tighter." Effie adjusted the way the lace veil fell over her tawny hair, fluffed at a flounce here, a tuck there.

Marguerite gestured to her son. Although his limbs were frail and twisted, he was a spirited lad. He'd appointed himself sentinel to the bridal chambers. Positioning his cane-backed wheelchair at the end of the corridor, he'd kept the men out of the hall. "Jeffrey, go tell your father we're ready to begin."

A little boy nodded excitedly and hurried from the room, careening full-speed down the hall in search of Bram. "Papa! Papa! It's time!"

Augusta turned from her reflection and gripped her sister's hands, so thankful that Effie's stubbornness had surfaced in time to take her from the fire and into town to help Augusta.

Blinking away a quick tear, she surveyed the other women present. Those who would soon become her sisters-in-law.

Micah's wife, Lizzy, was tall and slender with a no-nonsense attitude that hid a wicked sense of humor. She had dressed for the day in a simple gown of white lawn embroidered with tiny yellow rosebuds, but there was no disguising the fact that she would soon give birth.

Seeing Augusta's regard, she self-consciously smoothed the fabric over her middle. "I really think you should allow me to slip into a chair with the audience after the ceremony has started," she said frowning, guessing the thrust of Augusta's thoughts.

"Nonsense. I want you all there. I need you there."

Bram's bride, Marguerite, offered a devilish smile,

her dark eyes dancing. "Take it from me, wedding days are nothing more than a good deal of fuss and a chance to dress up. It's the wedding nights that are important."

"Marguerite!" Lizzy gasped.

Then they giggled, wondering why any of them bothered to act shocked.

"Are you nervous?" Marguerite inquired gently, adjusting the drape of her own elaborate plum-colored gown. Augusta suspected that Marguerite would soon be making an announcement of her own concerning an upcoming birth.

"No." And it was the truth. She wasn't nervous at all. She was excited, elated, and impatient. She wanted to live her life with Jackson openly and honestly, here at his home. Solitude.

"You know, that gown looks much better on you than it ever did on me," Marguerite commented, and they all laughed. It had been a running jest for weeks that Augusta's wedding ensemble had been remade from Marguerite's own bridal gown. One made—not for her wedding to Bram years ago—but for a marriage to another man. After being told Bram had died in the war, she'd meant to secure a home and a father for her crippled son. To her surprise, on the altar steps, she had discovered that Bram was very much alive and had come to claim her for himself.

Effie crossed to the window, pushing the lace aside. "They're giving the signal."

"It's time."

But none of the three St. Charles brides moved. Instead, they formed an intimate circle, holding one another's hands.

"We will always be close friends," Augusta said,

sensing that in these women she had found lifelong allies, an emotion she had never thought to share with anyone other than Effie.

"We'll have to band together against the St. Charles charm," Marguerite added.

"And the wickedness of those who would try to thwart them," Lizzy continued.

"Because none of you is as helpless as the men in your lives think you are," Effie added from her spot by the window.

As the laughter filled the room, Augusta knew that such comments were true, so very true. All of them were cut from the same cloth—the new breed of women who had been forged out of the fires of war. Never again would they allow themselves to be shielded from the "messiness" of the world. They knew well enough what hardships could be foisted upon them, and that they had the ability to survive. They would build a world far better than the one they'd experienced. For their children and their children's children.

"Ladies!"

Micah's impatient call sent them all scattering from the room, until only Effie and Augusta remained.

Effie touched her sister's cheek. "Thank you, Gus. Thank you for everything." Then, amid a watery smile, she commanded, "Be happy."

As she rushed from the room, and Augusta followed her to the garden at a more sedate pace, she knew that Effie's words would be prophetic.

For as she took Elijah's elbow and allowed him to escort her to the silken runner, then walked alone to the bower of blossoms where Jackson waited for her, she knew that her fate was sealed. In this place. With this man.

In his arms, she'd found her home. In his smile, she'd found her salvation. And in his passionate regard, she'd found the sweet decadence to tempt her from the lonely path she'd been doomed to follow.

Jackson took her hand. So strong, so warm, so real.

He was her life.

Her love.

Her husband.

Printed in the United States
By Bookmasters